Hemingway Deadlights

Hemingway Deadlights

Michael Atkinson

THORNDIKE
CHIVERS

This Large Print edition is published by Thorndike Press, Waterville, Maine, USA and by BBC Audiobooks Ltd, Bath, England.
Thorndike Press, a part of Gale, Cengage Learning.

An Ernest Hemingway Mystery.

This is a work of fiction. All of the characters, organizations, and events portrayed in this novel are either products of the author's imagination or are used fictitiously.
The text of this Large Print edition is unabridged.
Other aspects of the book may vary from the original edition.
Set in 16 pt. Plantin.
Printed on permanent paper.

LIBRARY OF CONGRESS CATALOGING-IN-PUBLICATION DATA

Atkinson, Michael, 1962–
Hemingway deadlights / by Michael Atkinson.
p. cm. — (Thorndike Press large print mystery)
"An Ernest Hemingway mystery."
ISBN-13: 978-1-4104-2116-6 (alk. paper)
ISBN-10: 1-4104-2116-3 (alk. paper)
1. Hemingway, Ernest, 1899–1961—Fiction. 2. Murder—Investigation—Fiction. 3. Key West (Fla.)—Fiction. 4. Large type books. I. Title.
PS3601.T496H46 2009b
813'.6—dc22 2009030538

BRITISH LIBRARY CATALOGUING-IN-PUBLICATION DATA AVAILABLE

Published in 2009 in the U.S. by arrangement with St. Martin's Press, LLC.
Published in 2010 in the U.K. by arrangement with St. Martin's Press, LLC.

U.K. Hardcover: 978 1 408 47734 2 (Chivers Large Print)
U.K. Softcover: 978 1 408 47735 9 (Camden Large Print)

Printed in the United States of America
1 2 3 4 5 6 7 13 12 11 10 09

For my wife Laurel and my children

ACKNOWLEDGMENTS

As thanks for all manner of help and support, a raised double daiquiri to Joseph Sullivan, Michael Magee, my eagle-eyed editor Peter Joseph, the ever-dogged Barbara Braun, John Parsley, and my first reader, Laurel.

1

Hemingway woke up on the floor of his bedroom, facedown, the bedsheets wrapped in a knot around his left ankle, which had a fat, heavy, slightly damp plaster cast on it, toe to knee. What the, Hemingway's face said, in a fisted scrunch. His eyes were, in Robert Capa's mother's phrase, pissholes in the snow. His cheeks, he could feel them hot with a few newly booze-ruptured capillaries. He became dimly aware that the inaccessible bottom of his foot itched. Outside, breakfast-time Key West fanned itself with coconutty tropical breezes like the queen of Sheba on a chaise lounge.

Early May, 1956. What had happened: Hemingway had been hunting geckos in his courtyard the previous afternoon, and hunting them meant rampaging around the gardens like a 230-pound kindergartner pretending to manhunt Iroquois with a popgun. An entire day's worth of tequila battering his liver, and a 1924 Winchester elephant-stopper in his sweaty hands. His favorite gun, if he had to pick a favorite. The house cats, only two of which had six toes on two feet each, helped, crawling low and melodramatically through the shrubbery and jungle grass, targeting a hapless lizard on the tile walk or high on a palm tree clearly enough so Hemingway would come to see it, too, and then open fire. Each shot from this gun shook the top of each tree even if Hemingway had not in fact shot that particular tree. As it was, one palm took a solid hit and promptly died. Hemingway would have to hire a local gardener and his crew of illegal Nicaraguans a week or so later to remove it completely, before it could topple and perhaps take the house's second-floor veranda with it.

The tile walk could be replaced, and so could the cats. The servants stayed in the cellar.

After more than a red-faced hour of this, Hemingway had, he thought, obliterated every gecko in the vicinity. But then, following a cat's sudden, twitchy head turn, he saw one of the sticky-fingered crawlers high on a gutter. As the two of them watched, the lizard scampered up and onto the roof.

Hemingway ran full bore into the house

and up the stairs. The cat followed, and ran underfoot on the second staircase. The feet came down on cat, let up, a split second, and then balance was lost. The man collided and grappled with the mahogany banister, kicking two of the balusters into splinters. Curses, some spittle, and then onward, to the third-floor study, past his old writing podium, and to the gable window overlooking a thin stretch of roof. Hemingway heaved his girth up onto the windowsill, atop a carved chest he had bought in Nairobi between safaris and in which, he remembered now for merely a second and then forgot all over again, he'd left love letters received from a Loyalist secretary twenty years earlier, what was her name, Camilla, when he was in Spain and just as Pauline was busy spending all of that money on the notorious salt-water swimming pool he was looking down into right now, kneeling and then standing on the steep, terra-cotta-shingled roof.

The pool was empty, Hemingway ruefully noted. If only it hadn't been. But good thing it was. A dive from where he stood was too tempting, and would've snapped his neck like an ice-cream stick.

The gecko was nowhere to be seen. The cat did not come out onto the roof.

Hemingway harumphed, stamping down with the butt of his rifle. Which broke two terra-cotta tiles, which cascaded down, over the edge and then, after a few pregnant seconds, shattered on the patio with the thick, startling concussion of first-rate skeets.

The cracked tiles around the first two began to shed heavy clay shards, raining down two and a half stories, and when Hemingway attempted to step backward, toward the window, every old shingle under his feet cracked, folded, came loose, and gave way. He landed flatly on his rump, which loosened virtually every tile on the roof, and a monsoon of deadly clay shrapnel poured down to earth. Hemingway instantly began sliding downward, and the rounded clay tiles he grabbed came off in his hand. He thought about the empty swimming pool again, too bad, and also how even if he managed to survive the fall, three floors onto baked tile and concrete, the storm of terracotta debris trailing behind him — featuring fractured chunks weighing up to two solid pounds — would surely finish him off.

He looked up. It was a sterling, pitch-perfect Key West day. I wonder who's fishing for what out there, he thought.

He had to let go of his gun, which was

soon airborne. As he closed in on the roof's edge, his legs made a decision, a decision his back and his head were certainly not in complete agreement with, to leap up and off at the last possible second toward the head of a young palm. Just a foot shorter than the roof edge, the tree stood almost fifteen feet from the house, but its fronds hung closer, like a dozing girl's hair. Hemingway's legs figured that if he was to land atop the tree, he could thereafter shimmy down its trunk and be saved. If he came anywhere near it, perhaps he could grab a frond and break his fall, at least to some degree. How the wrought-iron patio furniture beneath the tree would figure into the calculus of either scenario was not something Hemingway's legs had apparently considered. In the two and a half seconds it took for the whole ordeal to transpire, not every contingency could be properly weighed.

Hemingway leapt. Too far, as it happens — like a flying squirrel, the man's khaki-dressed, potbellied frame soared narrowly over the top of the tree, immediately beyond which lay a rock garden, rose bushes and more cement. So Hemingway grabbed one of the palm's long fronds as he nearly passed over it, and held on tight, swinging him back to the tree as if he'd grabbed onto a passing streetcar.

The first casualty were the phone lines, which passed near the tree and which Hemingway missed on his maiden voyage off the roof but in which he successfully entangled his legs upon whipping back. Desperately, he gripped the top of the palm, but the fronds couldn't support his weight, and so they snapped off. Hemingway proceeded to grip the tree itself, with both arms and phone-line-entwined legs. He started to slip downward, fast. The phone lines snapped off, the gun hit the pavement. The great man soon met the ground, hugging the tree with his eyes closed. His left ankle snapped on impact. He was largely unaware of this, soused as he was, and so he hobbled over to the wrought-iron patio furniture, sat down and yelled for Marisol, his favorite of the current kitchen help, who couldn't hear him until he was bellowing at the top of his lungs because she was in the cellar with the rest of the staff playing cards. Finally, she brought him a bottle, a glass, a lime and some cold crabmeat, but when she saw his ankle, which was already the size and hue of a ruby red grapefruit, she called the doctor. By the time the doctor arrived, Hemingway was asleep.

This was how Hemingway woke up the next morning with a cast on his foot he had no foreknowledge of, and how, when Peter Cuthbert called that evening with the dreadful sound of blood in his voice, no phone in Hemingway's house rang because the line was down. Nobody, therefore, even knew that Cuthbert had called except Cuthbert, and by midnight he was dead.

2

The police were in Hemingway's bedroom.

What the. Hemingway had been drinking today ever since Marisol told him about last evening's doctor's visit, and since Marisol told him to leave his hands off her or she'd tell the *Miami Herald* he'd raped her three years ago in a whiskey swoon and that her three-year-old son was his. The gecko hunt had been one thing, but Marisol hadn't even been working in the Whitehead Street house three years ago, ferChrissake. He didn't even *know* her then. Now that Pauline had passed on, the house was still 60 percent Hemingway's, and he could come and go as he liked. But since Hemingway actually lived in Cuba, with Mary, and since his pit stops in Key West to see his boys, Pauline's boys, Gregory and Patrick, now twenty-five and twenty-seven and rarely home in any case, and to drink and fish and do whatever the fuck else he wanted to do and not have to explain it, were irregular by any measure, Marisol's babblings were certainly idle threats.

Which didn't mean a rag like the *Herald* wouldn't publish them. Everything'll be fine as long as she keeps the clear liquor cold and the glasses clean.

The dicks in the bedroom didn't look comfortable, good. The bedroom had no chairs for them to sit in, just Hemingway's monstrous four-poster bed, made in Singapore from some bizarre Borneo hardwood he'd never heard of before or since, some bureaus, a desk with a Royal, and French doors open to the balcony.

"What happened." Captain Vincent Squiccarini was standing in the bedroom, pointing at Hemingway's cast. Hemingway had to swim out of his thoughts, which were as murky as a Detroit lake, to answer him.

"Uh . . . Fell."

"Is that right."

"Off the roof."

"Your roof? And is this all you broke?" Amused the moment he came in, Squiccarini was now getting into a sparring rhythm. He even tapped his toe on the floorboards by the foot of the bed.

"I . . . used the tree." Hemingway was still groggy, and it began to irritate him.

"I've seen you use trees." This was Lt. Gomez Maria, standing beside Squiccarini. Hemingway had been vaguely aware of someone else in the room. Whereas Squiccarini had the tan, the unkempt mustache, the belly and the bleached forearm hair to indicate years of life and service to the islands, Maria had the emphatic grooming and moist eyes of a cantina pimp.

"Fuck you, Maria." That was better. He began to sit up.

"Are you with us, Papa?" Squiccarini shifting into semi-official buddy-buddy gear. "You didn't *try* to hurt yourself, did you?"

"Why the fuck would I want to do that?"

"When I asked you that question last March," Squiccarini contentedly rolling his weight from one foot to the other, "after you told me you'd like to shoot yourself out of a cannon into a brick wall, you said it was because of headaches."

"Jesus Christ. You gonna vomit back up to me everything I ever said cocked to the gills?"

"And your back. Your back hurt."

"And I was wearing?"

"A straw hat shaped like a dinghy."

Hemingway brightened.

"Hey! I remember that day — you threw up on Joe's wife's shoes, and he punched you and made your ear bleed!"

"I don't recall that."

Squiccarini was Hemingway's favorite kind of supporting character in life — adept at banter, respectful but suspicious, capable at different times of both guileless tavern camaraderie and all-business resolve. He was a walking hybrid — a Bronx-lineage Italian with a taste for tropical anomie and tequila, a serious public servant who was corrupt only insofar as the system was corrupt, a reliable friend *and* an entertaining antagonist. He was labeled Captain Video for no better reason than he was a captain, and because it was thought that his thick, wavy crown of dark hair resembled that of the luckless actor who played the character on the kiddie TV show; Hemingway never saw it but Joe at Sloppy Joe's apparently had, and that was that. Hemingway'd known him for decades, but couldn't remember if it was first as a drinking buddy or as a cop. Didn't matter. By now they regarded each other as bastard cousins, perpetually indulging each other with attention because they were family, bitterly together in a bitter world. When Captain Video had to play detective, Hemingway felt it his obligation to play back, in the key of sour, gruff and colorful.

To Squiccarini's disavowal of the pounded ear, Hemingway could only snort sarcastically, something he regretted once a huge, hard plug of snot lodged deeper in his sinuses. He noted that his bedside glass was empty.

"Marisol!"

"We've got some questions." Maria.

Marisol walked in, her head angled, her hands on her hips.

"My lunch, girl!" She disappeared, returning almost instantly with a prestocked tray of gin, lime, bread and ice.

"Lunch?" Captain Video was now having the fun of a visit to the tiger cage.

"What, you eat yours?" Hemingway with glass to lips.

"Odd, isn't it."

"Your questions."

"That's right, Mr. Nobel. We have to ask you about Peter Cuthbert."

Hemingway stopped swallowing. Cuthbert was just a buddy, a Key West gin-mill fixture, fisherman, layabout, occasional Cuban dope, cigar, gun and refugee smuggler, lover of fine conch-fritters, which were hard to find, Christ only knows, and, incidentally, a superb watercolorist who never used white pigment and insisted on painting only on bleached sheepskin from Argentina, when he could find it. Hemingway knew Cuthbert since 1947 or thenabouts, knew him from Joe's and around the docks and, because Cuthbert seemed bullshit-free and simply admitted to never reading fiction at all, ever, Hemingway accepted him into his very loose circle. Like so many men, Cuthbert spent a lot of his time tiptoeing along the fringes of dead-serious crime looking for an easy, or sometimes even desperately difficult, buck. He could've crossed vectors with the law in any number of small ways, including a few drunk and disorderlies, but none of it would've brought Captain Video and *mucho* Maria to the foot of Hemingway's bed. Key West had only recently acquired a naval base and a bridge in 1955, the last in a string of bridges from the mainland, to Boca Chica. But it couldn't be said to have its own police precinct or team of detectives on call. Squiccarini was technically a Monroe County investigator *and* a Florida state police flatfoot, but mostly he was commissioned by the F.B.I. Who signed his checks, God only knew. Nearly everything that happened criminally in the Keys had something to do with foreign nationals, so for years the F.B.I. more or less declared unofficial jurisdiction over the whole spread. Squiccarini's had no beat per se: he could be investigating smuggling, treason, kidnapping, murder, espionage, Communism, fraud, parking tickets. But because the southern Keys were still a little wild then, with as many panthers as tourists, lawmen like the Captain actually investigated very little. Misdemeanors often went unremarked. Neighbors — people who lived in the swamps and on the beachfronts year round — usually settled disputes on their own, in ways that stayed buried. Only the truly serious problems warranted even the outward appearance of police work.

So, Cuthbert must be dead, Hemingway thought. He must be dead *bad,* in a cold-sweat-unleashing way that could not be ignored.

"Cuthbert knew a lot of people." Sip, gurgle. Half of Hemingway was determined to enjoy the day despite all this.

"But Cuthbert had your phone number in his pocket, written on a McLeerden's matchbook. McLeerden's in Miami."

"I know where McLeerden's is. Dolt."

"And your number, Cuthbert had dialed it last thing before he'd died."

"He didn't call here. I didn't talk to him."

". . ."

The three men waited out a modest but uncomfortable pause, in which the world-famous writer had to thumb back through the sodden pages of his life to the day before. Which seemed so long ago already. Captain Video first appearing in his bedroom, blocking the view of his bureau mirror, which reflected the 1932 Zaragoza bullfighting billet he had framed above his bed — *that* already seemed long ago. That bit about McLeerden's, when was that?

Oh, yeah. The geckos, the roof, the fall. The wires.

"Oh, yeah."

The drink to his lips.

"The phone company says he dialed the number."

"From where?"

"A pay phone on the docks."

Now, paddling around in his gin haze, Hemingway had a flash of cogency: what the fuck was all this? If this was Chicago, sure, the dicks would be talking up every acquaintance, following every lead, quizzing famous men about late-night phone calls. But this was the Keys, American Mile Zero, and Cuthbert was nobody. So he said so.

"What the fuck is all this? If this was Chicago, maybe . . ."

"What?" Squiccarini had started walking around the room.

"Cuthbert was nobody."

"Nice." Maria.

"What're you doing?" Hemingway sending up a defensive hand as the Captain picked up a Pygmy totem. "Don't touch that. Don't touch that. Hey Video!"

The cop dropped it on the desk.

"Cuthbert was nobody, we know," the Captain agreed. "Just askin'. What, you think because you're Ernest Goddamned Bestseller Nobel Prize Cover of Life Goddamn Magazine Hemingway, I can't come in here and pursue a routine investigation?"

"You just like busting my balls."

"Do not."

Looking at the draft page in the typewriter, Squiccarini distractedly hits the W.

"Hey! You horse's ass."

"C'mon, Papa." Squiccarini shrugged. "This isn't writing, it's just gibberish."

"Learning to type."

"Right. Sorry anyway. See, this is not my ball-busting face."

"Yeah so. I don't know any more about Cuthbert than you do."

"And we know scads."

"Sure you do. So? I don't know why he should call me, either. Maybe he was looking for a punchline to a joke so he could go out and wow some Cuban vacationer's wife. What happened to him, anyway?"

Took him awhile to ask that. Squiccarini shifted his weight again. Either the cop was playing dumb, playing cat-and-mouse, playing good cop, or there really was nothing exceptional about this interrogation, except that it could barely qualify as such. Maybe Squiccarini just enjoyed seeing his friends squirm, particularly if they were famous, famous for writing out a vision of the modern world in which they'd seen it all, had every kind of heartbreak, felt every kind of wound.

Squirmings. Hemingway remembered, actually, a time in either 1937 or 1938 in which Squiccarini told Wallace Stevens something Hemingway said during a full boat day of gin and tuna. Something about the poet being so incomprehensible and full of shit he might as well write upside down. And Stevens met Hemingway in the street and punched him in the jaw. Stevens was huge but insurance-office soft, and Hemingway regained his footing and kicked his ass. Then Squiccarini arrested *him.*

So Captain Video might have a little celebrity sadist in him. He might just live solely on oyster crackers, ginger ale and schadenfreude. Even if he could only define the first two.

"I know what schadenfreude means,"

Squiccarini said. Both cops had puzzled expressions. Hemingway froze: was he talking out loud? He hoped he didn't actually say the name "Wallace Stevens."

"Uh . . . You were saying."

"No, I wasn't," Squiccarini said. "Cuthbert — what happened. You're going to love this."

"No, I won't."

"Speared. A ninety-millimeter cannon harpoon pushed straight through his back. Found him in the basin besides Spangler's scoot — old Spangler Tosh. Looks like Cuthbert was trying to steal Spangler's boat, it's a mess. Jimmied out the ignition plate, cut wires, pissed on himself. Thought it was Spangler — imagine him hauling out a big old harpoon like that from somewhere to fix that boat-napper once and for all? But Spangler's in Baton Rouge. His daughter-in-law had twins."

"Huh."

"All we know is he wanted to talk to you. But everybody would like to talk to you, ain't that true."

"You do fuckin' enough of it." Hemingway looked to the veranda: a three-minute rain storm. He could see steam rising from the stucco outside.

"Yeah, boy, wind me up. Well, if you think

of anything, let us know."

"Now what?"

"Now what what?"

There it was: the merest outward appearance of police work. A man gets harpooned in the harbor, and the police take one morning on it.

"Tell me that's it for your investigation into a harpoon murder. Of a known smuggler, and watercolorist. In the middle of Submarine Basin. In the middle of the night."

"What, Papa, not getting your taxes' worth? Call your congressman."

The men resaddled their straw hats atop their heads and moseyed out toward the front door. As much as Squiccarini practically begged you to think that every word out of his mouth had two meanings, Hemingway knew from experience they usually had only one or none at all, and so there was no reason for him not to believe that Peter Cuthbert would be forgotten by nightfall in a chatty tide of tourists, evening drinks, black-market coups and Gulf breezes. The harpoon, wherever it came from, would likely find its way onto some local municipal officer's office wall. Spangler Tosh's new granddaughters would be happily chauffeured home, and his boat soon enough repaired. Cuthbert's body would be incinerated and dumped. Hemingway would forget the whole incident by lunchtime, when Marisol in the kitchen would kill a few lobsters and lay out their iced tails raw, with lemons.

3

Now, Peter Cuthbert had family, but that family didn't have him. Not for as long as anyone remembered. You spend too much time in Mexican jails, Florida bars and midnight Gulf barges, no wife or kids or even parents will continue to return your calls or visit your reeking digs. Hemingway knew as much; Cuthbert, because it was the only way he could say it, flaunted the fact that he was utterly alone in the world. "Just me, my boat and my liver," he'd whine sometimes; "I'd sooner pay alimony as drink creosote." This when he thought nobody was listening. He'd be stunned to learn that Papa, of all people, had noticed, much less remembered. But who knows why you remember things.

Hemingway seemed to forget little of this sort of thing in the long run, which was naturally a curse to him as much as a blessing, a blessing more so, you'd guess, if you measured, say, books against wives. Even drunkard musings came back to him months later, as if his blackouts eventually faded with time to clear sky. So after he'd drank and ate that afternoon in the absence of the Key's sad law enforcement, Hemingway realized that, first of all, Cuthbert would end up in some swampy upstate potter's field unless he, Hemingway, stepped up, and secondly, that unless he applied some pressure around town, that's all, just a little force, then nobody would ever find out how Cuthbert ended up in the basin impaled on a giant fish spear. Somebody should do that much, that's all. Some congenial muscle to unleash the island from its inertia, and let the system do its natural work.

And Hemingway was alone, he knew, not only in thinking something should perhaps be done, but also alone in being the only big fat global-celebrity poobah on the island, or in the county, that could actually exert the pressure required. He checked his inner calendar — wasn't he leaving for Cuba soon? When did he decide that? He'd remembered tavern talk from years before, but his own itinerary, day to day, was fish-slippery. Wasn't he supposed to have met his boys in Key West? When did he get here, anyway? The ordinary man, with a job and bills and a healthy fear of time's velocity, would find this airy, forgetful moment of lostness intolerable. But Hemingway did not grow anxious. He loved the present and always appreciated those boozy instances when it becomes disconnected from the past and future like an uncoupled boxcar. The past and future were terrifying; the present was all gravity and odors and what was on his fingertips and tongue.

If there was some place important to be, he figured, he'd've remembered it. Soon Hemingway was at the morgue. It was a squat little Alamo of a building, the half-dozen windows six feet from the floor and small, the size of loaves of bread, the wide-plank floor suggesting a century and a half of wear and tear as pirate-ship decking. This was first used as a jail for nineteenth-century poachers, then munitions storage, then nothing, empty, for forty or so years, then an office for the village clerk. Then a corrupt Key assemblyman used it as a fishermen's brothel, the main attraction of which was the assemblyman's Cuban girlfriend. Now it was a morgue, either temporary or merely lazily assembled, with humming portable refrigeration units that essentially turned the entire building into a freezer. The corpses lay out in the open, then, on cots. The windows were taped shut. The clay walls outside emitted a steady steam and dripped with condensation. Since this was May in south Florida, everybody liked it in that box, despite the smell.

Squiccarini was there, and Maria, along with the coroner, Wesley Tuggle, and a short-sleeved plainclothes cop named Tcheon. Hemingway had seen him around and heard his name spoken: the semi-silent *T* suggested a Russian line, but Hemingway smelled an affectation. Of undetermined Eurasian origin, Tcheon wore a Panama hat and had indigo burn scars covering his left arm and leg. Depending on his mood, his English was either quite adequate or non-existent.

When Hemingway came in, limping on his cast, Captain Video was typing up forms at a small desk in the corner. The other men stood around smoking.

"Hemingway, you're up," was what Squiccarini said with a brief glance. "How'd you come here? No doctor-ordered bed rest for you?"

"My scooter. I was wondering about the body. What's the gen."

Squiccarini turned in his seat, and the other men simply stared. Who the fuck are you, was the loudly unspoken response.

Hemingway could give two craps — these tropical hillbilly bullshitters. They could stare ominously all they liked. He took a few steps in, looking around.

"He doesn't have family."

"Yes, he does," Maria piped up. "But we can't find them."

"They don't want him. You'd have to hunt them down and rope them to your truck hood. Been that way a long time."

"Yeah, yeah, I know, Hemingway," Squiccarini finishing up with the papers. "Everybody knows. So?"

"So, I'll bury him."

The tense mood loosened slightly.

"Really." Tuggle.

"Oh no," the Captain said. "You've taken an interest. Haven't you. I've heard about this: celebrities taking interest in local brouhahas. What're you trying to do, Papa, take over? Solve the case? Step in and do the right thing. Make up for your sins."

"Go write a story about it," Tcheon muttered thickly with the contempt you'd reserve for a pedophile. Maria laughed, predictably. Hemingway would've swatted a mosquito, but he wouldn't acknowledge being annoyed by these humps.

"When are you going home, Papa?

Where's Mary?" Squiccarini.

"I only said I'd bury him."

"No, that's not true, you said you wanted to know what the gen with the body is. What'd the autopsy say. You want to be Hammett now."

He read the big man like a post-office poster. "Look," Hemingway said, having had it. He indulged in some diaphragmatic booming. "You pack of peckerwood nancies can sit around circle-jerking each other all day long for all I care, it's not as if you have jobs and it's not as if you're fucking doing them, and if you don't care why Cuthbert caught a harpoon in his back — and Vinnie, why you don't I don't know, he drove you home plenty — that's fine, you goddamned parasites. But somebody should know something about what happened, and somebody has to pay for his fucking grave. You gonna sit around and pick noses over that? Captain, do I have to call Miami?"

Captain Video knew it could happen: a) Hemingway was pompous and drunk and famous enough to actually get somebody important on the phone, and b) he'd done it once before, when the Whitehead Street house was broken into, and Squiccarini was in Cuba at the time, on duty but also on an illegal four-day weekend of whoring and roulette. Hemingway wouldn't let any of the staff clean up, and so they all shuffled around the overturned furniture and broken glass for three whole days before a cop showed up. Hemingway called the Bureau, stoked and fuming, and Squiccarini had his head handed to him. Apologies were exchanged, and the Captain bought Hemingway a new etched-glass panel for his front door. A few months later, it was admitted that three of the local Sloppy Joe's tribe had barged in when nobody was home, looking for a hidden bottle of absinthe Hemingway claimed to have bought in Cairo. Cuthbert was one of them, but Hemingway was sufficiently amused by the debacle by then, and broke out the bottle for the men, after which they shipped out westerly at 2 A.M. to speak to porpoises, and sank Greg Beaudine's skiff in seven feet of low tide.

"Alright, Papa. Don't get your belly in a crimp." Tuggle.

The coroner shrugged, strolled vaguely over to one of the three cots presently occupied. Pulled back the sheet, all the way.

Peter Cuthbert was buck-naked and the color of blue candy-tray mints. The gaping wound in his chest was just that — torn skin, blue, and a dark hole, no gore.

"You drained him already, where'd you do

that?" Hemingway sounding merely curious.

"We got a drainin' table out back," Tuggle said.

"No autopsy?"

"We know how he died, Hemingway."

"Where's the harpoon."

"In my office."

"What do you know?"

"Not much. Went in the back, came out here. Then it sank. He was in the water. The harpoon sank him, and it got stuck in the silt, and he was trying to float up against it . . . OK? If the tide current hadn't been clean, we might not've found him for a while."

"Who did?"

"A kid. Fishing for tommycots off the pier."

"Was the thing thrown? Pushed by hand?"

"Or what?" Squiccarini smirked. "Or was it shot? You think somebody has a portable ninety-mil harpoon gun they're lugging around the basin dockside, in case somebody dares break into a boat?"

"Rube. Who said he wasn't dumped in the basin?"

"We have no reason to think that might be so."

"I think a, what, seventy-pound harpoon

is a good reason. You can't throw that thing as a weapon."

"It's closer to fifty, fifty-five. If he was shot he'd a been torn in two."

"Maybe. But thrown? Fifty-five pounds?"

"C'mon."

Next thing he knew, Hemingway followed the four men out into the sun, behind the morgue, beneath a few bedraggled palms. He could hear the ocean. Considering now the foolhardiness of his visit, Hemingway tried to scratch the itchy inside of his cast with a stick. And he pined for a drink.

Tuggle had the harpoon: it did weigh in at nearly sixty pounds, a modestly sized whale spear from early in the century, after they'd decided swivel-head deck guns were the way to go, but before that Norwegian prick invented exploding spearheads. By which point whaling was history anyway. Then or since, anything less than one hundred pounds could be used only on orcas, sharks, marlins, not real whales, and therefore used only by butchers who couldn't be bothered to reel a modestly sized fish in like a man. Sixty-pound harpoons were never popular and are hard to find, if anyone ever looked.

Hemingway knew that Squiccarini knew nothing of the sort, that the Captain only knew that heavy, old gun harpoons did not commonly appear in people's backs. There seemed to be little point to Hemingway opening his mouth.

So Hemingway and four Florida municipal workers took turns lifting a medium-sized would-be-whale-killer-but-actually-a-chickenshit-shark-spear to see if it was throwable or somehow wieldable as a weapon against another human being.

"Throw it," Maria tossed. "Hemingway. Hit the Ford."

There was the shell of an old Ford sitting out by the swamp-edge just ten yards away, no windows or wheels, rust and salt-torn paint. Throw it? Whatever happened, Hemingway already knew in his heart, knew in his hands as they hefted the bolt of rusty cast iron, that Cuthbert didn't die this way. No one threw this stupid thing, and however it ended up plunged through the fool's torso, it didn't happen at the basin, surrounded by a hundred boats and nearby homes and late-night partiers. Hemingway wanted Squiccarini to realize this, but he could see that the Captain's tank of interest in justice in this particular case was already on empty. Cuthbert's story was wrapping up only a day after it'd begun. So he didn't stop himself. Lifting his cast foot in the air a little, Hemingway bowed back with the harpoon in one hand and heaved it at the derelict car.

My back, he thought.

After traveling an arc Jim Thorpe would've admired, the harpoon hit the Ford at 45-degrees and handily stuck with a loud *thwu-uungk* in its passenger-side door. It waved in the air for a few moments, then the weight of it slowly pulled it loose and it dropped to the sand.

"Let me try!" Maria, running over to fetch it.

Squiccarini looked satisfied. Hemingway didn't know what else to do. Except bury the guy.

On the road behind them, tourists were taking pictures of five grown men attacking a dead car with a giant spear, and one of the men was Ernest Hemingway. The photos would later be rejected by *Look* magazine as a hoax.

4

That was all a Wednesday; Wednesday night Hemingway spent drinking gin and coconut water, rereading old *Time* magazine and *Saturday Evening Post* reviews of his books, except for the demolition jobs on *Across the River and into the Trees,* which were indisputably motivated by tribal, kill-the-king spite. An old record he found, Pauline's, turned on the player. Fats Waller. Unsurprisingly, drink helped his ankle both ache and itch less, as it helped virtually everything else.

He also tried to write and got nowhere. It'd been awhile. He was always *trying,* but the sentences came in gluey clumps nowadays, hard to spit out and almost impossible to disentangle. The last thing he finished, *The Old Man,* spilled out four years ago, and it was the last thing Hemingway remembered being easy, in the way riding a fast horse can be tough but easy once you understand the rhythm. Was he blocked? "Blocked"? What did that mean, anyway? Was it a pipe blocked by a sludge ball or a dead rat? Or an artery gone arteriosclerotic, narrowing with fatty deposits until it closes altogether? "Fatty deposits" sounded right, that's what the thoughts felt like. But Hemingway couldn't help having them, they were second nature. Whatever: it wasn't the sludginess that was deadly, it was its consequence: the panic of having lost, somehow, out of view, the fulcrum upon which an entire lifetime and consciousness was built. If that goes, there's nothing left, nothing but habit, time, worry and weather. So far, Hemingway has been a champion at keeping the panic tamped down, whipped like a dog. It was worrisome but under control.

The next day, Thursday, was slated for a visit to the local grave master and Old Town boneyard, if there were spaces left that weren't taken up by tourist picnic tables. The place had become an obligatory stop for sightseers in the years since Hemingway first bought his house; it had some old stones and a few wiseass epitaphs. Cuthbert had said many times, amidst the usual toasted conversations about death, body disposal and last words, that he'd like to be buried as is, not, goddamn it, cremated and sprinkled out over the ocean like so much yacht ashtray ash, or over the islands like so much lily pollen. Buried in a tough wood box — teak, maybe — that'll last awhile, even in the Keys' salty soil, and beneath a gravestone with a name, dates and everything. Didn't want to be forgotten, Cuthbert — a desire that became pathetic once you remembered that very nearly everybody had already forgotten him long before he died. Who'd visit that grave site? Well, tourists would see it, maybe Cuthbert counted on that much. But it wouldn't be very old, and so would likely be unremarked upon. He should've come up with a witty saying to have cut into his marble, to ensure frequent visitors and snapshots. Maybe he did think of one at one point or another, in the pubs or on the decks, but if so, Hemingway didn't hear it. Wit was never on Cuthbert's to-do list.

But when Hemingway came to Bill Bolitho, owner of the island's monopoly on grave sites, caskets and connections for offshore stone-cutting, to his squirrelly storefront office on Margaret Street, he was told it was taken care of.

"Sort of," Bolitho said. "Haven't been paid or nothing."

"Then, what?"

"Some fella came in here, Lynch. Said he was a cousin of Cuthbert's and would handle the expenses. Cremation, urn. That's it. No service."

"It's a crock of shit."

"Don't I know. Cuthbert never had no cousin that would come looking to bury him. Poor fella."

"I saw Captain Video yesterday; they hadn't been able to contact anyone. Not that they tried too hard. What's your excuse?"

"For?"

"For taking his money."

Bolitho thought about smirking but decided no. "Told you, I haven't been paid." He was a jovial sort, round-faced and blond, fond of his fellow men only as a spectator sport, but fond all the same.

Hemingway huffed. He stood there with a foot in a cast, leaning on a cane. The morning light poured in like dusty butter. There wasn't any place proper to sit anywhere in this pissant office, just a few pine folding chairs with rain-stained cushions. How were grieving families supposed to come here and make interment decisions? Maybe Bolitho had it all worked out: make them fidget and squirm while they mourn, and they'll agree to anything.

"I'll pay it all right now."

"Sure! What'll you have?"

"I'll take the service, a nice big stone —"

Bolitho's eyebrows, both of them.

"— uh, what, four by four. Thereabouts. And a hardwood coffin. Teak?"

"Nah. You owe Peter money?"

"Billy? Fuck you."

"We've got mahogany. It's steep."

"There're plots?"

"Sure, we could do it tomorrow."

Hemingway nodded, looking down, pressing his white beard thoughtfully to his chest, thoughtlessly admiring the white hair on his own forearms, admiring it because, he supposed, his father had it, too. The cane was Dad's. But that broken ankle, that was Hemingway's. Christ, the roof? What the living hell was he even doing up there? My kidneys are *killing* me, he thought.

The tinny doorbell rang behind him; there, standing in the doorway, one hand on the knob, was a man in a silk shirt, sweat-seamed linen jacket and straw hat. He had a thin mustache, the sort of mustache that instantly inspires mistrust. His eyes were unforgiving, long-memory brown. He was thin, and moved cautiously, like a crab.

"That's Stanley Lynch," Bolitho piped up. The only man sitting, Billy was clearly prepared for a high time.

Hemingway turned and knew Lynch didn't need to be introduced.

"Mr. Hemingway! It's my honor to meet you." Shameless, with an outstretched hand. Hemingway took it and tried to be steely, which objectively speaking could be very steely indeed.

"Hmpf. Look, I don't know who you are, but you're not Peter Cuthbert's kin."

"Well," the straw-hatted man said plummily, obviously no stranger to being caught goldbricking. His expression didn't change, but his voice got sharper. "You don't know all get-out about it, Hemingway. You're just a drunk best-selling storyteller mucking around with real corpses and real lives when everybody in the world knows you're only good at making shit up."

Hemingway wanted to say, "I don't make anything up!" but knew it'd be beside the point. He also wanted to say something about what he knew of Cuthbert's history, which did not allow for the possibility of longlost cousins coming out of the woodwork — as in, Cuthbert wasn't even the man's family name. Squiccarini didn't seem to even know that, which Hemingway had always assumed was Cuthbert's point. He also wanted to ask this preposterous grifter why, why in Christ's name he'd want to bury Cuthbert — or at least, why he was willing to pay for the privilege so he could have at least temporary custody of the body. Or have it quickly incinerated, out of the public eye. A body with a hole you could drop a grapefruit through without incident.

But instead, the use of the word *shit* flipped a switch, and Hemingway pivoted slightly on the stony heel of his cast and threw his fist into the man's chin, which more or less crumpled under the strike like chicken bone. Lynch left the floor for a second and came down across the room. Blood spritzed from his gums. Bolitho hooted.

"I'm not done," Hemingway said.

Which now had Bolitho envisioning ambulances and cops and reporters, all of which might start mucking around in cemetery books, which wouldn't be good. "Whoa! Now, Papa, we don't need another body —"

"Take a breath, Billy, I'm just talking to the man."

Lynch stumbled to his feet, weeping. "You fuck," he sputtered. His words came out now like sounds out of a horn stuffed with gravel.

"Yeah. Did I break much?"

"I don't know, never had my jaw broken.

What's it like?"

"Hurts," Bolitho.

"Like a sonofabitch," Hemingway offered. "But you're talking, so."

Lynch seemed okay and was checking for loose teeth.

"So, tell me, without insulting me again. What's your line to Cuthbert."

"Uh . . . yeah, his father was my grand uncle."

"That's Old Man Cuthbert."

"Right."

"I oughta hit you again. Lying to my face."

"No, not at all."

"There was no Old Man Cuthbert. Cuthbert's a name Peter found in a newspaper."

"That's not what the police said." Did he just say that? And when did he talk to the police?

"What the cops don't know could land you on the moon with a lounge chair and a fat martini."

Good line, he thought. Land you on the moon, lounge chair, fat martini. But he could never use it. Thurber could use it, but not him. Too much color. But why is color a bad thing, just because James and Wharton and Fitzgerald go big guns on it? Why can't I use a funny line every now and then? Moon, lounge, martini . . . Maybe it wasn't so great.

Bolitho moved only his mouth, looking Lynch down. "You know you just admitted you're a fraud."

Hemingway grinned. Lynch glanced toward the door.

"What we need to know," Hemingway rumbled, now rather happily playing with the weight of his cane a little — it wasn't light or fragile, "is why you wanted to bury Peter. What were you looking for. That's what I'd like to know. He had no inheritance. Did you think he had money somewhere?" Why'd I say that, Hemingway thought. Always showing off, laying my cards out every time. I'm definitely not cut out for this detective crap.

Lynch's minuscule hesitation could've been read as reticence to fess up or something else. It was all Hemingway got for his question, and he tucked it away for later.

"I, uh . . . yeah. Up I-ninety-five, I heard he had some stash, and that nobody else would come after it because he had no family."

"Heard from who."

"Uh. A con, that said he'd met Cuthbert on a run down here." Vague — very nice. Lynch was regaining his composure, and his lies were getting smoother.

Hemingway shifted again. "You've done this before, haven't you."

"Maybe. So."

A moment before, Lynch had the wired tension of a cornered weasel. Now he was affecting a smug amorality. Hemingway wasn't sure if he'd just given this bottom-feeder a reasonable, larcenous, alibi that seemed relatively harmless compared to the truth. Which was? Hemingway had no guess. But at least he'd scotched it.

"Get the fuck out of here, off this island. If I see you again, I'll beat you till you piss blood."

"That'd make a nice headline." Bolitho, muttering.

"Hey, whose side you on?"

With a "well, good day, gentlemen," Lynch straightened his hat, held his jaw, and walked out into the shady street.

"Papa, that's some weirdness," Bolitho finally said. "Who coulda gave him the idea that Peter had treasure somewhere?"

"I did. Just now."

"Then what the?"

"Helluva question. What I think, though, is that man isn't long for the world. He's setting something poisonous in motion. I'm not going to hurt him again, Billy, but you are going to bury him."

5

The evening sounded like other evenings, singing with palm whispers and lizard skitterings and distant waves and rigging clinks, but also clotted with the laughter and idiotic conversation of tourists. Hemingway had liked the occasional Key tourist way back when — there was an innocence to them, and mostly they wanted to fish — but now they were thick as flies, buzzing, smug from too much money in the years since the war and nothing to spend it on but restaurants and souvenirs. They didn't fish, they just walked around in spiffy outfits, looking for something to buy. And they were loud, loud as if they were in a Brooklyn beer hall and not the Gulf tropics, where you could hear a motor boat on the water before you could see it. Each year it got worse.

Ah well. At home with a glass of ice and booze in a Malabar wicker chair so strong it could hold up a farting silverback. Here's what there was to it: a body, killed in a way nobody could properly explain, with a weapon that's not really a weapon but a freak of a nautical antique, from God knows where. What law there is isn't terribly interested — which may or may not be a matter for suspicion, since they're rarely interested in anything. But this was a bizarrerie — where was Squiccarini's line in the sand drawn? How berserk does a killing have to be to draw flies around here? Perhaps the good Captain is paying attention but is keeping his cards uncharacteristically close to his breastplate — unlikely, given the man's public record, but not impossible. But no autopsy?

And then there's the Mysterious Stranger, coming from nowhere and trying to get rights to the body and/or its nonexistent estate, for what are professed to be greedy reasons that are pure bullshit to the naked eye. And there's the phone call, and the proximity of Spangler's boat, both of which might be irrelevant. It might all be irrelevant. Except the things on the list no one's seen yet: the place where Cuthbert was actually killed, the person who actually killed him, with the harpoon or otherwise — who knew, without a forensic peek-and-see — and of course, the circumstances under which such a thing could happen in the first place. That stuff was relevant if anything ever was. Hemingway heard a headache coming, and he dropped off before it pulled in.

Then: a jostling hand on his shoulder — how he hated a jostling hand on his sleeping shoulder, more than virtually anything, more than Wallace Stevens, Philadelphia and the idea of cold breakfast cereal. More than television, "fish sticks," Baptists, Volkswagens, the way Mary — the ugliest woman he ever loved — smirk-frowns like a menopausal Bible salesman when she's angry, Mickey Rooney and calves' liver.

Who knows how long he'd been allowed to sleep.

"It's twelve." Patrick. Tanned, strong and already balding a bit at twenty-seven. Stopping in from Tanganyika by way of Lisbon and Miami.

Twelve? Three hours' sleep, then. For the love of Pete. Wait: bright for midnight.

"Lunchtime." Oh: noon. Fifteen hours. That was OK. But slumped in the chair, Hemingway knew he'd pay for the sleep in back pain all day.

"Oh shit." Hemingway heaved himself up like an old whale through silty water.

"How's goes it, Pop?

"I've got a funeral, in an hour."

"Miss it! Haven't seen you since last year, after the plane crash. You look all healed and pink and ready for rumbling."

Crash? Oh, *that.* Where *is* Mary? How long is it since I've been back to Cuba?

"Can't miss it. I'm paying for it."

"Holy shit, why?!" a startled Patrick virtually hollered. For a split-second: *family.*

"It's nothing, just a local fellow. Nobody else to do it. Murder."

"Jeepers. Can I come? What kind of crowd are we looking at?"

"Just you and me. Billy Bolitho. And the coroner."

"Huh. No drama. No Italian mothers clawing at the casket. No short-skirted young widows already scouting out her future options."

"No. Maybe a few fishermen. But I doubt it, they're all out after swordfish now."

One meatball. That song, awoke with it inexplicably burbling away in his head. *One meatball!* Jesus.

"Wait — what the fuck is that on your leg?" The cast had just fought its way out of sweat-cold sheets.

"A cast, boy, don't you know anything?" Hemingway was in a unshakable state of irate disgust with himself and the world, but it was also right about now that he realized how happy he was to see his youngest boy, his nerviest, funniest Indian fighter.

"Ha! What I know is that old idiots with kidney, liver and blood pressure ailments shouldn't be doing anything that might result in the shattering of bones. Who's the horse's ass. Let me guess: you decided to beat a local Olympic champion at pole vaulting. On asphalt."

"Funny." Did Patrick have to be *this* goddamn spunky? Hemingway got up and started rifling through his closet.

"I know: you ate an agave worm and decided you could fly off the roof."

"Close. If you're coming to this burial, you'd better put on something other than that Zanzibar smock." Patrick was wearing an African thing, wrapped all wrong, like an Arab, almost. It was black and purple.

"Uganda, actually."

"Then you got gypped."

Ever since he was a boy, Patrick had been determined to maintain a cavalier zest about things despite his father's behemothic egomania, judgmental bullying and macho histrionics, and unlike Greg, he'd been largely successful. It wasn't that difficult — a sense of humor and a sense of distance together did the job. Expect nothing but shenanigans and pratfalls, and you won't be disappointed.

"Gypped, huh? Gee, that dollar meant the world to me." The sarcasm hung pleasantly in the breeze-free air.

"Go, go, go. Or stay here, all I care." Hemingway had found his black suit, which he began to put on unpressed. But the cast wouldn't fit through the pant leg. He tried at least one more time than a normal person would have. Patrick watched, saying to himself, see?

Hemingway tossed it aside with a harumph — something wouldn't let him slit the leg of a $400 silk suit for one Key West burial. He hobbled about the clothes-strewn bedroom in his briefs, retrieving his khaki shorts.

"Well?" Looking at Patrick.

"Sorry," Patrick said. "W. C. Fields came to town suddenly."

"Aw, go fuck a duck."

After a quick molestation of the icebox downstairs, Patrick dressed as sincerely as his Key West closet would let him: pleated safari shorts, dress shirt, leather shoes with argyle socks. Hemingway resorted to much the same; a bystander might've thought he'd devoted no time to his funeral attire whatsoever. But he did, and that was maddening to him. At least it seemed so until Patrick started talking books on the walk over to the cemetery.

"Didja hear? Faulkner just got the Pulitzer." Patrick just putting a lit match to it, that's all. Around them the palm and beech shadows kept the gardens and the sidewalks cool.

"Christ!" Hemingway sputtered on reflex. "He must've finally written something someone could understand."

"It was for *A Fable.*"

"Didn't read it."

"I thought it was quite remarkable."

Hemingway gave his son an eyebrow raised to the heavens.

"Did you understand it?"

"Believe it or not."

"When they gave me one of those awards last year, nobody had to ask if anyone could understand the damn book."

"*Old Man was* pretty simple."

Hemingway liked a good-natured taunting as much as anyone, but he still stopped and glared a moment.

"Is this the only entertainment you get? Working me up?"

"Not the only." Patrick smiled. They

walked. “Anyway, you won yours two years ago.”

“What? Yeah? Oh yeah. Who won last year?”

“Nobody.”

“What?! Why didn’t I know that? Where was I?”

“In Africa.”

“They didn’t give a Pulitzer last year? Why?”

“Nobody said. No good books, I guess.”

“No good books! In 1953? What the hell was I reading . . . That Nabokov book was new, that uh . . . *Pin.*”

“*Nin.* The *P* is silent.” Patrick packed that satisfaction away for a rainy day.

“Is it? Are you sure? I read that in Nairobi, didn’t finish it, though. I think the maid stole it.”

“That’s likely.”

“But it was a dilly. That crazy Russkie can write a fire.”

“Really?” Patrick never remembered hearing his father praise another writer, besides Flaubert and Chekhov, and only then when he’d been drinking Pernod by the case. “You must be getting old.”

“Well, I am, aren’t I.”

“You miss Cuba.”

“I’d be there if I did. It hasn’t been the

same there, this time of year, since the Dodgers stopped training in Havana. Used to drink and shoot with those fellas."

"Jackie Robinson, too?"

"No, not Robinson. He was having too much fun with the women, and I don't think he was a sportsman, generally."

"Hey, so, who looks good, Papa?"

"I could say the Dodgers. But that'll never happen."

The walk was short. The day was already growing hot enough for a pitcher of frozen booze and a book — maybe *The Custom of the Country* again, which Hemingway'd had a bookmark in since 1921. Can't — shit, that's in Cuba. He'd have to look at the shelves here, see what he left. Maybe *The Possessed.* That'll cut the sunshine.

"Do you realize the most obvious and useless entry in a dictionary is *dictionary?*" Patrick was saying.

"C'mon."

The cemetery smelled like tequila-spiked sweat and had the slightly drunken, dizzy-from-the-heat disorganization of tropical public places. If it was Billy Bolitho's task to keep it weeded and tended, then Billy was saving some money. In spots, the grass was as high as a teenage boy.

"Nice crowd," Patrick said. Hemingway

squinted in the sudden lack of shade.

True enough: there had to be twenty people standing in the stones, all of them either dressed up like professional mourners or suited up in a half-assed but earnest effort to appear solemn. Bolitho was there, in the same suit he's used for these things since 1944. Squiccarini, too, in his official black cotton and striped tie. Maria the sardonic flatfoot underling wasn't around, but five fishing buddies were: Jean Fumereaux, Guy Williams, Scotty M. (still, no one's pulled the last name out of Scotty, and wouldn't right up until G-men took him off the dock in 1961 and spirited him away), Angel "Rick" Villareal, and, of course, Joe Taurog, who almost unconsciously made sure there were two or three standing bodies between him and Squiccarini at all times, in case the cop decided to repay Joe's 1953 haymaker. Also, a waitress from Sloppy Joe's, Cuthbert's 275-pound landlady, and four complete strangers, one of which — a yacht-owning Cuban plantation owner named de Oliviera — Hemingway knew for certain didn't know Cuthbert as any more than a face in a bar mirror.

Who called all these people, he thought. One other stranger was a woman, Cuban also, who Hemingway noted immediately was the scene's obligatory Bruno, which was a private piece of nomenclature Hemingway used after seeing Alfred Hitchcock's *Strangers on a Train* a few years earlier in Miami, a movie in which Robert Walker's smiling sociopath Bruno stalks Farley Granger and, at a tennis match, is seen as the only person in the audience staring straight ahead, at his prey, instead of following the ball with his eyes. After that, a Bruno was that individual who sticks out, if you're paying attention, from the social web, unable to mask contexts or intentions that differ radically from those around him. During the film, sitting beside Mary, Hemingway remembered a Popular Front organizer in Spain who stood in the center of a heated rally — hundreds of faces upturned to the rostrum rabble-rousers — with his eyes level, scanning the edges of the crowd. Hemingway didn't think much of it then, but sure enough the guy turned out to be an Army mole, and the rally was soon thereafter attacked by guerrillas. Six people, including a nurse from Leeds that Hemingway liked enough to *not* sleep with her, were killed. That was Hemingway's first Bruno; there've been others.

This Cuban woman, tall and strong-boned and Indian-shawled in a formal, going-to-Mass kind of way, was this hot day's Bruno;

everyone else either looked genuinely solemn or faintly exasperated with the effort to fake it. She was *waiting,* and she had a fighter pilot's grip on her emotions, so there was no telling what she was waiting for. She could've been waiting, neurotically, for the whole ordeal to be over so she could privately explode in grief . . . *Unlikely,* Hemingway thought. She didn't seem the high-strung or troubled type. And everyone knew Cuthbert hadn't given anyone a reason to be terribly upset at his graveside, not for decades. She didn't take her eyes off the mahogany box, which was worth more than your average Cuban peasant earns in a year. If Peter wasn't already dead, Hemingway might've been convinced this woman was intent on killing him.

"Can't believe you're not late," was all Bolitho said, sweating like a banana picker.

"Hello to you, too, Billy," Patrick chimed in with an edge.

"How could I be late," Hemingway growled. "It's my funeral."

Everyone within earshot thought of a snappy riposte to this, but no one said a thing. Hemingway nodded to and handshook a few of the attendees, and then threw a nod at the reverend that Billy had called down from Dade, who began his eulogy.

Knowing nothing about Cuthbert, he kept it vague and simple. "Kind, generous, friendly . . . ," etcetera. Instantly, everyone was bored and tried to hide it by squinting up at the sun and thinking about how humid it was. And it was, the air rich with gluey moisture.

The Cuban woman didn't budge, and Hemingway kept the corner of his eye trained on her. Hemingway couldn't help it — he nudged Patrick, and then pointed his chin subtly at the woman.

"A Bruno," Patrick whispered immediately. "Hey, what happened here, anyway. With Cuthbert."

An hour later, he thinks to ask. Hemingway blinked slowly: *Tell you later.* The eulogy, rote and by formula, lasted eight minutes, but if you'd polled the crowd, they would've guessed that it was between thirty and forty minutes long. When it was over, they began to disperse. Hemingway walked slowly off, too, with Patrick, Jean, Captain Video and Rick Villareal, all the while keeping a bead on the Cuban. She took a few steps closer to the grave, knelt and appeared to pray.

"So, Captain, how's the case. It's been a day and a half." Hemingway said it without actually looking at Squiccarini.

The cop snorted. "Fucking novelist. What would *you* do."

"Jesus Christ. I'd trace the harpoon. You're such good for nothing."

"Harpoon?" Patrick piped up in alarm.

"What, you think that spike was registered somewhere?" Squiccarini whined.

"It's an antique!" Hemingway said. "It's not a common item, or didn't you even bother to find that out."

"No one's reported one missing, Papa."

"Cuthbert was killed with an antique harpoon?" Patrick couldn't get enough.

"What about Peter's digs."

"Nothing," Squiccarini said. "Like a junkie's room. No address book full of mysterious initials and dates and meeting places."

Hemingway looked toward the Cuban woman again. She was standing now, and walking toward them, to the exit.

"What about Cuthbert's whereabouts last week, or five days ago?"

"No ideas. We've talked to people."

"Just here, downtown, right? C'mon, Vinnie. What about up the islands? What about in Cuba?"

"You've got to be fucking kidding."

"That's probably where he'd been." The Cuban woman walked right by, glancing into Hemingway's eyes, absolutely without the minutest glimmer of an expression on her face.

"Whatever you say. We have no leads, and we cannot go spend weeks interviewing Cuban gangsters because of Peter Cuthbert. We can't even find any next of kin."

"That's because his name isn't Cuthbert, jack-off."

Squiccarini eyed him. Hemingway turned to see the Cuban woman exit to the street, and then saw her do the most remarkable thing: she lifted a small camera to her half-lidded eye and took a picture of the five men standing in the sunshine. Hemingway's jaw dropped open and the woman hustled out of view.

"That woman just took our picture . . ."

"The Bruno?" Patrick asked.

"What woman?" Squiccarini.

"Who's Bruno?" Rick Villareal muttered.

"You're some damn cop, Vinnie." Hemingway took a step toward the exit.

"She's probably your biggest fan, Hemingway. Go give her an autograph."

Hemingway stormed out onto Angela Street as best he could with a cast and a cane, and saw the mystery woman already a block away, walking quickly.

"Patrick! Go follow her!"

"What if I catch her?" Everyone was in the street now.

"Ask her How Much They'll Pay to Find Out Where It Is."

Patrick broke into a bolt.

"Where what is?" Squiccarini shook his head.

"Who knows. But this is about something that somebody's trying to sell for a crapload of money. I can smell that much."

"Hemingway, you don't know what the fuck you're doing."

"Maybe. But I'm *doing* something."

6

Patrick did catch that Cuban woman — or, rather, two blocks from the cemetery gates, he ran around her, turned to her with a practiced smile, and asked, "*Hola,* can I take *your* picture?"

She tried to dodge him, never meeting his eye. "*Señora,* please, I have a message from Peter."

She stopped but did not look convinced.

"No, you don't."

"He said long ago, 'If you see a beautiful Cuban woman by my graveside, buy her a strong drink. She deserves it.' "

"You are a jackass." Her accent was sharp, but her English was cool and clear.

"That's no distinction around here."

"You are right about that, at least."

"OK, honestly, I'm supposed to ask you How Much They'll Pay."

"For what? Who's 'they'?"

"You know."

"No, I do not. I'm just *una turista.*"

Patrick's turn. "*Señora,* you couldn't pass for a tourist in Key West with a thirty-ounce rum drink in your hand, a boat-shaped hat on your head and a map stuck in your belt. You are something else: someone with business, a proxy for something or other, a messenger, a widow with a vendetta — I have no goddamn idea. But you are no tourist."

"Not all tourists are like American tourists." Now she smiled. She liked Patrick.

"Yeah, some pray inexpressively at local funerals and then take pictures in cemeteries, after a man who's been mysteriously murdered has just been put in the ground."

"Murdered?" She rolled the *r*s and the *d*s together like glass marbles in her mouth, a little melodramatically, Patrick thought.

"Uh-huh. I bet it's the first you've heard of it."

"Young man, who are you, anyway?"

"Not telling. You first."

The woman shook her head and seemed to think she could just walk away. Patrick was on her like a hungry salesman.

"Alright! My name is Patrick. You?"

". . ."

"I can tell you one thing, you're a Bruno. Ever see *Strangers on a Train*?"

She nodded. "I love Farley Granger. So,

what, I'm like that Bruno guy, a psychopath, then?"

Her English was good enough for *psychopath.* "No, no, that's not what I mean, no, it's just, uh, in the context. . . . Sometimes, there's —"

"Patrick, you go tell your people you learned nothing, that I was just an old Matanzas whore who flirted with you and who knew nothing."

"But you knew Peter."

"Not really."

"You knew his name."

"Shut up."

"Give me your camera."

"What camera? I don't have a camera."

"We all saw you."

"Why don't you frisk me, gringo, in front of all these people?"

Patrick glanced around. The street was fairly thick with passersby. "I could have you arrested. Several of the men back there were policemen, and as you probably know it's not difficult to get them to lock up peasants and Indians, and then conveniently forget why."

"Go ahead. With the fuss I'll kick up, right here in front of these people, your father will end up on the front page of the *Miami Herald.* He raped me, for one thing. Five times. So did you."

"C'mon."

"Try me. See how it reads."

Patrick paused. He couldn't touch her, couldn't frisk her, couldn't out-talk her. Being his father's son, he was quickly developing a crush on her. The morning sun began to blister on their skin.

"Alright. I'm just looking for a number. Peter left that part out."

"So full of shit. I'll say this much: you're better off not knowing." And she walked. Patrick had used up everything he could think of to say to stop her.

The school of mourners gravitated to Sloppy Joe's by instinct, ate a long table's lunch of conch fritters and purple tomatoes in the porch shade, and spent the afternoon running up a monstrous bar tab Hemingway was eventually expected to pay. He paid it in the end and did not grumble. They drank Pernod, English gin, Milwaukee beer, tequila, and Scotch blend and soda. Bolitho stayed behind at the graveyard, but Squiccarini saw no reason to favor duty over booze and came. Patrick went back to the house in a suddenly descended jetlag swoon. Of the fishermen, only Rick and Scotty M. realized an entire day of free drinking was in the offing and came along. The next day, 285-pound Cajun shark hunter Jean Fumereaux fell into a daylong black mood of enraged disappointment because he'd unthinkingly decided to clean his boat instead.

"I know Peter's real name," Rick said five or so hours into this debauch, gazing dreamily at the beach-hut-and-fishing-canoe sketch on the bottle of San Luispo tequila and wondering in a slurry way why his life, which largely consisted of beach huts (a bungalow, anyway), palm trees, fishing boats, agave worms and sunsets, hadn't seemed to coalesce into the kind of lazy paradise the picture suggested. Maybe it had something to do with his not having had sex in nineteen months, or having to work fourteen-hour days in season in order to pay his meager rent, which was in arrears a few grand as it was. "It's Kovarick. It was Kovarick. Kovarisky. Kavinsky. Ka . . ."

"Rick, hump off," Hemingway said. "You've been drinking like a Scottish widower. What you don't know."

"And Vincenzo, that was his first name."

"That's *my* first name," Squiccarini said, at which point Rick couldn't buy attention with a yard and a half.

"There's a book, in there, dontcha think, Papa, about Peter."

"C'mon, Scotty."

"You know, a lost guy under a fake name hiding out from civilization at Mile Zero . . ."

"That's you, Scotty." Squiccarini.

"Yeah, but it was Peter, too. What was his story? What was he running from?"

"C'mon." Hemingway was shaving the white meat from inside a coconut shard into a short glass of tequila, so it looked like tiny iceberg hunks floating in oily water.

"Coulda asked that right to him when he was alive," Rick croaked.

"He wouldn't've answered, he *couldn't've* answered, or else he'd spoil his own story." Scotty's imagination was beginning to hyperventilate. "Dontcha see? You gotta write it! It's only a question you can ask when he's dead, when the mystery grows . . . exponentially." Squiccarini's eyebrows went up, as they tended to when a flat-out souse pronounced a five-syllable word clearly.

"C'mon." Hemingway, rousing, his beard flecked with coconut, his famous Santa Claus eyes virtually lost in the red inflammation of his face. "I'm not talking stories with you muttonheads. I'm in the middle of something. Scotty, *you* write it. I promise, I'll get it under an editor's nose at Scribner's."

"Me? I can barely fill out a check."

"Anyway, Peter's story ain't no story — it's just bad luck and mistakes and hurt feelings and fear."

"That's a story."

"Shaddap. You guys should be talking about how he died — there's a half-sour pickle for you."

"Poor guy."

"We've been there and back," Squiccarini said, struggling for a chestful of air over far too much beer. "It's a crazy thing. But just a bit of dockside violence, it happens. Maybe not like that, not often, but still. So, what can we do? Awful way to die."

"If that's how he died," Hemingway said. "What if: not. What if he was blasted open with that fucking thing to obscure the real deal. What if it's some kind of absurd cover-up."

"Excuse me . . . Papa?"

Hemingway turned. A woman, a tourist, had silently infiltrated the four men's invisibly but unmistakably demarcated social zone before anyone noticed or had the foresight to hurl a drink at her before she got too close. Before she called him *Papa.*

"You *are* Ernest Hemingway. . . . I knew it! It's so fantastic to come here, after all I've read — read all of your books — and find you here, just like in *Life* magazine! Charlotte!"

The men's reactive reflexes were for shit by this point. They froze like point men in a war, having just heard something suspicious in the night. Rick was actually crouching, as if listening for distant rifle clicks. Charlotte, a rotund redhead who was a bit more reticent than the first woman, joined them, flush with celebrity lust. "Oh my God, and he's drunk, too!"

Luckily, Hemingway couldn't obey his instincts because the drinking had coated his nerve endings in shoe-sole rubber and had slowed him down generally to the thoughtful, blank-eyed pace of a chameleon reaching for a branch. So he turned and smiled obscenely, without moving his glass from his mouth.

"Can we have your autograph? If it's not any trouble!"

Trouble isn't what witnesses called it later, but that may be because they, most of them, lived in Key West and were as surprised by Ernest Hemingway creating a scene in a bar as a pasture cow is by passing cars.

First he boomed, "Can't without talking to my agent first! Bob?" This to Scotty, who was caught speechless.

Then: "I'll sign only on your asses, in

grenadine! Barkeep!" McCaffrey the bartender had already stationed himself at the far end of the bar, and there he stayed, looking grim.

Finally: "Look, ladies, we're mourning the death of a compadre here tonight —"

"Still afternoon," Squiccarini couldn't help but say.

"— and there will be no traffic in cheap celebrity or token-taking or ass-kissing or low-down tourist crap whatsoever, no pictures, no signings, no kissing of ugly babies. You *can,* however, drink with us. Take a bumper for the poor sonofabitch. You up to it?"

"Why of course," the first woman said gravely.

"McCaffrey, Bartolo for the ladies."

"Who died?" Charlotte.

"Einstein. The old bastard."

"He did?!" The first, nameless woman was horrified. "You go on vacation, and you miss all the news."

The men all nodded solemnly. McCaffrey poured the two double shots of grappa, which none of the men, not if they're standing for a good bit of drink, would touch.

The women hoisted the tiny glasses with earnest importance and knocked the liquor back without caution. The first woman gagged, sputtered, spit out the grappa in an angry spew on the sawdust floor, and ran out to the street. Retching. Charlotte, on the other hand, smacked her lips, and looked Hemingway in the eye with a calm that deliberately avoided displaying outrage but of course has the effect of displaying outrage rather incisively. "That was a mean trick," she said evenly. "You should be ashamed of yourself."

"I have been, baby, long before you showed up."

By dusk they were on the docks. Hemingway was saying something about how Cuthbert died for their sins, their laziness and affluence and the whole shit-storm society, set up so as to reward lawyers and publicists but not real men who just want to be left alone to work and take fish from the sea.

"I wonder what really happened." Scotty M. said it for the fifth time in an hour.

"Oh, Peter probably got mixed up with some badasses from somewhere," Hemingway said. "Cubans or Colombians or Nazis or Klansmen or something."

"I know his name. Kerouac." Rick was trying to skip clam shells on the water, but because he wasn't water-level, they just plopped.

"Rick, we know."

"And I know where his second boat is anchored."

"His what?"

"His second boat. The one he didn't tell everyone about."

"What are you talking about?" Squiccarini wasn't even listening, but Hemingway was.

" 'On the *Em,*' he said. That's how he said it."

"The what?"

"The *Em.* Twenty-five minutes or so north, north-northwest, off Little Mullet, he said."

"That's the name, the *Em — Emily?* North what?"

"Off Little Mullet. I think. And his name was definitely Kovarick."

7

The next morning, the hangover wasn't any nastier or any more gentle than usual, and Hemingway battled it appropriately with aspirin, chili peppers, bacon, eye drops and orange juice with a few slugs of gin stirred in. After he'd showered and scrubbed the asphalt off his teeth, he felt ready to wrestle the world. He wasn't ready, however, for Patrick, who had slept for fourteen hours and was bounding about the house like a housecat that had just had the bowel movement of its life. Whatever excess élan Hemingway might've felt was dissipated by Patrick's irritating ebullience.

Maybe it wasn't élan that was moving him, in any case, so much as motivation, for Hemingway awoke with a headful of questions about Cuthbert's death, and a set of fact-finding tasks poised for implementation. It was clear that if he wasn't going to do something, *something,* nobody would, and better than that, there were some things he *could* do. Or so he thought. This is better than reading that Christie dame, or Simenon, he thought. This is real, and vital, and heroic, and goddamned *fun.* If *fun* was the word. Yeah, sure, why not: fun. It was, for that morning at least, more fun than writing. Or hunting. Or fucking.

More *fun* than writing? "Fun"? Writing. *It was already midnight when Cuthbert found the telephone on the dock.* No. *Midnight already, and Cuthbert found the dock phone. . . . It was late, but Cuthbert found the phone by the dockside.* Ach.

Patrick was done with breakfast, of course, and was out in the back garden, doing chin-ups on the high bar Hemingway put there in 1939 and had scarcely looked at since.

"Don't hurt yourself." Hemingway with a second juice in his hand, squinting in the morning shade, which dappled in a way that could make you dream about dreaming of spring. He was joking, but exercise like that did remind him of nothing but pain.

"C'mon, Pop, it's not as if I'm leaping onto it from the roof and tearing branches off as I fall."

"Stop it. Mouse, we've got work to do."

"Well, I'm leaving." He dropped down, sweating.

"You're not leaving yet. I mean today. We've got to look into Peter."

"Yeah? OK, but why, exactly?"

"Why? Because Peter was a friend, who never hurt anyone. That's not enough for you?"

"We're not talking about me. Sure, it's enough, for all I can do about it all. It reeks of a dubious quest for justice — you're going to find out that he fell on that torpedo, or something. Something stupid and ordinary."

"Hardly ordinary."

"But stupid. I'll betcha."

"That'd be alright with me. If that's what it is"

"So, where do we begin? I take it Vinnie has done nothing."

"Less than that. First, we try to find about that harpoon. Whaling nuts, antique people, they keep records."

"Let me go put on my monocle."

The Hemingway men were soon hammering on the door of the lighthouse on the end of Whitehead Street, true American Mile Zero, rousing Jack Scatzberg, the keeper since 1931. Like virtually anyone who decides to sequester themselves in a lighthouse, Jack was a chipper recluse with obsessive interests and a ballooned notion of his responsibilities, many of which he adopted himself rather than see them go undone. Because of this, Hemingway — who had always felt that the largest reason why he'd written particular books was because no one else was going to write them — had always liked the obsessive old coot, empathized with him, even if conversations with him could quickly become as pleasurable as urological exams. Jack's self-created duties included cataloging the varietals of Key West seaweed (thirty-six species, so far, though the marine lab at the naval yards on Fleming Key Road said there were only seven), documenting the tides in order to prove the uselessness of the *Farmer's Almanac* as well as Florida's few fishing industry tabloids, stuffing various neighbors' mailboxes with prints he made from conch shells and squid ink because "people get such boring mail," and pacing along Flagler Avenue watching for tourists' station wagons, quickly making a note of the car's make and color and then reporting this to Keith Karcher, a bartender at the Dogfish Pantry on Atlantic Boulevard, who couldn't have cared less. But being bookish in a very particularized way, Jack was a caretaker of nautical history, with a front-of-the-brain working knowledge of every sunken shipwreck, every major storm to hit Key West since 1622 (when the Spanish *Terra Firma* fleet was hit by a hurricane off the Dry Tortugas and sank like rocks), every market price a grouper or stone crab was ever sold at in his lifetime, and every progressive stage of whaling and fishing technology going back at least a century.

Squiccarini probably didn't know that Jack knew much of anything besides the shape of the wood paneling on the side of a Buick Roadmaster spotted at three hundred yards. But Hemingway, who'd had his share of headaches listening to Jack prattle on about Spanish galleons and conch reproduction, knew that he might be the only man in the state who'd know where a fifty-year-old cannon harpoon might have come from.

"Have no fucking idea," Jack said, wrapping himself in a terry-cloth robe that smelled of shrimp.

In Jack's kitchen. "I'll get coffee," he said. Jack's age had more to do with seaside weathering than time; his skin was brown and creased a thousand ways like a mummy's, but whether he was fifty or eighty no one could say. Lighthouse life both wears on the body and preserves it, it would appear.

"Jack, you're the only one. It doesn't happen every day. You don't see these things outside of museums."

"Sure you do. The bays are filled with them. This one have rust? Was it weathered?"

"No, it was aged, but it wasn't dug up from the harbor. It looked like an antique, like it'd been wiped down every now and then."

"Fifty-year-old harpoons aren't necessarily antiques. You go back to 1875, or early 1800s, there you have real weapons, made with care, objects that speak of another day and age, when it *mattered,* aerodynamically, how well-crafted your spearhead was . . . the Spanish blades, the Bahamian harpoons of the 1820s with walnut handles —"

"So they're not worth anything?"

"What's worth? Some antiquers, daytrippers from Naples, might pay for them. Who knows."

"Jack. Think. Who would have something like this laying around?"

"I'm telling you, Papa, could be anybody. Anybody with a granddad who was a whaler, or a tackle seller, or just a crazy collector. Anybody with a shed."

"They're not that common."

"I didn't say they were. I just said it *could* be anybody. I'm looking at the question in

Cartesian terms. Do I know what people have in their garages under tarps and chipped garden statuary and rotten fishing nets? I have no reason to think this thing is a common item, but I have no real reason to believe otherwise, either. And neither do you."

His head in his hand, Hemingway was beginning to regret knocking on the old man's door. Patrick was reading old newspaper front pages pinned to the wall.

"OK. But how many have you seen?"

"A few, but not for at least twenty years and none ever on this island."

"So . . . Cartesianally speaking, who'd be the most likely candidate?"

"Somebody wealthy. No one else would care."

"Well, looks like I might've spent the morning better trying to get Marisol's panties off," Patrick said.

"You'd've gotten nowhere. But now what."

"Maybe we should find out what Peter was doing that day."

"Who're you going to ask? Nobody pays attention to anyone's business down here. Except mine. I think we first have to find that second boat. Rick Villareal told us where."

"Oh-boy. Rick said this yesterday? He could've been having an agave hallucination. Suddenly, this sounds a lot less fun."

"It's a lead, as they say. Shut yer trap and take a ride."

Since Hemingway's boat was in Cuba, he decided to call Rick and use his skiff, knowing that the fallout of a day's drinking would've kept him in bed and off the ocean until the midday tide, which meant off for the whole day. Rick wheezed and grumbled on the phone but gave in quickly.

At the dock, he was already straightening up his boat — piling the nets and traps in one corner of the deck — when the Hemingways showed up.

"Y'know, Papa, you're going to have to drive. I'm not sure I'm done throwin' up just yet." He looked gray, no question.

"OK, Rick," Patrick said soothingly. "But you have to stay conscious."

Rick stopped, looked up from unleashing the dock ropes from his cleats. "Why?"

"So you can show us where that boat is," Hemingway chirped. "Peter's boat."

"His boat's lashed up right over there." Pointing south, through masts.

"His *other* boat. Remember?"

"No."

Patrick clapped his hand over his mouth

and turned red.

"You said you knew where a second boat was anchored. West of . . . some shit or another."

"Nope. When'd I say this?"

"Last night, on the docks, you stupid greaseball!"

"Last thing I remember was that lady spitting on the floor."

The three of them stood, simmering and choking and shrugging. Rick was still holding the rope, hanging on to the shore.

"You wanna go out anyway?"

Rick fell asleep on his boat all the same. The Hemingway men walked southeast, away from the water. They would, it was decided, next try to talk to Pedra Whatever Her Name Was, a Mexican woman who lived on Sunset Drive with six other Mexicans, and whom, Hemingway alone knew, Peter visited now and then.

8

Pedra Whatever Her Name Was was not a pleasant woman, not welcoming nor tolerant nor patient nor charitable. Too sexy than was seemly for her age — fifty if she was a day, Patrick thought, but years can accumulate slowly on Mexican women who don't farm, so a closer guess would be fifty-seven or fifty-eight — she had all the charm of a coastline boulder. It took her eight whole minutes to come to the door, and then she spoke to the Hemingways through a crack a half-inch wide. The men stood their ground, and eventually she opened the door for them and took a single step back, by way of inviting them in.

Hemingway thought she was a regal beast; he understood why Peter came to her. There wouldn't be a lot of pesky conversation, for one thing. And she could probably screw a man's entire head of hair right out of its roots.

He had begun, outside, by asking her about Peter — facts, details, places — and got nowhere. Half the time she just stared mutely back, but with a mean squint. He changed tones, as if he'd reached an emotional moment.

"*Señora,* why did you not come to the service yesterday?"

Shoulders slumped — she did not like the question. At least she responded.

"*Señor,* no one needed me there."

"I was looking for you. I know that Peter came to you. It was important for him to come to you, sometimes."

"I prayed, in my own way."

"Of course you did."

She narrowed her eyes again. "Shouldn't you be writing or something?"

Whatta bitch. Nobody understands that when you walk around, talk to people, drink in a bar, cast a boat out, you're always writing the whole time. What was that Thurber anecdote, his wife barking at him as he daydreamed at dinner: *No writing at the table!* Hemingway was, in fact, working on something at home, a few things, stories he hadn't now looked at for a week because all of these fucking distractions and because, honestly, he was getting nowhere with any of them. There was that lumbering thing about last year's safari, but the story was shaped like a drunken camel's walk up a dune. Another thing he'd written a few lines of was about a Pinkerton in Savannah; another was about John Brown. There were also notes and (mostly unfinished) outlines about Normandy, a manhunt in Madagascar, the making of *The African Queen* and what a lot of bullshit it was despite Bogart being there, two Russian spies falling in love with a Cuban girl, a Danish woman farming coffee in Kenya (based on Karen Blixen, but in the story she'd be an abortionist running away from the law back home), the Battle of San Pietro, cockfighting in Havana, an Alexandrian executioner guiltily unable to spend the money he's paid, a soldier returning from the liberation of Treblinka to Alabama segregation, a Congolese gorilla poacher lost in the jungle, and a Manhattan secretary during the war forced to buy and sell black market prosthetics. Or something like that. There were also, strewn around on his desk, hints of a wartime love story between an AWOL American and a German widow on the Polish border, a ghost story — holy mackerel — set in the French trenches of WWI, a Chicago-based reworking of Gorky's *The Lower Depths* (in fact, that note in its entirety read "rework Lower

Depths, in Chicago") and a something about the Iditarod.

Hemingway suddenly had a headful of unwritten fiction buzzing in his ears; all he wanted to do was retreat from this loathsome woman's doorstep and hightail it back into that tailored cocoon he loved so well, of clear liquor and cool tile and wicker chairs and compliant servants and white paper and a pen and a typewriter and time, time, time to be left alone and blissful with stories that don't exist yet, but then do. There, in that space, you could ignore not only the cataract of everyday crap that threatens to burst through your door like firehose water, but also the facts of being an author — publishing, talking with agents and editors and journalists, worrying about sales and reviews and reputation, wondering if in fact you were washed up, an orca gasping on an empty beach, with no way to regain your grip on whatever it was you once had firm in your fist. That stuff was hell, but the mornings and afternoons alone with paper, that was grand. Even when nothing much happened. Hemingway always seemed distracted — even to himself — because wherever he was, he wanted to get back there. But right now, he was positively pining for it, like an opium eater stuck in a line at Town Hall.

The face-off in Pedra's entryway didn't last forever. Eventually, the Hemingways were inside her cramped, damp stucco hacienda, anole lizards flying like roaches. No place to sit, and no lights. A few more volleys about Peter and the funeral, and Hemingway decided in a new sweat that he couldn't stand much more of this hoary interrogation routine.

"*Señora,* I'm trying to find out how Peter died."

"Who the murderer is."

"Yes."

"Why? Isn't it probably just a . . . dock bum or *borracho?*"

Cuthbert knew the shadow was no one he knew. Cuthbert didn't know the man, he could tell that from the shadow. Cuthbert —

"No, it probably isn't."

"No?"

"No. The cops aren't pursuing it, the weapon is a freak, and Peter was too secretive. No. Not probably."

"So, you are the hero, then? You will solve the mystery? You will do right. Bring justice."

Hemingway bristled. The woman didn't seem to care about anything but her own opportunities to make life tough for everybody else. “Don’t worry about me. Tell me about Peter.”

“Worry about you? What’s to worry, Mr. Bestseller.” She said this with a tripled-up *l* that sounded like a bird call. Patrick looked around wearily again for someplace to sit.

“Peter.”

“Fuck Peter!” she barked suddenly. “He never so much as brought me a dollar or a fish or a bottle of *cerveza.* He gave me nothing. He’d come, screw me, talk till I couldn’t stand him no more, breathe on me like a horse, and then leave. I don’t know anything about him.”

“What’d he talk about?”

“Oh, fuck all, boats, business shit. Dreams. You.”

“Business?”

“Yes. Deals. I never believed any of it.”

“Smuggling?”

Pedra shut up. Then, “Sure. So what.”

“Names, *señora.* Anything.”

“Oh yeah? Castro and Guevara. You like?”

A sigh.

“Anyone else?”

She shrugged, getting tired herself.

“Sure, what . . . Galko . . . ?”

“Galko? Ferenc Galko?”

“*Si.* So?”

9

The day was overdue for food and drink, and so, after putting a call into the Harvey Government Office over on Truman and asking about a boat registered as the *Emma* or *Emily* or *Emilsen* or *Emmet,* and coming up zilch, the men sat at a table outside a café on Seminary Street, ordered a martini pitcher, rolls, boiled shrimp and steamed asparagus. The shrimp were undercooked, which was fine, and boiled with cloves, which was better. The martinis were extraordinarily cold.

"Mom would've liked this, you on a crusade."

"No, she wouldn't've. She'd have been worried there'd be danger."

"Naw. She would've thought it was all chasing windmills. But she would've liked to see you committed to it, for a friend's sake."

"Nuts."

A lot he didn't know, Hemingway thought, and a lot she never knew, about commitment and friendship and crusades. There was that story, about José Robles Pazos, that will remain untold.

"Martha, on the other hand, would've been beating out a path in front of you, spyglass to the ground."

Hemingway didn't love lining up the wives and comparing their stats like pitchers, and Patrick did. The molten core of fondness, regret and guilt he cached away in his chest for each of them was a private matter. So Hemingway snorted. "What do *you* think?" Without lifting his eyes from the table.

"It's not windmills," Patrick said. "But I'm not sure it's anything else. Who's Galko?"

"A gangster. Hungarian. Made a fortune selling munitions to the Communists during the war. Now, he makes a new fortune every day just taking his morning crap. Lives in Miami, but he owns the Audubon House, too."

"That place is a dump."

"I think he thinks it gives him a low profile. With a fleet of pink Isottas parked out front."

"He should fix it up. It's the Audubon House."

"He's got ten other houses. That's what Captain Video says."

"What's your next move?"

"My? Where are you going?"

"I'm leaving. Going to New York."

"Why?"

"None of your beeswax. Investors, meetings. I need capital."

"Shit, I was having fun with you here, Mouse."

"Is that right? You didn't look like you were enjoying yourself."

"You know I never look that way. But most of the time I am."

"Even when you're pissed at the world."

"Especially then."

They ordered more shrimp.

"Talk about books some more, Pat."

"Yeah? What. I reread *A Farewell to Arms* in February."

"Yeah? Why, you heard Selznick's making another movie out of it?"

"Well, not really, but yeah, Mary said that."

"And."

"What the fuck is it with that book."

"Jesus Christ. You want me to explain it?"

"The distance there . . . It's like trying to watch somebody through a soaped window. Yeah. Go ahead, explain it."

"Lies. Lying to yourself at wartime."

"That's it?"

"That's it. And eating and drinking and fucking. And reading. Words. Other people. And lying."

"Oh. But not about love."

"God, no."

"I see."

"You know, I meant talk about somebody else's books."

Patrick took a cab to the mainland and Hemingway, tired of humping along with his cane, took the minute-and-a-half cab ride back to the house. His ankle was starting to ache in its itchy darkness. He paid the driver with the quarters in his pocket, got out.

There was Tcheon, the secretive, burn-scarred dick of undetermined Eurasian blood, sitting on the front step. He was usually, as he was when Hemingway last saw him in the Key's ersatz morgue, a background character, deliberately keeping to the visual margins of whoever's talking, so it was notable that here he was suddenly situated on Hemingway's stoop, prominently and alone and looking for confrontation, smoking, sheathed in Panama hat, sunglasses and kerchief around his neck, as if he were a movie star hoping not to get recognized shopping in Macy's but in fact intending to be conspicuous. Hemingway hobbled up to him and past him.

"Hey Papa," the cop drawled, his accent today a snappy but vague admixture of Indochinese and Russian. He stood up. "A word, big sir. For your own protection."

The door was open, Hemingway turned. He was inside but not far enough inside to implicitly allow the cagey dick to step inside, too. So the man stood outside.

"My protection?"

"Yes sir. We don't want to see you get hurt. Doing something other than writing and fishing and keeping the island's bars in the black."

Hemingway looked at him — it was like looking at a basilisk. "I'm touched. Go away."

"What I don't understand," Tcheon began, shifting his weight, gesticulating a little, suggesting everyone should brace for a smidgeon of theatrics, "is not that you suspect there's some solvable fishy business going on around your friend Cuthbert's death — I mean, I understand that this is something you think, everyone knows it, and I understand why. That's not the question, the question is why you think that whatever fishy business it is, it is on one hand unusual fishy business, out of the ordinary fishy business, when down here, as you well know, everyone's got little fishy . . . things. Shadiness. Off the books. It's the way things are here, right? On the other hand, or at the same time, what I don't understand equally as well, or equally not as well, is why you do not realize that whatever . . . thing it is that Cuthbert got fooling around in, or with, that it, because it is shady or fishy or what have you, it is dangerous. Maybe to you. These things I don't get. These are things you should know. But you don't seem to know them. You don't kick sleeping dogs, Mr. Hemingway. Right? You were there in the boat when Jean Fumereaux strangled Alejandro Echevarria in 1938, I'm told. And still it is a secret, an unsolved case. You did nothing. Is my information wrong?"

It wasn't; Squiccarini was in that boat, too. Vinnie was a flagrantly corrupt Coast Guardsman then, paying off family debts by running rum, while Jean Fumereaux was exactly what he is now — a genial mountain of a Louisianan fisherman who looks for shit from no man and takes just as little. Echevarria was a nasty Puerto Rican thief who'd pulled a snubnose out of his pants and stuck it up Squiccarini's nose, hollering macho bullshit. Hemingway was drunk and sleeping in the hold. Later, Fumereaux said it was a smuggling argument and that he didn't like guns and didn't like Echevarria and simply put him into a headlock Fumereaux had learned wrestling on a New Orleans orphanage team, and the guy's necked snapped. Before Hemingway woke up, the two standing men had chummed the water with trash fish, waited for the bull sharks to come, and then slipped Echevarria over to them. Fumereaux and Squiccarini have had a quiet bond ever since, naturally, but they've avoided each other in public.

"I don't think you're even a real cop," Hemingway growled. "What kind of policeman walks around saying shit like this? You ask Captain Video why that was different. Anyway, he can hardly threaten me with that."

"Nobody's threatening. But if the Captain might get indicted, your name would be in every newspaper in the world."

"You wormy little blackmailer. I oughta beat you with an axe handle. The problem with your plan is that you don't know anything about the newspapers of the world or what people think. Let that old story out. You'd be selling a half-million books for me."

"Nobody's threatening. I'm just asking, why you're kicking this sleeping dog this time."

"Because I fucking want to," his face reddening, his body moving an inch closer, "and I'll be goddamned if I'm going to explain myself to an oily little turd like you. But now that I know for sure that there is a sleeping dog, I'm gonna kick the fucker good."

Tcheon took two quick steps through the doorframe and suddenly there was a revolver in his hand, a Smith & Wesson J frame, rising up in a half second to Hemingway's eye level. Hemingway took a step back, a small step but a step, which germinated a sprout of shame he was instantly determined to crush, and soon, come hell or high water.

"You have a wife, Hemingway, all by herself down there in Havana."

"You can't touch her. I *own* Havana."

"You are its privileged guest, Papa, for now. But things will change. Your connections could disappear in a gunshot, and your house burned to the ground. Your wife tossed into a pit."

"Don't sell me that Communist crap."

"I'll say it again, more clearly: you're not too big to kill. There are men here that are too big to kill. You're not among them. You're just a *writer.*"

Hemingway, without moving his shoulders or face, swung his walking stick up from the floor and nailed the cop between the legs, in a movement as decisive as a baseball player whacking a soft pitch. Tcheon crumbled, Hemingway grabbed the gun and tossed it skidding across the tile behind him. He hit Tcheon once in the left ear, a full hook, and the cop's head snapped over and smacked against the wall by the door jamb, leaving a dent in the plaster.

Hemingway dropped to his knees, quickly thudded a right knee on the man's chest, and grabbed his hair with the left hand, pounding the policeman's face with the right. When the skin on Hemingway's knuckles began to break and bleed, he stopped, bent the man facedown by his neck, pulled his left arm down and behind his back, and pulled it up to the nape until it broke. The sound reminded Marisol, who was the first of the house staff to show up in the foyer, of a carriage axle snapping in a pothole.

"Point a gun at me," Hemingway said, getting up, holding his back. "Jesus Christ. Marisol? Have Eduardo pull him out to the curb and call him a cab. Give the cabbie five bucks. I'd like beer, very cold, and tortillas on the back deck, please."

10

It was about at this time, when Hemingway tried to vent his system of adrenaline by calmly drinking beer under the whispering palms in his own backyard, that he caught the smell of disaster wafting in. Tcheon's visit had only told him so much about the Cuthbert Affair: that Tcheon was a stooge, and that there was wealth and power steam-rolling along behind the scenes, something Jack Scatzberg had already said, in his mad-dening way. This wasn't news, really, to Hemingway; he'd whiffed it in the grave-yard.

No, the scent of disaster was Hemingway's own, because on one hand he knew that he should matter-of-factly pack up and go home to Mary. Bury Peter, get done mixing it up with the local rats, call it a week. On the other, he knew that because somebody leveled a gun at his septum, he would have to ride the mystery train to its last stop. He couldn't walk away, his ego and sandlot pride wouldn't *let* him walk away, although he knew it was the only sensible thing to do. And how, he thought, can you possibly imagine a scenario with these ingredients that isn't a catastrophe?

The beer was, in fact, ice cold, and the fierce fusion between alcohol and frigid carbonated bite exclusive to decent beer — in this case, good Mexican beer, none of that St. Louis shit — began to mollify his overworked system. The beers disappeared easily, like stupid soldiers into the battle, and soon enough Hemingway was calm and emboldened enough to want to talk to Squiccarini. But he couldn't — he got some paper and a pencil. *The boats that brought opium in from Guanabacoa came drifting in from the south channel before dawn, and Cuthbert knew —.* Hmm. *The man waited on the dark dock. No one knew his real name, or asked. The Mexicans called him Orleanos because they thought he was Cajun. He wasn't.* Paper crumbled, thrown. *To the white men in the waterside business and to the captains he was just Jake — nothing more. He had, of course, another name, but he was anxious that it should not be pronounced.* Wait, that's *Lord Jim.*

There was no focusing. Time for Captain Video.

"When the fuck are they going to fix the phone wires!" he bellowed into the house.

"Yesterday," one of the staff answered.

Cesar, the Cuban cook, brought the phone out to the spot in the shade.

"Vinnie?"

"Papa. I was just going to call you. What happened."

"As if you didn't know."

"What, Tcheon questioned you, you lost your temper. Been drinking all day, right?"

"I owe you a few broken teeth, chum. No. He threatened me, and Mary, and then stuffed his revolver in my face."

"You're kidding."

"No. I still have the gun. I don't think I'm giving it back."

"I have no idea what to say."

"Where'd you dig him up from, anyway."

"He's F.B.I. Assigned, not my choice."

"By Hoover."

"Somebody. Don't tell me you've got bad business with Hoover."

"You would've heard about it if I did."

"Suppose. But if he threatened you, he's also a perfect idiot, and tied in and dirty."

"That seems to be it."

"Look, I apologize, Papa, for whatever

good it'll do. He was not on police business when he went to your house."

"I know. But tied into what?"

"Who knows."

"Don't give me that lazy-dick shit, Vinnie, that asshole's broken arm is proof that Cuthbert's death is . . . what, part of a bigger criminal whatever-it-is."

"Maybe. It could just be proof of what a dick you are. But anyway I don't have the resources to pursue it, you know that. And what if I did? It'd be arms or opium or some other smuggling deal, and I already have sixteen cases just like that on my desk right now, from the last four months alone. A few bodies, too, and a few disappearances. There's no shortage of this kind of crap."

"And."

"And, that's right, there are quite possibly feds or Coast Guardsmen or C.I.A. involved, doing some kind of covert operation or side deal, you know that's common, and I'd probably be told to lay off it, let the State Department handle it, which they would do by forgetting all about it. So I'm preempting them, I'm walking away. Do you understand? Will you stop riding me?"

"I get it, Vinnie, but whatever it is, they stepped through my door and aimed a gun barrel at my head. I'm sure you understand that it can't stop with that."

"Or with a broken arm?"

"No."

"I'll arrest him. But the feds will lawyer it out. It'll come to nothing."

"Don't arrest him, just tell me what's fueling this horseshit."

"I haven't a clue, Hemingway. C'mon. You're going to persist, and I'll try to protect you, but you're launching out into night waters, man, stuff I have no control over."

"You know, I do journalism sometimes. They love it, the glossies. Maybe I should call *Life* magazine right now and write a piece about this — homicide, cover-ups, corrupt cops in the tropics. 'Dark Ideas of Law and Order in Key West.' "

"Why don't you go ahead and do that thing. Put me out of my fuckin' misery. Knowing you and doing this job at the same time is no Easter parade, I can tell you. *Life* magazine! Go ahead. Peter will stay dead, stay forgotten, and whatever faint residue of conspiracy is left in the air for you will vanish in an instant. They'll make sure of it. Whoever they are. You'll get a check, and I'll be reassigned to a penitentiary in Alaska."

"He mentioned Echevarria, Vinnie."

“Oh.” Silence on the line. “You’ll never see that guy again, Papa.”

“OK, Vinnie, but —”

Squiccarini hung up. Hemingway called back; no answer.

It was getting late. The shade was swallowing the yard.

11

The next twenty-four hours were exhaustingly busy. By the end of the next evening, Hemingway was so tired he slept with his head on the kitchen table, as if someone had assassinated him while he ate and strode away. First, the night before, he was dreaming, terrible, clotted, anxious narratives about Mary (catching him sniffing her bras, looming fifteen feet tall above him); driver ants; getting lost in Illinois (a colored-only saloon stood where his childhood house was, which was panic-inducing because he had to pee in his own potty, badly); not being able to outrun a zebra that for some reason wanted to bite him; and Joseph Stalin, just eating but making a mess of his mustache.

That morning Hemingway felt like he'd already run a race when he woke up to an inappropriately loud ferry horn, but he did wake with a line in his head, something about the pelicans *slapping their buckets shut,* which sounded more like a line in a poem but he turned it over as he brushed his teeth. *Buckets, shut.* Whatever: just that he wondered why he could never get the Key West kitchen help to make him those red onion sandwiches he'd grown addicted to for breakfast in Cuba, he realized he'd never inspected Peter's boat, the boat everyone knew about, moored at the basin. Surely Captain Video had gone over it initially, but it has become clearer with each passing day that Vinnie's shrugging attention to his duties wasn't just laziness or ineptitude but a conscious effort to treat the case with tongs, lest he discover a larger matter he'd have to get seriously involved in. Better to send a neat, simple report up north and never bother with it again. It was frustrating, Vinnie's laissez-faire approach: while it made him an optimal dockside booze buddy, it was far from helpful when business got serious. In this case, Vinnie's big mistake was talking to Hemingway in the first place — the dockside phone call needed to be followed up, but still. Something should've told the Captain to steer clear and not tempt Hemingway's sense of righteous indignation. The odds were good that the famous bull goose American artiste might've just rolled over in his hangover and forgotten the whole thing. But that's not the way the cards fell: Hemingway's mother could've told the flatfoot that her boy never could quite tolerate situations in which authority called the shots and left crucial questions, like why, unasked and unanswered.

The boat was worth a once-over, and so Hemingway went down to the docks on the Cushman Road King motor scooter that remained at the house after being discarded by Gregory in favor of a Fiat.

It was a filthy deadrise workboat that Hemingway would've bet hadn't been hosed down since 1945. You could see the policeman's desultory footprints on its deck, stamped in the years of fish bones, salt, sand, cigarette butts and raggy wisps of seaweed. Smelled, too, as much of body odor as fermenting sea stuff. It was morning, and the docks were empty; the fishermen had left and the tourists had yet to arrive. In the pilothouse, Hemingway saw the planks, left loose for smuggling storage, lifted and tossed about by police, revealing nothing but dank wood in the darkness.

That was it as far as the cops were concerned. Hemingway knew, as Vinnie should've, since he'd spent off-hours time in Cuthbert's company over the years, that Cuthbert was no sloppy scofflaw, but an off-the-grid paranoid of perhaps dubious outlaw skills but possessed nevertheless of a certain secretive cunning. So, with the morning warm over him, swinging his plaster-cast leg in wide circles, Hemingway checked every instrument face on the dash panel, every screw, every crevice, every seam of the coaming, every cleft in the woodwork. He sifted through the trash on the sill and on the floor: notes, bills, collection-agency declarations, dime novels, pamphlets for everything from the American Socialist Party to Baton Rouge whorehouses to camping grounds in Tahoe. Cuthbert also had covered the inner surfaces of the small pilothouse with pornographic pinups and publicity images snipped from newspaper-pulp fan magazines: Rita Hayworth, Carole Landis, Faith Domergue, Alice Faye. The cops had barely touched them, apparently, and amid them was a shred of paper reading out a Chinese proverb in Peter's spasmodic handwriting: *he who chases two rabbits catches neither.* It was Scotch-taped heavily on all four edges, and it had a faint bulge — Hemingway remembered Peter saying the proverb out loud once or twice, when it had struck him as memorable and,

God knows, truthful, and so Hemingway was impelled to look at the paper for more than a second, and put his finger to it. There, something underneath: lift the yellowing tape, and pull out a thin locker key.

This wasn't going to be easy, or pretty. There was only one possible home for such key on the island, if it was in fact a locker key — the bus depot at Mallory Square, where tourists swarm like an invading species, bursting the seams of cartoonized taverns, curio shops and the nearby aquarium. For a local poobah with international face recognition, it was the most dangerous spot in town.

He scootered home for a hat and sunglasses, which he understood would be only nominal protection, and made his way up to the square. The buses were parked in rows like sunning alligators; the people, innocent as individuals but, as a milling horde, ravenous and stupid as termites, bustled about in their striped shirts, strawhats, knee-high socks and sunglasses, wallets in hand. Hemingway sucked in a deep breath, parked his scooter, and forged into the crowd, his face turned down, his cane rapping alongside.

Inside the old depot building, roaring with caged fans bolted to the ceiling beams: so far so good. His hat and shoulders hunched, Hemingway beelined it for the wall of old lockers, thinking only now to look at the key's number: 16. A lanky fellow who looked like Robinson Crusoe and smelled like a mountain of pig shit stood one locker over, stuffing a filthy duffel bag into the space. Hemingway hung back uncomfortably, every moment he stood in the open stranded without an apparent purpose leaving him more exposed, a lame antelope on a veldt of lionesses. The smelly sand bum showed no signs of progressing in his task; Hemingway walked up. The man glanced over, Hemingway did not glance back. The man glanced again.

"Holy crap, you're . . ."

"No, I'm not." Fiddling quickly with the lock. The cane fell, loudly. "I'm just a look-alike."

"A what? Why would you be a Hemingway look-alike and then deny that you're him?"

Hemingway turned and growled. "You smell like a dung pit. Go clean yourself up."

The man frowned and put renewed energy into kneading his duffel bag.

The key and lock didn't match, not even remotely. The unlocked door on locker 16 swung open, revealing emptiness. The sand bum noticed. "You sure you know what you're doing there, Mr. Hemingway?"

"Shaddap." Hemingway turned on his heel, picked up his cane, and headed for the exit. A dead end — the key could mean nothing, a worthless keepsake, or the only way into a public locker in Trenton containing twenty-five-year-old socks. Should've known better — Cuthbert had always been such an almighty mess, how could it have been that he might leave clear clues behind to his own absurd death? Or even clues to what his life had really been like?

It took a second or so of hurried walking, halfway to the door, for Hemingway to realize he's strode right into a schoolgirls' field trip — a dense, perfumed army of teenage girls, pouring in from the buses and chaperoned by a few tight-looking adult women. The girls' hair was shaped into alien helmets that bounced when they walked, their overdeveloped breasts heaved out of their necklines, their pink hands all held guide maps and, holy Jesus, Hemingway books, scores of them, paperbacks, hardcovers, some new, some manhandled over the years and taped back together — *Green Hills of Africa, The Sun Also Rises, For Whom the Bell Tolls, Men Without Women, Winner Take Nothing, The Old Man and the Sea, The Fifth Column, To Have and Have Not,* et cetera —

each volume clutched to these new and ardent bosoms like twined packets of wartime lovers' correspondence. Hemingway noticed a few Georgia State College for Women jersey shirts, and lots of legs, before one or more of the coeds noticed him.

It may've spanned only a minute or two, but the siege that followed hit him, in a sonic boom of squeals, like a Pacific wave. There was even an undertow, an invisible force that sucked his balance away, as the college girls assaulted the man, pressed in on him, brandishing their books, their eyes shining with readerly lust, their voices rising in a trumpeting, choral wail of pleadings, swoonings, autograph beggings, flatteries and panting exclamations. "OMIGOD, it's him!"; "Sign my *Bell Tolls,* Mr. Hemingway!"; "Holy fucking Kee-rist!"; "We *just* got off the bus! How lucky is that!"; "This was my father's book, he died at Iwo Jima!"; "I have a flask!"; and so on.

Hemingway resisted as best he could, pushing away nubiles to get a foothold, trying to raise his cane as a defensive rail, but it was like a bad dream, he could move only slowly, sludgily. He found himself trying to accommodate them, talk to them twenty or thirty at a time, scribbling his name in their books, nodding, forcing a smile when he could catch a breath. Then they began to touch him, his shoulder, his back, his hat, his fist gripping the cane handle, one even plucked a white chest hair. The loud public spectacle of a very large and very famous man completely subsumed by a mob of college girls spiraled down into an entropic fury once one of them — Hemingway could not see who — grabbed his cane and yanked it out of his grasp.

He thrashed out, through baffled midriffs and sleeveless arms, *"HEY! GIMME MY CANE, YOU LITTLE BITCH!,"* brushing by the occasional jutting breast, and then, when the crowd would not thin, fell to his knees, grabbing ankles, shoving calves, hunting for sight of his cane, inciting a new, higher, nearly inaudible pitch to the enthusiastic screams. This is the point at which the others in the depot, travelers and workers, stopped merely glancing at the melee and simply stared.

He faintly heard one girl call another "you idiot bitch," and a moment later a small but strong hand came under his armpit and tried to lift him upwards. He stood with the help, and holding onto his arm was a freckled teen with eyes so wide her eyelids did not touch the edges of her irises, smiling and holding his cane. Another girl — the cane thief? — began screaming in a completely new register, about her ear and blood, refocusing the crowd's crazed attention, and in that brief instant the saucer-eyed coed pulled Hemingway from the crowd's distracted orbit and out the side door.

No one followed, quiet took a miraculous hold, the girl handed the old man his cane under an old melaleuca tree and then stretched up and kissed him and pressed the pliable arc of her body to his from thigh to chest. Her reward, she doubtlessly thought, for her take-no-prisoners heroism. A folded paperback of *In Our Time* poked out of her skirt waistband. She fetched Hemingway's scooter, and they zipped home on the side streets, Anne, Elizabeth and Caroline — the daughters of George II — and in no time he was on the four-poster, and she was kneeling between his legs, blowing him.

What the, Hemingway thought. How old is she? Fuck it! Clearly, she'd been training in her dreams for this very moment. Her name was Germaine, she was from Arkansas, and she hated the GSCW because they wouldn't let boys into the dormitories, meaning they'd have to sneak in, fuck the girls crazy and then creep back out, and so

Germaine never once in her whole college career got to cook a Western omelet for a boy she'd screwed, Western omelets being her specialty. Her top was pulled up over her breasts, which also had freckles. Her left hand was under her skirt, working.

Age is only one of many factors, Hemingway decided, but even if she was young enough to be his grandchild, she was still legal. The girl's mouth, and in fact her whole body, her whole pulsing, peachy being, was a salve — if I was Iceland, he thought, she'd be a scarce and priceless hot spring, secret and lovely and evanescent. Already he was wondering when she'd leave. She lifted her head and climbed up, spreading herself over his cock and settling onto it slowly. They grunted together.

The phone rang, Hemingway let it ring, someone else in the house picked it up: Mary. *"Señora!"* Marisol hollered. Bull's eye. There's the one more thing needed to make the morning an unarguable trainwreck. A bit light-headed, Hemingway decided to ride this risky episode to one more station and reached for the phone while Germaine was squirming on top of his midsection, sweat coursing down her breasts like tiny avalanches.

" 'Lo, Mary."

"Papa, what in the name of God have you been doing? You should've come home weeks ago."

"Yeah . . . I, um —"

"You said you'd be home weeks ago."

"Uh-huh. Patrick was here."

"Great. Is somebody there with you?"

"Yeah, the staff is cleaning up. I knocked over a pitcher."

"Of."

"Water."

"Look, you have to come home soon."

"Why, is there a problem?" Hemingway's mental trolley instantly jumped tracks to the Cuthbert megillah, and Tcheon's big mouth. Have they descended on Mary already?

"Problem? Yeah, the bathtub leaks. No, there's no problem, except we live here, ferChrissake, and when you travel you should be traveling with me. God knows what you're doing."

"What I'm doing? I'd tell you what I've been doing, but you wouldn't believe me."

"What."

"Peter Cuthbert died."

"Oh yeah? What a loss. What've you been doing, losing sleep?"

"Well, fine, but he didn't just die, he was

murdered, and they've since threatened me."

"Threats? Who's they?"

"Don't know that yet. Some F.B.I. cretin pulled a pistol on me."

"Ernest, get the hell out of that country right now."

"Oh don't be a hen, Pickle. I'm alright, I'll be home in a few days, I promise." Germaine was biting her own braided pigtail, coming. Hemingway had to cover his eyes.

"Are you drunk already? It's not even noon."

"Nope. Couldn't be more sober. Not a bad idea, though." Germaine shuddered, collapsed forward and begin to milk him with wave-like undulations. She was serious good.

"Jeeez. Don't beat anyone up, Ernest."

"Too late."

"Damn it. Don't get caught up in something thinking you'll use it later in a goddamn book. Maybe I should come up there."

Hemingway bit his knuckle and came in the girl. All he let out was a mule-like exhalation.

"What the fuck are you doing."

"It's my ankle, I bumped it."

"Bumped it. So?"

"Oh yeah. It's broken. I broke it last week." Germaine slumped to the floor, Hemingway covered the phone to take big gulps of air.

"How'd you do that? And after last year's crash! You're walking around getting threatened by corrupt feds who already have something to do with murder, and you're doing it with a broken ankle?"

"It's alright! Jesus. It's in a cast!"

"I feel like I'm talking with a three-year-old."

"Mary, just leave it. I'll be fine."

"Yeah, sure. I know, it's man's man's business. I'm just a dame, I don't know the first thing about it."

"Well, you don't, you haven't been here, but it's nothing to get all worked up over. I shouldn't've mentioned it. I'll be home in a few days."

She hung up.

Germaine lay on the floor immodestly splayed, toying with her braids. Hemingway sat up and hiked his shorts back on.

"Christ, I barely knew what I was doing," Hemingway muttered, as he began to contemplate just a few of the possible consequences of his day so far, including divorce, Church-group protests, and Germaine's father, in overalls and with a shotgun.

Germaine shrugged with her nose. "I have that effect on people."

"I'll bet. I shoulda . . . We should've used a rubber or something."

"Or something? Like what?"

". . ."

"Don't worry, Papa Hemingway, I'm not going to call you nine months from now with bad news. I'm not even going to tell anyone — I'm going to save this for my memoirs."

"That's a relief. But accidents happen."

"That was no accident, mister. You humped me famously. You've got a nice thick pecker."

Hemingway was not consoled. Germaine rolled over, grinning, her bare ass yellow in the midday sun. "I won't get knocked up! And if I do, I'll take care of it. 'Hills Like White Elephants' is my favorite story. It's a masterpiece. Meant the world to me, no kidding."

"Gee, great. Thanks. When do you think you'll be missed by your chaperones?"

"Probably am already, they don't ride easy, those bags. But they should be out front soon, your house is the main attraction. What time is it?"

"My God. Eleven-fifteen."

"They should be here already."

Hemingway went to the window. Yup, there was the crowd of forty-five red-cheeked college damsels, clustered on Whitehead Street around his front walk, being lectured at by one of the older women.

He rubbed his eyes, scanned the room for a drink, found none. The gears began to turn. Hemingway was at least moderately certain that Germaine, as hare-brained and reckless as she was, was also a girl of her fanatic word; the key move now was to get her back into the complacent embrace of the American university system before anything worse happened. The spry little thing seemed no worse for wear, that was for sure. She'd make some college boy an exciting if troublesome wife someday.

Germaine got dressed, and Hemingway, whose skull had been hot with thoughtful percolations of all varieties since the micro-second *after* he came, told her to exit out the side, scurry behind a hedge and join the group at the back. He, in the meantime, would meet them out front for a special tour. She ran out without so much as a smooch.

Feeling guilty but not a little reenergized, Hemingway donned his safari chapeau, grabbed his cane and strode downstairs, threw open the front door and thrust his arms welcomingly toward the mob.

"Ladies!," employing his best gin-mill boom. "Fantastic to see you again! I've decided to give you my own Key West tour! Alright? Fasten your seatbelts!"

They squealed anew and followed him like a giant brood of ducklings. He small-talked a bit with the head matron, who was as flushed as a Macintosh. He was suddenly aware of being thirsty — too much activity for one day already without a single snort.

"Who said they had a flask?" A girl's arm immediately volunteered a monogram-embossed silver pint out of the cloud-layer of young hair, and Hemingway swiped it, patting the now-scowling head matron on the shoulder, belching "It's part of the whole ambience, right? That whole hard-drinkin', hard-livin' writer deal!," and then swallowed a half pint of wretched blueberry schnapps in one gulp. Handed it back to the crowd empty.

Hemingway took them down Whitehead, using his cane as punctuation in the air, making up absolute bullshit all the way about great white sharks and pirate ships in Submarine Basin and so on, until he was standing in front of the Audubon House, its railing and gables and porches decaying in the way that reminded everybody who looked of a Southern plantation gone to seed and inhabited by insane and incestuous ex–slave owners. Only one of Ferenc Galko's near-magenta Isottas was parked out front.

"Dames and damsels, this is the Audubon House! This is where James Fenimore Audubon lived and did all of his research and those paintings and books and shit! It's been carefully maintained to look *exactly* the way it did when he lived here, whatever it was, one hundred years ago! Except for the car! Ha! He was an eccentric fella, so the house might look messy or lived-in or whatever, but don't worry, that's part of the exhibit. And the caretakers are a bit eccentric, too, but you don't pay them any mind! Go on, have the run of the joint!"

Forty-five feckless young women stormed into the old house, and Hemingway paused out on the walk, waiting for the inevitable fireworks. Ferenc Galko, besides being a millionaire who was compelled to make quarterly bribery payments to the State Department so as to not be extradited to any one of six countries looking to prosecute him, was also notorious in Key West for being a dismal failure at being a local aristocrat. His tastes were awful, his manners were confused at best, and his attempts at spreading his wealth and making donations and greasing palms so someone, ferChrissake, would finally give him the key to the Keys, as they had to Hemingway decades earlier, have almost always been short-circuited by his flammable temper. Once, at a Rotary function, he spit on an assemblyman's wife's cleavage, after she professed to like some Czech writers and knew of no Hungarians. Another time, he pulled a gun in a restaurant on a waiter who delivered an overdone ribeye after Galko had sent it back for being too rare, and then brought a Bananas Foster to the table that wasn't even warm. When he explained that cold Foster was the house manner, Galko pulled his pistol out of his waistband in such a fluster of rage that he knocked over a bottle of cabernet, which fell and broke, sending a small wave of wine up and onto the white linen dress worn by Grace Kelly, who was having baked sole at the next table. She politely asked for, and got, a replacement dress, tailored after the original, delivered from Fifth Avenue by airplane the next day. Galko himself would be the first and proudest to note the old saw about Hungarians: Given a room where among one hundred people one individual has an ingrown toenail, a Hungarian walking into that room will always step on the inflamed toe.

Germaine lingered on the sidewalk, gave Hemingway a look. A mounting buzz of mayhem emanated from the windows.

"What're you playing at, Mr. Hemingway? This isn't a public building."

"Don't worry your pretty head about it, Germaine. It'll be a story for all concerned."

"Yeah, well . . ." She looked up and down the street, antsy and thoughtful. "Y'know, fuck all this. See ya around." And she walked north, away from her compatriots.

Hemingway watched her go, and a sound like a fire-bombing erupted from the second floor of the house.

"WHO-DA-FOCK-ARE-ALL-DESE-FOCKING-GIRLS!" Galko, caught perhaps coming out of the shower.

Hemingway took the cue and hobbled in, smirking. The main hall, carrying right through to the back gardens, was massive but cluttered with columns, ferns, statues, velvet-seated Victorian chairs, massive ceramic pots from India, threadbare rugs and unopened wooden crates, housing God knows what, with stamped manifest IDs from dozens of countries, including Yugoslavia and Korea. The elaborate trim, windows, plaster and woodwork throughout the house didn't look as if it'd been painted or even cleaned in half a century. Upstairs, Hemingway could hear the crazed clopping of several dozen school-girl tennis shoes, the buzzing roar of excited chatter and the deeper rumble of Galko, cursing like a miner and barking orders: "Every last one of dem, OUT! Zbignew, do your focking job! Are they crazy?! Hemingvay doesn't leef here!"

Weeks later, Hemingway heard that one of the girls caught Galko masturbating on the toilet, and that they went through his closet, his underwear drawer, his nightstand and his refrigerator, emptying it of good French Chardonnay. One of the little skirted monsters even snagged his corkscrew. The girls of Georgia State College for Women spent the next twelve hours haunting Key West like a platoon of Legionnaires on leave, drinking at the taverns, pushing each other off the piers, vomiting on the sidewalks.

At last, Galko appeared at the top of the stairs, hurriedly buttoning his shirt, his kinky hair wet and uncombed. And then he saw Hemingway, his mouth falling open. Hemingway had been meeting men like him ever since he left Illinois: fifty-somethings with too much money and a manner of talking to you as if they were toying with the idea of foreclosing on your home and feeding your children to their crocodiles. Men whose very unscrupulousness and success gives them the preposterous idea that they are epitomes of the species, warriors of commerce, and whose unscrupulous success makes them honestly hope they can stay young and virile forever. Tans, ropey muscles, clothes so expensive the cost of an afternoon's outfit could keep the Congo in cornmeal for a year. Too much overstyled hair, teeth too white, manicures. Galko came down the stairs, chewing on the scene in his house, and by the last step, he'd understood what Hemingway had done.

"You could've called, Hemingvay. Why did you invade my home with these . . . vixens."

His naturally dishonest smile took awhile to stretch, but then it did.

"Your flunkies would've hung up on me. Since when do you take phone calls? And this was fun."

"My phones are all bugged."

"I know. So."

"So, what, you've corrupted all of these nice American girls already."

"Not all of them."

"For what. What is your mission, buddy. With a broken foot. I try to live discreetly."

"Sure you do. No small talk? No 'how

about a drink?' "

"It's noon."

"That's just what I was thinking."

Galko let a little shrug loose and hollered at a harried henchman to get Mr. Hemingway a cocktail, ferChrissake.

"I don't know, Ferenc, you've lost what little manners you used to have. Don't forget I saved your ass once. What about lunch?"

Meaning, as Hemingway had put it more than once, Grace Kelly, in her wine-stained dress years earlier, was angry enough at the idiot Hungarian's behavior to want to get him deported, and Hemingway talked her out of it that weekend by taking her to bed. Anyone who knew Kelly, a famously, and perhaps tragically, indiscriminate nymphomaniac, wasn't too surprised by the story, but Galko never believed it. He didn't believe it because he knew that Hemingway had nothing but fun-loving contempt for him and if sending him back to Budapest was the price he had to pay to screw Grace Kelly, he would've put on a boat that Monday. Which made sense, except for the possibility that Hemingway and Kelly might have, probably were going to, rut like minks in any case, given their personalities and fame and proximity that autumn. Who knows the truth of it, but Hemingway always found a way to joke in every conversation since that he'd balled a movie star for Galko's sake, and that the pirate was in his debt.

"Get de Betty Grables out of my house."

A cold gin and tonic came, with a lovely slice of lime. Hemingway asked for a second immediately, then took a moment to drink half of the one he held.

The girls began to filter out through the central hall of their own wayward accord, waving as they went. The chaperones were nowhere to be seen, but Hemingway wasn't looking for them.

"C'mon." Galko led his guest to the back library, which was filled with books Galko never read, in floor-to-ceiling oak bookcases. Hemingway couldn't help but roam the shelves with his eyes. Most of it was abject garbage: Reader's Digest Condensed Books, thick romances, multiple copies of *Anthony Adverse;* the volumes seemed to have been bought by the foot, just to fill the space. Hemingway kept roaming — "Hemingvay?" — in hopes of finding something rare and ownable accidentally caught in the dump shovel.

"Hemingvay? C'mon, I have verk I must do today."

"Verk?" Hemingway turned. The second g-&-t came, accepted blissfully. "You don't work, Ferenc. I don't know what it is you do, but don't call it work."

"If it's not play . . . Look, let's go out back and do some hunting."

"Hunting? In Key West?"

Out on the lawn beyond the gardens, Galko walked up to a woven wicker table and chairs, and picked up an ironwood bow with horn tips that Hemingway figured must be a century old, and probably authentically Kickapoo. Out amongst the greenery sat an old Hungarian, in a strawhat and vest, on a folding chair; Hemingway couldn't quite see what he was doing, but he could see that there was a large cage nestled in the bushes almost out of view, and he could see that the man watched Galko with a relaxed diligence. When Galko pointed upward quickly with his chin, the man bent over, fiddled with something, and a skinny fox ran out onto the grass. It stopped quickly to look around and smell the air, but it didn't need to pause for Galko to fire an arrow directly through its ribs, sending it careening in a bloody fit across about ten feet of the grass. Then it was dead.

"Fucking hell," Hemingway belched. "That's not hunting."

"Who has time for a trip, a vacation, Hemingway. You, right? Lots of vacations. This, this does it for me."

"That's because you're a cretin." This without thinking ahead: he *was* there to get information about Cuthbert.

"I'm a Greek now? Oh no, cretin as in like idiot. Of course."

"How many foxes you got caged up out there?"

"I have four or five drove in every week. It pays to know how to shoot an arrow deadly-like, for it is so quiet. But I know this doesn't live up to your safari experiences. Tell me about your last African trip, Hemingvay."

"No thanks. I wanted to ask you some questions about Peter Cuthbert."

"Who?"

A minute was spent by Galko blandly denying ever having heard the man's name in his whole life, and Hemingway steadfastly maintaining that that was a lie, a rondo that ended finally when Hemingway reminded the Hunkie that he'd introduced them in 1948, at a governor's soiree held in Hemingway's own courtyard.

"I don't remember."

"Look, Ferenc, I know Peter was smuggling, Christ *everyone* smuggles something here, and I know you do, too, and I know that you know a lot of people. And I know Peter did business with you. So I'm just looking for connections, who Peter worked with, what he was messed up in. I'm not a T-man, for God's sake."

Galko fired an arrow haphazardly into the trees. It hit wood with a thwack. "Hemingvay, if he did do business with me, dat would mean he did business with some employee or contractor of mine, and I vouldn't know him from dozens of other riffraff. I can't, unfortunately, give you a list of people under me who do dat kind of work. They like privacy."

"I know . . . Give me a what, then. It wasn't rum or refugees. Unless —"

"I told you, I don't know vhat it was. Now, please get the fock out."

A pair of bulky Hungarians, with faces like sea cliffs, were suddenly standing behind them. One had a broken nose and two black eyes. He had his jacket buttoned, but the other didn't, and a Beretta stuck out of that man's belt. Hemingway had only a tenth-of-a-second's glance, but he could swear that where *"beretta"* should have been pressed into the slide's metal, he saw Arabic lettering. "You know Tibor and Jacint, yes?" Ferenc didn't even turn around.

Hemingway threw his glance upward at the goon's faces, and knew immediately, by their expressionless expressions and body English, that this wasn't the last conversation he'd have with Ferenc Galko about Peter. These guys, probably ex-AVO torturers, weren't nonchalant like their boss — they were tense, bristling, standing on the balls of their feet. Hemingway could almost hear the flesh in their fists rub and squeak with the tightening. There was, in other words, a sense of violent emergency in Hemingway's visit that Galko managed to convincingly downplay in his swarthy manner, but which his unschooled bodyguards could not. Something undisclosed was unmistakably at stake here. The big boys with the odd guns gave the game up.

Hemingway caned it back through the center hall. At the corner of his eye, to the left, he caught a dark, brooding figure: on the staircase was the Mexican woman from Peter's funeral, the Bruno, posed so the sight of her was unavoidable. She was wearing a deep purple peasant dress, but wore a pearl necklace Hemingway could see from where he stood. Hemingway stopped gape-mouthed, she nodded, and disappeared upstairs. That was all she needed to say.

Hemingway used up the afternoon quaffing tequila and beer at a tiny off-road bar stand he knew on the south side, accompanied by only a few Cuban boaters who knew no English and paid him no mind. The breeze outside was relentlessly tropical, soft and hot and eucalyptic. The next time he went to Galko's, he'd better bring a gun or a squad of National Guardsmen, that was plain. But in the meantime, Hemingway had no idea what to do next. The more he drank, the more he reclined emotionally in a figurative wading pool of mournful despair, and for the first time, he grieved for the loss of his friend. No tears or anything, just brooding and sad thoughts, heavy and clumsy like obese chain-gang convicts slogging down the line. The walk home, after dark, took a long time, bedeviled by high curbs, tree-heaved sidewalks, garbage cans and tourists. And then he was asleep in the kitchen.

12

Midday: a backache to go with his hangover and itchy foot, a tendril of worry growing in the brain's inky sepsis about Galko — did I just foozle my own safety and well-being there? Are the dropping dominoes headed downtown? What the lazy fuck am I doing? — and a name, caught in his thoughts like a burr: Kovarick.

But first, worry about Galko? Was Hemingway too big to be in danger, or, as Tcheon put it, *just* a writer? *Just* a writer, that's how he'd said it. Or was it, just a *writer?* Which was worse? But writers don't end up pitifully, suddenly murdered, except by their own hand — unless in the Soviet Union. Ambrose Bierce ended up in a shallow grave in Mexico, and he was pretty big, in a 1912 kind of way, but that was war, and he shouldn't't've gone. No, it was so rare that one could regard a certain size of readership of books to be a kind of insurance, an accepted bribe to the fates. Presidents have had something like a 10 percent chance of taking a bullet, but writers of fiction are virtually inviolate.

At least, that is, in countries where publishing is a legitimate industry. In Cuba, anything could happen.

Kovarick. Rick was sure about the name, Cuthbert's real name, after seven hours of drinking, which was unusual because Rick hardly seemed certain about *anything,* under any conditions or influence. He was a paradigmatic Mexican drunkard, forgetful, gentle, light on self-esteem, always distracted by a mescal-sodden *corrido* floating around in his head.

Hemingway felt ridiculously low on real information — all Peter's fault, that *rotten fucking sonofabitch!* If only Peter had stuck to tobacco or rum, illegal imports nobody cared about, and if only he'd stuck with the ordinary, run-of-the-mill Gulf runners, the guys everyone knows and who pay off the Coast Guard like clockwork and never raise a red flag on anybody. If only he'd stayed upstate, where he belonged. Or used to belong.

After cleaning up, eating, dressing, scratching inside his cast with a yardstick, and looking for eyedrops, Hemingway scootered all the way down Flagler to 18th Street, where Rick lived in a collapsing stucco hacienda with his mother, his ninety-nine-year-old great-grandmother, and two sisters, both of whom were near thirty but unmarried, and at least one of whom was, as they say, a bull. No one wondered why Rick drank, and some wondered why he didn't drink more.

"The thing about book writers," Mrs. Villareal began saying practically the moment she opened the door, her tanned scowl and hair dusted with cornmeal powder, "is they don't work like normal men so they're always around in the middle of the day. Drinking, making spectacles . . . knocking on doors . . ."

"Rick's around, and he's no writer," Hemingway said this already walking in.

"Yeah, he don't work at *nothing.*"

Rick stood up from the kitchen table, tilted his head to the back door, and he and Hemingway vanished out back. Neither could stand more domestic comedy than they'd had already that week. Around a rusty mismatch of lawn furniture, under a sky so blue it seemed to hum.

"Rick, the name. Kovarick."

"Told you, I can't remember. Saying it or why I might've said it. Sorry, Papa."

"This is a bitch, this whole thing." Hemingway was scratching his beard, then his scalp, then his belly. "I told you about the guy who came to Billy before the burial and claimed to be a relative of Peter's."

"Yeah. You busted him."

"Why would somebody want Peter's body?"

"You think there's something *in* the body?"

"Like what? No. There's a hole the size of sewer pipe running right through it, there's nothing left to it."

"Maybe this guy thought he'd get Peter's remaining, y'know, stuff. Papers, his boat."

"But there's nothing, I've looked."

"Maybe he didn't know that. Maybe he's just a bunco louse from Miami. . . . Where is he now?" Shrugs. "You could call the cops. Call a detective in Miami."

"Good idea. But I don't know any cops in Miami."

"So what. You're Ernest Hemingway. Call one up and make friends. They'll kiss your ass."

"I do know a fed."

"There you go."

"Rick, what exactly did Peter do?"

Rick knew a bit. Peter would run his boat back and forth from the Cuban shore at least three times a week, during fishing trips and "fishing trips," and cart nearly anything his contact would ask him to: cocaine, raw opium, hashish, guns, grenades, 181-proof rum, revolutionaries, casino cash for American politicians, Mafia men running from extradition, counterfeit dollars, prostitutes, stolen gems and antiques and women's shoes, even fruit and sugarcane, the loads of which were always so massive and heavy Peter worried about making it back to port without having to throw much of it overboard. Always cigars, duty free. Peter's boat was small, and so he struggled, fought to get the jobs and fought to support himself with how little they paid. But he was dependable, apparently — "Say what?" Hemingway harumphed — and his shipments were always intact. And he was safe. The fact that Peter said so little about himself was taken as demonstration by everyone that he would never squeal if caught, but just do his time with his lip buttoned. Smugglers were usually nervous, amoral bumfucks you wouldn't trust to tell you if the sun was hot. But Peter inspired trust, like a border collie. His local police record began and ended with a few sleepovers in Captain Video's drunk tank. He appeared on Key West with a boat in 1944; who he was or what his life was like before that,

Rick knew as little as everyone else. Who his contact in Cuba was, he didn't know. Whether he worked for Galko, he didn't know that either.

"I can't imagine why someone would've offed Peter," Rick mused. "He never betrayed no one. And he had nothing that anybody would want."

"Except information. Faces, names. Maybe the F.B.I. has a new task force gearing up, and somebody got wind. So he was suddenly an expensive man to leave alive."

"Wow. You think? You should call Miami."

Hemingway went home, with Rick behind on foot thanks to a promise of drinks, and called. His Bureau buddy's name was George Kwaak, which Kwaak maintained was a Scottish name. Hemingway didn't know what it was, except a cover for another name, probably. He'd never met him, but spoke with him often during the war, when Kwaak was a State Department liaison and Hemingway was spending his undrunken afternoons in Cuba with the gang of amateur-spy buddies he'd labeled the Crook Factory, sailing around the Caribbean looking for German U-boats. Kwaak was taciturnity personified, his pauses frequent, his voice flat, and his jokes unleashed with a mortician's solemnity. Hemingway didn't know what he looked like, but imagined him to be extremely tall, gloomily thin, half-lidded and big-nosed. He hadn't spoken with him in years.

"Mr. Hemingway. Congrats on your Nobel. . . . Another break-in on Whitehead?"

"Thanks, George, and no. I've got a few, uh, investigative questions I was wondering if you could help me with."

"Off the record."

"That's right, off the record."

"This doesn't . . . entail Captain Squiccarini?"

"Eh, not so much. Really. Number one, I was wondering if you could tell me, unofficially, if there's a push around the office up there about, y'know, Cuba and smuggling and shit like that."

"This is about Cuthbert."

"Fuck!" Hemingway found himself getting nervous. "Yeah. It is. But I'm just fishing here, just sport fishing."

"Why?"

"C'mon, George, I don't want to talk in detail. He was a friend. Maybe, I'm thinking, if there's something coming down, that might've initiated the thing. That would explain things."

"OK. But . . . nothing new, as far as I know. It's not my county, but I haven't heard anything. I don't think fear of the feds is a large motivating factor down there . . . right now."

"Shit. Then I've got nothing."

"Keep looking."

"What . . . did you just say?"

Rick's heavy eyebrows raised up like a drawbridge over the rim of his glass.

"Keep looking."

"What do you know?"

"C'mon, Hemingway. Nothing . . . But don't give up."

"Who's Stanley Lynch?"

"A . . . Savannah blackmailer, extortionist, wannabe racket guy. Been out of Georgia State a year and a half, made an appearance in New Mexico this spring. Heard he'd been down to you. He went to the precinct down there . . . with his jaw busted, and they laughed at him."

"I didn't know that."

"Well."

"Where is he now?"

"Cuba."

Is that right, Hemingway thought, stunned. Kwaak is tossing grenades *and* feeding him rope. Rick was still listening intently.

"And a name, George, could you nose around with a name for me?"

"A little. What is it."

"Kovarick. No first name."

"No first name. I'll see."

"OK, George. Thanks. I think. I didn't call you."

"No you did not."

"Wait — one more question. Why would a Beretta have Arabic etched on the barrel?"

"It'd be a Helwan, a copy. Made in Egypt."

"It's not a common gun, is it."

"In Egypt it's common. And Tunisia, and Libya. You don't see them over here. But I guess you did."

"Uh-huh."

"Good luck with that."

13

"Are you drunk yet, Rick?" The phone hung up, the hot breeze was invading the house, the dusk was on its way.

"No, why."

"I'm still hoping you'll get as drunk as you were after Peter's burial and remember what you said about his boat."

"Beside the *Em* part."

"Right. For all the good that's done us."

"Sorry, cap'n."

"Keep drinking."

Hemingway knew it could take hours. Come six, the two decided to launch out into the Gulf anyway on Rick's skiff, toward Little Mullet Key, the mention of which is all Hemingway could remember now from his friend's dockside babblings. What significance the fabled boat could be Hemingway could not guess — it might only yield more nudie pinups, beer cans, soggy cigarette butts and, maybe at best, traces of smuggling jaunts long gone. But a fed had told him to not give up — not that he would have anyway, at this point, but Kwaak said those words, lean and steely and bundled with undeciphered meaning, and so Hemingway would press on. Goddammit. What else was there to do, this spring, anyway? Mary waited in Havana, but so what. He didn't want to land a new wife any time soon, but he knew he could if he absolutely had to.

Little Mullet wasn't that far, heading up the Northwest Channel and then veering west, miles past Big Mullet, but it was, significantly, off-limits. The Navy used it for flight exercises, and the conservationists upstate had been in a row for years about *anyone* going within two hundred yards of the thing because of its reefs. Between these two opposing ideologies, there was a semi-official moratorium on fishing, beaching, boating, any activity at all that wasn't either military or, let's face it, illegal. Which made it at least a semi-discreet place to park a mystery vessel. Not that the Navy B-12s wouldn't spot it, or even bomb it out of the water if they had a mind to. No, if Peter had anchored a boat up there, it had to be some distance away from the sandbar proper, in which case who knows where it could be.

The Gulf was in a good mood, and the gloaming on the horizon was crayon-box hot orange, just for the New Yorkers who drove down in station wagons to watch, standing on the beach with straw hats still bearing price stickers and tropical shirts suggesting at least a wishful but fatally unconvincing realignment of lifestyle.

"Urp," Rick said, the alcohol rising in his throat.

"Wyatt," said Hemingway. He was steering, Rick began throwing up overboard. Spanish sardines began peppering the stained water.

Soon they were in open water, making a big, comfortable berth around Big Mullet, which they could barely see what with the sky purpling up and the magic hour slipping away with the minutes. Hemingway was wondering how in hell they'd even find their way back if both of them kept drinking like they were.

Then something flew by him and moved a few of the gray hairs over his left ear. A second later, the moist evening air carried a sound, like a big hand slapping a linoleum table a mile away.

Rick looked up. "Papa?" Hemingway stood, wavering for a moment. "Papa, you hear that?"

"Yeah . . ."

Rick looked at Hemingway as he touched his ear, and then glanced at his fingers, which were clean. "Somebody shoot at us?"

Hemingway gunned the engine. Rick rolled, smacked his head. A second engine, in the semi-darkness, answered with a gunning.

Boat chases at night are funny things: you have little idea of where you're going, how far you are from your pursuer, or even your own relative speed, until it feels like a current of dream suspense, as if you're both walking up a down escalator with a blindfold on. Anyone who's run through a dark house in a fright and cracked their head on a wall corner knows the sense of it.

Hemingway had no idea now where he was, but he kept weight on the gas. The swells bucked him: *wathump, wathump, wathump.*

Who knows who we just got mixed up with, whose path we crossed, Hemingway thought. Pirates, dope shippers, Communists, anybody.

Rick's head was bleeding, and he tried to staunch the wound with a gasoline-soaked rag that made him howl in pain. Hemingway looked back — the other boat turned on a spotlight, which for a second was directed down, illuminating the boat, before it was aimed out at Rick's.

"Oh it's them. They're not smugglers. They're following us," Rick said.

"What? How do you know."

"I saw them on the dock. Before."

"You're drunk."

"They were eating sno-cones."

"Fuck. I thought they were just crooks out here, looking to get us out of their way."

"You hoped."

Hemingway knew if he cut to the starboard he might eventually run up on sand; any other direction went into miles of dark waters. Get lost, use the North Star if you could, veer around the east Gulf until you ran out of gas, and wait until morning light. Rick's boat had only the empty cavern in the dashboard where a radio would've sat, so then you hope you don't have a heart attack baking in the 110-degree heat as you pray for a Coast Guard vessel to wander by, and hope they won't have too many questions about why a famous celebrity stranded himself and a ne'er-do-well Mexican fisherman out past the Mullets, where nobody was supposed to go.

Wathump. The light from the other boat wavered around in a big, clumsy torrent, only occasionally catching Rick's boat and casting Hemingway's shadow ahead of him. It took awhile for a second shot to *thwap* across the night air; taking out Rick's little windshield, which instead of shattering simply broke tiredly into three large, stale shards and fell in, onto the floor.

"Ricky." Blood still dripping into his eye, Rick couldn't see well as he tried to stand, which elicited a puke and a poisonous fart at the same moment.

"Jesus," Hemingway groaned. So Rick crawled over, gingerly picked the glass up and tossed it all overboard, just as Hemingway jerked the wheel, weaving in the blackness, for what reason he could not say. He squinted at the gas.

"This work?" Tapping the dashboard. Rick didn't look up but knew what he meant.

"No."

"Are we gonna run out of gas, Rick?"

"Yes."

"Fuckit fuckit fuckit."

Hemingway abruptly eased the throttle and let the boat slow and die. "Papa," Rick said, sounding scared for the first time.

"You reek." In a hoarse whisper — the ocean was suddenly quiet.

"Papa?"

"I don't want to get stuck farther out at

sea. We need enough to get back. *Those guys* probably have a full tank of gas. They'd outrun us and leave us for dead where no one would ever look."

"As opposed to here."

"Ricky, quit bitching, and pick up that gaff. If we die here, it's because we were drunk-stupid enough to come out here at all, without gassing up."

The men waited in the dark in the belly of the skiff, crouched with rusty tuna gaffs like Watusis with spears. Hemingway's head began to pound.

But nothing — silence, not even a distant, retreating boat engine.

"What the. We can't be alone out here now."

"Papa, you ever got shot at before?"

"Yeah. Three or four times. I was in Europe in 1918, the 'thirties. Scary."

"Sure."

"Hm? You?"

"Oh, sure. My brothers and me were strikers and fighters against the Valdes administration, 'forty-eight, 'forty-nine, 'fifty. It was only interested in foreign investors, and workers like us were getting fucked. We were jailed, shot at, whipped. I was shot three times through — twice through my belly here, on the side, and once up here, where it broke a rib. My brother Miguel was shot dead by police in 1950. Eulalio we never found."

14

They did run out of gas, after delicately backtracking in the dark for only ten minutes. They woke up at sunrise, bobbing and tossing, miserable as dehydrated lizards, but they didn't get back to shore until just before noon, after a Coast Guard boat finally sidled alongside their drifting vessel, berated the two men for being such goddamn fools, talked Hemingway up about *The Old Man* a bit too much, and then gave them a few gallons of gas. No one mentioned the chase or the shootings — Rick assumed Hemingway would if it were the intelligent thing to do, and Hemingway decided not to, certain that a mere patrolman could and would do nothing but shuttle the case right back to Squiccarini, who's already decided to ignore it. If Hemingway wanted to persist in his investigation, which he had to admit was what it was, he had to go his own way — and he did want to, sensibly or not, more than ever, an effect that being shot at has on a certain type of person, the kind that as a schoolkid smiled at sadistic teachers after getting slashed with a steel-edged ruler.

So now Hemingway had a sunburn to go with his broken ankle, bum back, throbbing kidneys and scabby knuckles. Mary's gonna be pissed off.

Back on Whitehead Street, he needed a bath and had one, and it was good. It wasn't quite as good as the bath he had had in Milan, with Agnes that nurse from Chicago, damn he still thought he'd missed the express, letting that woman go, or letting her slip away, or escape, God only knows, but the bath, in Milan, was triumphant, in a big alabaster tub alone on an empty ward, only him and her and his first erection since Schio, over three weeks later which is an eternity without an erection when you're nineteen, warm water, a bottle of *zubrowka,* and though it was technically his second experience between a woman's legs, the first a beery late-night high school tramp dalliance he couldn't quite remember, this was really his initiation into the feverish secrets of intercourse, the boggling instant when you realize a woman *wants* you to touch her where she's moist; the lost feeling of doing something unconsciously, skin on skin, membrane on membrane, with a beautiful woman who if you were to be standing aside and watching her do this would compel you to, as the kids say, whack off. And he'd never forget it, though of course nineteen was too young to have held on to Agnes even if he could have. He would've eventually moved on in his jumping-trains-at-night way, and so she was probably better off as it was. She would be, what, sixty-three now? He hoped she'd married a nice doctor.

He got hard now in his bath, thinking, but it didn't last, and he wasn't comfortable enough with his plaster cast hanging over the edge to take care of it anyway. He wasn't frustrated, but was once Marisol simply walked in — why wouldn't she want to fuck the world's most famous writer? What better option does a semi-literate Mexican woman with an illegitimate kid, working as a maid, have? — and told him he had a caller at the front door. Who?

"Una señora." Marisol looked lazily at his wet nakedness, pulling himself out of the tub, as if she were looking at a pig sitting in mud.

Hemingway dried off and dressed as quickly as he could without trying to seem, even to himself, hurried and excited, and the reality of it was actually not very quick at all. By the time he came downstairs, the front door was closed, the foyer was empty, and the woman, the Cuban woman from Galko's, the Bruno, was standing in the parlor sipping a gimlet.

Her dress had the same halfway fusion of traditional peasant and gangster's moll chic, and her dark, sharp-edged features were still alarmingly interesting. Hemingway thought of Dolores del Rio, but this woman had a more commanding presence, as if she were the queen of a lost country.

Hemingway came at her with his hand out, affecting a nonchalance appropriate for old friends, but with an ironic smile that let her affect it as well. She did.

"I'm so glad you found me," Hemingway said neutrally. He silently and with his pointing finger and his eyebrows requested an identical gimlet from Marisol, who had looked in.

"Find you, I'd have to leave the island to get away from you, Hemingway," she said. Sipping, and smiling a little. He was hoping for a sporting good time of flirtatious dialogue, and tried in his manner to aim her in that direction.

"Matilde Pirrin."

But why would she have come, if not for

sport? Hemingway was a little on edge — he'd seen too many guns this week and heard too many threats. The gimlet came.

"Matilde, does Ferenc know you're here?"

"Galko doesn't know about anything that doesn't sit on his lap and scream." Her English had a little New England in it — Hemingway guessed that she'd spent a little time in New Haven or Cambridge.

"Galko has known enough to make a lot of money."

"So? What was it the guy in the movie said: it's no trick to making lots of money if all you want to do is make lots of money."

"*Citizen Kane.*"

"*Si.*"

"I met Hearst."

"I'm sure you have."

"Unhappiest man who ever lived."

". . ."

"So what's your story, Matilde? Why have you come to me?"

"Going to pull it out of me that easy? Is that all I get?"

Hemingway smiled: that's what he would've said. "OK. Is Matilde Pirrin your real name?"

"Of course. Why wouldn't it be?"

"Who knows. How long have you been in Key West? In the United States."

"I'm not. I come and go. It's not far."

"I know. You are Cuban — what are your feelings on the Twenty-sixth of July Movement?" Hemingway was reaching, perhaps — it had just occurred to him — but maybe Cuthbert's death had something to do with Castro's nascent rebel movement. But perhaps not. It would account, one way or another, for the raised stakes and menacing secrecy all around, all of which certainly seemed to point to something other than just another everyday smuggling homicide. But he was throwing darts now, blindfolded.

"I almost forgot, you have a house in Havana," Matilde purred. "The rebels are, I think, presumptuous, self-serving hoodlums."

"And the Moncada Barracks attack itself?"

"Slapstick." The question remained: was she anti-Castro, or lying?

"President Eisenhower?"

"We'll see. What do *you* think?"

"I'll handle the questions, *señora.* Did you know Peter Cuthbert?"

"No."

"Honestly."

"Yes. Honestly. Never met him. My condolences, by the way."

"Thanks. Do you sleep with Galko?"

"Never. Though I do fuck him occasionally."

"Why?"

"Because I have no money." She said this with pride in her voice, which sounded fishy.

"You're a liar."

"I am?"

"Tell me I'm wrong."

"You're right — I've just told two lies. Which are they?"

"You're still lying. You've told only one. You're from old cigar money, you've never worked a day in your life, not even as a whore. Not even as a rich man's wife."

"Mr. Hemingway, you are deft."

Hemingway was sweating, he discovered, as if from sexual exertion. Laughing, he bellowed to Marisol not just for two more drinks, but a pitcher.

Neither wanted to sit, they wandered around the room as they talked, in circles as if bullfighting.

"And what of you, Hemingway."

"Call me Ernest."

"Hemingway. You are world-famous. Maybe the most famous writer, novel writer, in the world. And you are on what number of wife?"

"Four. And you ask as if being a writer and an unsuccessful monogamist should be, and normally are, mutually exclusive occupations. I would suggest the opposite."

"You'd be neither right nor wrong, of course. For every *comemierda* you name, I can name a devoted husband."

"I doubt it. One out of four, maybe."

"But I wasn't suggesting that. I meant, being famous has done you no favors. You cannot find love."

"You're wrong. My days are filled with love, more than I can normally stand. I'm not looking for love, so I can hardly be unable to find it. Women aren't my problem."

"Then what is?"

The gimlet pitcher arrived, right on time.

"Right now? I'll tell you. A blank page. Sentences that sound just like other sentences, that sound more and more like bullshit the more time passes. Sentences that aren't *truth.* Stories that aren't stories really, but just outlandish ideas, because I can't seem to think of stories that *should* be written anymore. My back. My ankle. Taxes. Alimony. The fact that my sons are all grown up and aren't terribly interested in me any longer. The fact that Paris and Spain and Africa and the wars are all behind me, and what's in front of me looks dull and unchallenging. A world that doesn't understand the meaning of concision and restraint and nobility. A readership that thinks I write the way I do because I'm charmingly emotionally impacted, as a man. Critics whose pitifully paying profession compels them to whip at me like they would an old mule for shitting in the barn. Friends I've insulted or offended while soused and can't figure out how to apologize to. Other people, not friends, who aren't insulted or offended no matter what I do. And a friend's body, in an expensive wood box I paid for, with a hole in him no one can explain, and a strange but lovely Cuban woman in my house that wouldn't be here, it seems, unless Peter was murdered and unless that killing was more than just a dock fight between crooked drunks. *That's* a problem."

"Strange? Me?"

He shrugged.

"Do you miss any of your old wives?"

"What."

"Your three previous wives."

The fun Hemingway was having had begun to abate somewhere in the middle of his monologue; still headsore from sleeping on that wretched skiff, he was getting tired and antsy, and that was cutting into the gimlet-fueled sexual tension.

"Hadley. I miss Hadley. What I can remember."

"Maybe write about her."

"I have been. Bits and pieces. I think I miss being that young more than I miss her. But don't worry about what I'm writing — there's another problem I've got, being surrounded my whole livelong day by fishermen and bartenders and cops and Cubans and hookers and wives and bureaucrats and lushes who all think they should tell me what I should fucking write about."

"That's not too much of a problem."

"No, of course it isn't."

"Well, Hemingway, in any case, if your problem is not women, then it is a bigger, deeper thing."

"If I knew I was going to be psychoanalyzed today, I'd've stayed in bed."

"Not alone, I trust."

"Very much so. What's Galko's big business in Cuba?"

"He has lots —"

"I know, lots of business everywhere, nobody could possibly say. What I mean, what was so different or important this time?"

"With Cuthbert, you mean? You think Cuthbert worked for Galko?"

"C'mon, Matilde."

By now he was rebounding, he'd had enough gimlet to make virtually any situation buzz with congeniality.

She paused. "Hemingway, I would've thought it was obvious. I'm here to get information from you, not the other way around."

"Really. What could I know?"

"That's the question, big fella. What *could* you know?"

"About what?"

This pull-my-daisy crap would've tried Hemingway's patience under normal circumstances, but today he was juiced on it. Could've bantered with this rangy elk of a woman all day.

"Your investigation."

"So, Galko's interested in my investigation."

"You brought it to his house, and he's still cleaning up after the schoolgirls."

"He's got staff for that. Admit it, admit that Galko knew why I was there the moment I appeared. Admit that I scared him. Which is admitting that he knows something about Cuthbert."

The woman had exhausted her resources, and suddenly, imperceptibly, slouched.

"Oh, Hemingway, it's Cuba. We're on an edge, a precipice. Can't you see that?"

"I can see that. And Galko wants to help."

She shrugged. "Of course. Don't you?"

She had stepped a fraction closer to Hemingway, and he felt warmer for it.

"Yes."

She finally stepped closer, placed an extraordinarily warm hand on the skin of his arm, and kissed him. She smelled faintly of both pine tar and sarsparilla. His hands moved to her waist, which was slim, and to her back, which was smooth and muscled. She pressed her body inward and crossed the invisible line that told Hemingway that he needn't do virtually anything else to get this woman naked and on her back in no time at all.

Which is what happened: her long legs seemed to almost touch their toes to the ceiling, her dark Latin skin was baby smooth, the grip of her vagina was only firm and expert enough to be mistaken for seismic passion. She was in fact thinner, bonier, than Hemingway generally preferred, but the sense of fucking her to get at, somehow, what was *really* going on, in her head and heart and in the world at large, kept him flushed and engaged even after he'd decided, during the sixteenth minute of coitus, that he was exhausted and would rather just nap. She did, however, lubricate more effusively than any woman he'd ever had. He heard splashing.

Afterwards, he did nap, fell asleep in mid-sentence: ". . . not lying, Marlene Dietrich is a good friend of mine . . ." When he awoke, it was evening, Matilde was long gone. Hemingway lay in his still-damp sheets, listening to the clink of rigging from anchored boats. There was a hollow feeling in the room, and Hemingway immediately tried, in vain, to steer his thoughts away from the nothingness that faced him in the form of meaningless sex with strange women, dull wealthy comfort, writing that wouldn't come, and the fact that he was now old, dammit, old and getting older and able to look forward to nothing much more than distraction and tedium. Reaching the point of only finding significance in the looking backward, at his life and at his work and at the world, terrified him more than any violence could. Actually becoming "Hemingway" the international symbol of gun-toting, truth-telling ramrod writer-hunk terrified him even more. Did he really miss Hadley? He certainly missed being young and on the verge of figuring out his two worlds — fictional and real — while in Paris. Just as he found himself capable of vanishing down the crumbling country well of evaporated happinesses he could never regain, Hemingway realized that the bizarre, long-legged Cuban woman whose secretions he could still smell on his beard had told him something he hadn't known for certain before: "It's Cuba." That's why Peter died — the Batista regime had been fending off Castro's little insurrectionary force, fueled by expatriate funding in the U.S., for several years. Peter must've brokered a deal, of either arms or contraband to sell, for the revolutionaries, or *thought* that's what he was doing, or tried to scam them in the process. Or something. Hemingway had no clue if in fact the woman learned what she came to learn; he didn't recall saying anything revelatory. But this megillah, it's definitely Cuba. That's where the jungle paths will lead.

15

"Kovarick."

Hemingway first squinted and then exhaled. So *that's* why he'd been dragged away from his pot of coffee and his typewriter, through his own front door, by three dark-suited, dog-faced feds in a black car, and driven up Fleming Key Road to the Naval Reservation, its gray boxy installations defiantly grim before the gentle turquoise lapping of Key West Bight to the west. Parking lot, checkpoints, electronic doors, hallways: and then Hemingway was seated in a spare room full of chairs, and faced with four G-men, introduced as Elam, Barclay, Roope and Jergens, asking about "Kovarick," the name Hemingway had dropped to Kwaak. Squiccarini appeared after a while, and sat in the back, saying nothing.

"Yeah. One of my bar cronies mentioned it, thought it might've been Peter Cuthbert's real name. Remembered Peter mentioning it years ago in a tequila swoon. How much do you guys know about all this?"

"Everything," Roope said, out of lips that rolled back over gray teeth like cracked leather over a cobbler's bootlast. "Almost. Which bar crony?"

"I don't remember."

"Don't lie to us."

"What're you gonna do about it?

"Why'd you call Agent Kwaak?"

"Because I know him, a little. It was off the record."

Three out of four gave a look: off the what?

"So," Jergens began in a more congenial mode, "we'd like to know if you have any, well, corroboration of this, the name, then. Besides your drunken crony."

"Not until right now, no. That was his name, wasn't it? Obviously. You guys have a first?"

". . . Marco."

"Marco?!" Hemingway's lonesome guffawing went on for only a few seconds.

"Is there anything else you can tell us about Kovarick, things he might've let slip during drinking bouts, whatever?"

There was, of course: That he once let a Brazilian pimp drown deep in the Gulf on a fishing trip after the pimp had beaten a local whore with a hose. That he'd once been in love with a Mexican girl, in Texas, named Idalia. That Idalia had a twin sister that Peter had mistakenly mounted in her sleep after a tequila day, which scotched the relationships every which way. That he'd never been to Canada. That his father trained hunting dogs to attack black men, until they set on him after a training session and ate pieces of him while he was still hollering. That he had five brothers and sisters, whose names he said he couldn't remember.

"No. But I'm sure you can tell me plenty. Can't you. If you fill me in a little, I might be able to help."

Elam laconically opened a file on his lap. They were obviously prepared to divulge a certain amount of information.

"Marco Kovarick the third, born 1915 in —"

"*Nineteen-fifteen?!* He looked ten years older."

"— in New Brunswick —"

"New Brunswick?"

"— ahem . . . Old addresses to his family keep cropping up, including Phenix City, New Smyrna Beach, Corpus Christi, and Tuxpan, Mexico. We can't find any of the family now. They're likely alive, he's got a slew of siblings but all probably living incognito. Something of a family tradition, it seems. Before he came to the Keys, he belonged to the longshoremen's union in New Orleans, did time in Bostick up in Georgia for stolen goods, had a bank account in a small Mississippi bank for six months, under another name. Not Cuthbert."

"What was it."

"Can't tell you."

"That it? Does this mean you guys have been actually investigating his murder?"

"Not really. Kovarick was wanted on multiple warrants, smuggling across state lines, stuff like that."

"Bullshit. The four of you ironed your suits today and put on your ties and kidnapped me here and have compiled who knows how much classified documentation, so as to get to the truth of a penny-ante backroad runner you have no hopes of catching because you know he's already dead? That's why the name 'Kovarick' rang the fire alarm? Does the F.B.I. have so little to do these days?"

Jergens shifted uncomfortably in his seat. "Well, we also have reason to believe he was a Communist and was providing material aid to Soviet-supported movements all over the subcontinent."

Hemingway entered into a tremendous,

derisive snort but it got caught midway up his eustachian tube. He remembered that Socialist Party pamphlet on Peter's boat, and of course Matilde's koan-like utterances the day before. Was Peter just smuggling for money — and for whom? — or did he actually get himself committed to something, and something so unlikely as a tropical Communist revolution? Would it matter to the feds what his motives were, for whatever he was pickled up in? Hemingway had been half aware of the last few years of the televised witch hunting led by the wormy Wisconsite McCarthy, and many of his Hollywood friends — including John Garfield, who made a great and unclichéd Harry Morgan in *The Breaking Point* — had watched their careers wither like sick saplings because out of curiosity they had attended a meeting or had received a newspaper twenty years earlier. He realized immediately that as far the government was concerned, Peter was a Communist and that was that. Never mind that he couldn't have told a dialectic from a phone dial.

"Cuthbert was a Red, eh? Whatta you know."

"You don't seem surprised."

Hemingway didn't see them lean forward in their seats, but he smelled predatory instincts in the air, and he knew he had to choose his words carefully — wouldn't that be fine for them if Ernest Hemingway implicated himself in the great Communist conspiracy, even by association.

"I am. Surprised. I just don't show it well. I frankly don't believe it. He wasn't a man of broad and passionate convictions, though he had definite views on watercolor painting, you know, not using white pigment because it's a translucent medium, and on his own right to live like a bum. But whatever, he's dead. Whether you're right or wrong, you can't hurt him now."

"We're not looking to hurt anyone. We're working for the good of the country. We want to trace his network."

Now Hemingway rolled his eyes. "His network? He had no network! He was a low-ball smuggler, mostly, and those people don't keep books. Good luck."

"You seem to know a lot about it."

"I know a lot about a great many things. Ask me about baseball."

"So why did Kovarick call you the night he died?"

"Haven't you spoken to Captain Squiccarini? I didn't talk to him, the lines were down. I have no idea why he called."

"Uh-huh."

This fishing trip was just about over, Hemingway thought. But he was stunned to find himself uneasy — the scent of witch-hunt suspicion hung in the room like a dog's mild fart, detectable but unmentionable. He knew, from what little news he read nowadays, that the Pope himself wasn't safe from being hauled up in front of the Red-scare inquisition and having his livelihood and reputation obliterated. This wasn't something Hemingway would be able to bare-knuckle his way out of if it came down to it, or ignore, or lawyer to death. But Hemingway was no Commie — or was he? He'd seemed to be when he was in Spain, though that position seemed predominantly anti-Fascist, and he's never cared a spit gob for the corporate economy or the welfare of American politicians, whom he thought all resembled Irish priests with dirty secrets. What was going on in Russia and China wasn't that Marxist stuff, anyway, not the way he'd heard about in Spain; it was dictatorship leavened with jargon. So maybe, what, he wasn't sitting here before a firing squad of taciturn G-men by accident? Was this really about Peter? Or was he the big fish they were looking for? Would persecuting Hemingway as a Red be anything more than a publicity coup for HUAC, or would that be more than enough for these sons of bitches? It was nothing to sneeze at, he knew: Hemingway wouldn't be Hemingway for long if no publisher would take him and no bookstore would sell him. Like anybody who has achieved anything, his life was a straw shack of perception and whim, and could collapse in a breeze.

Fuck, he thought: paranoia didn't suit him. The situation chafed at his inner folds like wool underwear. Shit on them, he thought. Let these pencil-wristed humps suit up and come hunting.

"You *did,*" the fellow named Elam slowly let loose, "aid and abet the Republicans in Spain . . . ?"

"I was a reporter!"

"Munitions training, no? John Dos Passos told us you did."

"Oh, *fuck* Dos Passos! He can barely tell a nursery rhyme, that guy, you're going to believe him? He was barely with me in Spain, he doesn't know *shit* about me."

"Well . . ."

"I'm not a Red. That's enough of that. Is that all? Gentlemen? Was this the extent of your plan? To toss some idle accusations? Why don't you figure out who murdered this horrible, dangerous dead Communist smuggler bum you're so concerned with, and maybe you'd learn something substantial."

"We don't care about who killed Kovarick. It's incidental; we'd be more interested in who wanted him alive. If anyone. You should go to the F.B.I."

"What?" *What?* "I thought you guys were the F.B.I."

"We're C.I.A." Hemingway couldn't help himself, he let his big jaw hang open for a second.

"I didn't realize the two agencies shared so well."

"Kwaak didn't call us." Roope was being very smug about what he wasn't saying.

"Which means you listen in to F.B.I. phone calls?!"

"The F.B.I. isn't bugged, Mr. Hemingway." They all smiled at this.

"Oh. So I am. Y'know," he said, "if you guys wonder why I may not have all that much faith in the American bureaucracy, just look in the mirror."

Squiccarini stood up in the back and left before anyone, without a word.

They drove him home, silently, and by the time Hemingway was through the front door, he was fuming and grabbing for the phone. Dialing Kwaak.

It wasn't so easy to get him this time: the

D.C. phone banks kept rerouting him to the general info desk, and then to the public relations wing, and then back again. Only after Hemingway used his name and then mentioned Roope and Jergens explicitly — the only names he remembered from his morning — did they connect him to Kwaak's office. Even then he had to wait five minutes before Kwaak deigned to put the phone to his ear.

"Mr. Hemingway, hope you are well. Any . . . developments in the Cuthbert case?"

"C'mon, Kwaak, don't give me the stonewall. You know perfectly well what the situation is."

"So the Company boys asked you a few questions."

"Yeah, and essentially accused me of being a Red."

"Puts you in good company, right?"

"Kiss my ass, George, I don't need good company, and I don't need spooks sticking their noses into my jockstrap and asking John Fucking Dos Passos what I did in Spain twenty years ago. If you knew, you could've given me a heads-up."

"Excuse me? I don't work for you, Hemingway, I work at the pleasure of the President. Do you know how many people work for American intelligence right now?"

"You're not allowed to tell me, I'm sure."

"A number just shy of the population of West Virginia. And they all have their own ideas about how to do their jobs. I knew they were planning on talking to you, somebody told me as a courtesy. But you know I didn't send them. I've got enough on my docket."

"Which means my house is bugged, pretty much."

"Pretty much."

"And they don't care about Cuthbert. Kovarick. I can't figure it out — if they think Cuthbert was a Commie smuggling for Castro, why wouldn't they think his murder would lead them somewhere, *anywhere?*"

"That may be a naive question, Kemosabe. They are covert, after all. Perhaps they're investigating and don't want you to know. . . . Perhaps your Mexican housegirl is an agent."

"Get outta here."

"Perhaps they know already. Or perhaps they're just waiting to see what you'll do next. To follow you."

"Follow me? Where am I going?"

"I'd think you were going to Cuba. Am I right?"

16

I'll make it up to you, Squiccarini told Hemingway when he came to the house that afternoon. Let's go.

It'd been awhile, but the two men went to Joe's, which was virtually empty on account of the crab traps were filling up out in the water and it was a Tuesday. They had fritters and avocado and bread, and tequila, and a bucket of ice to put the bottle in and to cool their glasses. It was a table under a window, and the gulls yammered outside.

Hemingway had ten thousand questions for the shady, never-entirely-on-the-up-and-up fed, but he was already tired by one P.M., and was happy for the moment to avoid the briar patch. The tequila was old and from Oaxaca and had a perfume like a lily.

"I wouldn't worry, Papa," Squiccarini started with, "they accuse anybody and everybody, they're like the Stasi. Or, really, like a typical bureaucracy — they exceed their necessity and help create the problem they're supposed to address because they want to stay funded."

"And powerful. I don't know how much those cretins are making a week, but I know they're digging their sense of power. Swinging their dicks around."

"Yes. There's juice there. Money buys a lot. Power buys the rest."

"Who said that. You?"

"As far as I know."

"I knew some real Communists, Vinnie. In Brunete, in Madrid. I knew Max Eastman."

"Good guys, right."

"No, some were unholy bastards. They'd sell their mothers for meat if the ideology called for it. Others were very good. They actually saw through the theory to the community stuff. They weren't far from the Masai. *That* was a real community, everyone helping each other. No one stole, no one had more than anyone else. You kill a zebra, you make sure everyone eats. 'Cause tomorrow someone else might kill the zebra."

"You are a Red."

"Fuck off."

"I'm calling Hoover this minute. This avocado is Cuban, isn't it."

"Has to be."

They enjoyed a silence spent chewing and swallowing. Then they talked some more, about the Prio years, about how both men felt a touch guilty, in their own ways, about the liberties and indulgences and gambling profits they've enjoyed in the last three years of Batista's reign.

"Have some brandy, Hemingway. It's on the F.B.I."

"Maybe. Later. I remember you told me you met Hoover. In D.C."

"Hoover? Well, it wasn't a meeting, really. He came in to address a bunch of us — Coast Guard officers who were suspected of 'independent operations,' they called it — to recruit us as feds, believe it or not, something about resourcefulness and tactics, and he simply screamed at us for sixty seconds about how if we defiled the name of the Bureau he'd have the memory of us scrubbed from the planet."

"Those must've been his words."

"Oh yeah."

"You told me you met Hoover, shook his hand."

"I must've lied."

"I remember, you told me this in 1938. We were on that boat with Echevarria."

"I don't remember talking."

"You were making a point. Drunk, to Echevarria. About your connections. You were swinging your dick around."

". . ."

"I fell asleep after that. Was that really all about smuggling, Vinnie?"

"Why are you trolling there, Papa?"

"No reason."

"No, Papa, it wasn't smuggling."

"Jean always said it was."

"Jean's Jean. No, Echevarria pulled his cap gun after I said that Carlos Mendieta y Montefur was just a gigolo for Batista. Echevarria couldn't argue about that today, but in 'thirty-eight he did."

"Fucking Cuba."

"Hmpf."

"So Jean grabbed him."

"OK, Papa, let me say this. Since you're fishing, just like those spooks at Naval. Jean grabbed him, but he didn't kill him."

"Jean said he did."

"Jean Fumereaux is a better kind of man. He thinks he owes me."

"Does he?"

"No. I owe him. What happened was, Jean had him, and I took that gun and put it to his left eye and fired."

"Shit. Why didn't I wake up."

"It was a mess. A mistake. I was drunk. It

took hours to gather the sharks, and we never knew if someone was going to spot us. I'm still waiting for someone in the Bureau to uncover something and come to my door."

"Which is one reason, right, you'd like this Cuthbert thing to disappear."

"Sure. With you involved, the circle gets just a little tighter. And Jean, coming to Peter's burial. And getting our picture taken."

"There's no circle, Captain. You should relax."

"You don't know, Papa."

"You're right, I don't. Why'd you tell me this, anyway? Damn fool thing to do."

"So you'd trust me. Trust me when I say there's nothing to be done about Peter's murder on American soil."

"OK, Vinnie."

"But . . ."

"I know, Vinnie. Cuba."

17

The next day, Hemingway packed up his single suitcase, bid adieu to the house staff, and caught the 9:45 A.M. ferry to Cuba.

The morning was unseasonably cool, and got cooler every time small roving clouds would smother the sun. Crossing the 24th parallel, the light Gulf spray thick in the air, Hemingway tried his best to steer his thoughts away from the grim fact that he had no idea what he was doing. Cuba in 1956 could be a king's roost for an indulgent white man with money, but it was also a warren of thieves and exploiters, organized gangs and rogue grifters, most of whom essentially tithed a percentage of their take to the government for their right to function. Nothing was authentically prohibited from becoming commerce: stolen goods, dope, women, babies, weapons. For the rich, the law under Batista was reliable, but for ordinary citizens it was arbitrary at best, outright felonious at worst. This worked fine for Hemingway when he had only donnybrooks and disorderliness to deal with.

But now, it was murky waters indeed. He'd be asking big questions about people who don't want to be talked about, and Hemingway was anticipating several things to happen: the street-level people he knew would run scared, and eventually he'd get warned, by large men with no scruples, and he might end up in a hospital. Which in Cuba was its own kind of dangerous. Hemingway sometimes wondered about such men, having seen them in action in Illinois, in Madrid, in Nairobi as well as Havana — how did they occur? What kind of violence did they know and at what tender age, to empty them out so thoroughly that they could break a woman's fingers to make her husband pay fifty bucks, or clamp jumper cables to someone's armpits so he might not tell the law what he knows about the henchmen's crooked boss, who surely underpays them for such work? Hemingway wished he could just look at men like that and simply see brainless evil, but he couldn't; he saw boys that got punched by their miserable fathers, who were punched or whipped or what have you themselves, and so on.

Anyway, perhaps he'd be lucky if that's *all* he'd run into while digging up the garden bed. He knew, from bar chat and from the newspapers, that the 26th of July Movement had regrouped and was rearming in Mexico, after its disastrous assault on the Moncada Barracks a few years earlier, and that Batista and his infrastructure were on hot alert for another offensive. Obviously, Cuba was some sort of nexus for ideological conflict in the hemisphere, for whatever reason — though the reasons, as always, probably came down to money, to who had a lot of it and what majority had next to none at all and therefore nothing to lose. He thought: should've moved to Costa Rica.

Once he was in Havana, Hemingway would have very little idea where to start. Find Omar Gargallo, an engaging street weasel who maintained a precarious criminal existence in Havana selling information to both the police and the gangs, and find out what he knows. About? Smuggling todos for the sake of the revolutionary cause, not the usual boatfuls of luxury items and fugitives, but something big enough to a) involve Galko; b) inspire the participation of that Lynch fellow (all the way down from Georgia), whoever he is; c) provoke Tcheon to pull a pistol in warning; d) pique the interest of the C.I.A.; e) and create a bloody debacle on an American tourist dock that resulted in someone being impaled on a giant harpoon. Of course, the pickle of it was that Hemingway wasn't terribly sure that he didn't set this absurd machinery in motion, Chicken Little–like. How much of this half-seen story was actually created by his presence, as if he were an agent of the Heisenberg principle writ large? Would the C.I.A. be watching otherwise? Maybe, if it involved politics. But maybe it didn't — was it, in fact, just an ordinary, albeit ridiculous, criminal incident before he got involved?

Hemingway paid a dime for a can of ginger ale out of a crate of ice carried by an old Cuban man in a red kerchief and drank it at the railing. The ferry crossing was smooth, the wind was not unduly cold, the sky eventually became characteristically blue, blue enough to hurt your eyes. He saw Cuba coming at him, low atop the morning turquoise of the Gulf. He tried to remember the last time he'd been home — a month? six weeks? — and where he'd been in Mary's graces when he'd left, but drew no conclusions. When he'd married Mary, he was under the semiconscious impression that she was the most masculine woman he'd ever married — which he felt to be a good thing, a relief from the fickle, nagging, sensitive women he'd known well and, eventually, left behind. He'd always been conflicted about male camaraderie, always desiring instead the company of a good woman but then quickly growing frustrated with the fact that they were, in fact, women, and couldn't quite fathom him or his instincts. The men he'd known fathomed him fine, but soon grew dull and unmysterious in that understanding.

Mary, he'd hoped without ever articulating as much to himself, would be an ideal middle ground, and true enough, she had been a staunch and good-natured soldier on all of their trips, even the ones that were launched in a boozy swoon and stalled early on because no one knew why they were where they were. But otherwise she turned out be, well, a wife — Hemingway could count on her to doubt his common sense, to expect him to forget things that were important to her, to carp about his desire to take off on his own (to do, she must merely suspect, unhusbandly things), to care what others thought of their marriage even if the people in question were odious morons. And she had the temper of a rabid animal, one of those things a certain kind of man can find bewitching and nervy in courtship but come to regret thereafter, especially if by that time he's aging and tiring and fighting off a horrible gloominess.

She'd be storming about Finca Vigia as she probably has for weeks now, kicking at the glass-eyed heads of the animal-skin rugs, rasping at the servants, maybe thumbing through his books for forgotten love notes or receipts. When he arrived, she would demand a full accounting of his weeks away (the story of how his ankle was busted would alone garner an hourlong harangue about how stupid men can be), and then some time for them to spend alone eating and talking about the Havana house, how much work it needed and how many things about it she wanted to spend enormous amounts of money to change, and then she'd complain about his sons, and his surviving ex-wives and their alimony, and then she'd more than likely, with enough wine, get sullen remembering the baby she lost in 1946. If Hemingway even mentioned Cuthbert again, or the fact that he intended on pursuing the matter in Havana, Mary would hit a tirade of wild-eyed ferocity that no man would choose to witness over, say, catching a stingray barb in the throat.

As the ferry sidled up to the dock and threw its ropes, Hemingway decided he would not go home, not just yet. With a finger in the air he summoned a gypsy cab driver, handed over his bag and told him to drive to the Hotel Sevilla on Trocadero, where he knew of a neat, private room with windows that open only to the back garden.

He had no trouble securing the room, or bribing the desk clerk to deny to all inquiries as to whether Hemingway was a client of the establishment. In the room, which was quiet and well-ventilated, Hemingway changed and washed up, quietly, feeling as if he were a spy in a strange city, under an alias. He almost was, he supposed, but somehow the secrecy of what he was doing now — even if it was only secret from Mary for the time being — made his mission feel genuinely hazardous for the first time. He'd lived in Cuba for years, but it felt unknown to him now, foreign and frightening and hidden, happening outside his window oblivious to him, in all of its iniquities and invisible risks. Bierce *did* die in Mexico, after all, because he left the writing to someone else and got involved. He left his typewriter and joined a fight, in one manner or another. And paid for it. Without Hemingway's fame to protect him the way it could when he's the Loudmouth Artiste Icon, anything could happen.

He had lunch in the garden, during which the hotel staff generously seated no one else outside. A soufflé, red potatoes and a Pouilly-Fuissé from just after the war. Then some English brandy, several in fact, and after that Hemingway had gathered enough steam to venture forth and make trouble.

In a wide hat and sunglasses, he taxied down to Malecón, on the water where boats both legal and shady arrived. It was a long run of tortilla booths, mango stacks, goat sausage ropes, hearts of palm, *cubilete* games, silent doorways, roaming dogs, men selling Mexican beer bottles out of wooden crates, men selling American cigarettes and American paperbacks and American handguns, napping streetwalkers and dice. Looking for Omar — in the year or so since Hemingway last spoke to him, the skitterish runt could be embroiled in anything at all. But Hemingway knew that Omar's wife, Zanaida, who hated Omar and hadn't lived with him for more than ten years but never divorced him for fear of being left penniless in the event Omar did actually strike it rich one day, faithfully manned her *pastelito* stand each day and might respond to an American ten-dollar bill. She did.

"*Señor* Ernest, I would help you without the money."

"I know, Zanaida."

"Really."

"Sure."

"But *gracias.* He's at *numero doscientos treinta.* You have to knock and say, *Bolivar.*"

"That's a password?"

"*Si.* They haven't changed it in twenty-five years."

"What're they doing there?"

"Pelea de gallos."

Maybe there's a story here, Hemingway considered. When he moved to Cuba, seventeen years hence, he saw his first cockfight, and after that he'd diverted a few nervous white men, journalists mostly, to see one on Malecón now and again, to watch the blood run from their complexions. But he'd never taken to it; he'd always thought it was something cheap and stupid and reliant on the betting losses of very poor men, more pig race than bullfight. In any case, he hadn't seen one since he'd married Mary. At his age, and weight, and present sense of weary aimlessness, he doubted he'd find it very entertaining.

A copper-skinned old man with five-days'-worth of white beard answered the door and let Hemingway in without asking for a password or even looking once at his face. Then he sat back down at a table beside a kitchenette in the next room, and continued to do what looked like boiling up opium on a hot plate. Trying not to make much noise with his cast and cane, Hemingway found his way down a hallway lit up only by the light coming from open doors, and most of the rooms were empty except for mattresses, beer cans, cigarette butts and, in one, a rooster standing on the floor and tethered to the window sash by a length of knotted shoelaces. The whole place smelled like a neglected coop.

Hemingway could hear the noise of the fight, the yelling, down the hallway to the left, through one room to another hallway. He finally came to the door, beside which sat a sleeping man in a straw hat, a shotgun lying across his lap. Hemingway tried to wake the *hombre* gently, with a tap and a jostle, thinking he'd give the fellow a chance to do what was apparently his job. But the man only began to snore.

Inside was the *gallera,* fashioned out of four or five smaller rooms simply by ripping out the adjoining walls, creating a large, bare-bulb-lit open space, enough for a hundred men, the bowed ceiling of which threatened to collapse in at any moment. In the middle there was the pit, around it were the forty or fifty bettors, in it were the cockfighters and their birds, and one of them was Omar.

Did Omar get embroiled in actually owning a bird? Men have lost homes and families fighting cocks, but Omar had neither, which led Hemingway to conclude that Omar was just handling another's man life investment, which itself was obviously risky business. Omar, wily and skinny and cursed with teeth that stuck so far out of his mouth his lips could never cover them, was crouching down over an ink-black Cubalaya rooster, which already looked as if it'd been hit with a shovel. The other cock, a larger red-and-black game bird, looked worse. The match was at a pause and had already been going on for a few minutes; Omar's cock wouldn't stop squawking or flailing, the trimmed razors strapped to his feet whipping about frantically. The noise was deafening and seemed to be getting louder.

Hemingway stayed to the back, not interested in being recognized by anyone, much less Omar, until the money had changed hands and the birds were done.

Omar was breathing in his bird, goosing him, doing all the right things but sweating so badly he looked unarguably guilty, of something. Hemingway could smell the panic in the room, as the noise escalated, more and more of the Havana lowlife surrounding Omar yelling their heads off about something being wrong, about Omar not being forthright, about wanting their money back. Omar's watery eyes were widening like sunflowers at noon. Hemingway unconsciously shifted his grip on his cane, so he could raise it as a club.

Just as the birds were once again thrust at each other, it happened, Hemingway was braced for something like it: Omar's Cubalaya shat out a red *banos* pepper into the sand. It's an old cheat, irritating the rooster so badly from the inside with a chili that it turned into a homicidal maniac among poultry — most cockfighters by then considered it a brawlable insult to have their rooster's rectum checked for peppers, it was that old. But Omar had tried it nonetheless. The room exploded. Omar's bird immediately relaxed, exhausted, on its haunches; the other bird immediately swiped at it and nearly cut its head off with its right-foot razor. Omar's instinct was still to jump on his bird, pick it up and run, but he didn't get much of an inch past the spot where the Cubalaya squatted, bleeding to death. The crowd grabbed the guy, held him up like a lynching-party victim, and began emptying his pockets for anything it could find.

Before he'd weighed the downside — again with this? — Hemingway stepped in, booming *alright, alright, break it up!,* holding his cane up like a riot stick and prying the crowd away from Omar, grabbing him by the hair and pulling him as mercilessly as he could away from the men that were already coming close to drawing their knives and cutting up what would be 140 pounds of human meat to toss into the neighborhood's various pigsties. Hemingway outweighed everyone in the room by eighty pounds, and the crowd relented a little in its grip as he knew they would; what would happen one moment after that was anyone's guess. Omar went to his knees in the sand, wet with chicken blood.

What a debacle. Hemingway scanned the brunt of the red-eyed mob, all of a foot away from him, their breath fog reeking of tequila, and saw a few knives and one screwdriver.

"Hombres, you've all won! *¡Usteads ganan! ¡Acéptense su lucro!* No harm, no foul! *¡No perjuicio, no crimen!* Omar *es mi asistente,* and *mi* Ernest Hemingway! *¡Gracias!"*

The logic of this was pointless under the circumstances — cheating at cockfighting places you distinctly beyond the pale of redemption in most regions — as was Hemingway's attempt at impressing them with his celebrity status. They remained for a second stymied, until one — a blue-eyed hoodlum holding what looked like an oyster knife — piped up.

"You are Ernest Hemingway? The book writer!"

"Si, señor."

The men quieted, deferring to the *hombre* with the oyster knife.

"You bet on chickens?"

"Me? No. I just came looking for Omar, my assistant. I need him to do work for me."

First Omar had heard of it. He went to stand, but Hemingway's hand kept him down.

"Omar, assist you with what? Research?!"

"Si!" chimed in a snaggle-toothed cohort to the left, the one with the screwdriver, "Research how to get your own balls cut off!"

The crowd began snickering.

"I've read you, Hemingway." The fellow with the oyster knife.

"My books."

"*Si.* I liked, what's it called, *For You a Bell Tolls* very much."

"That's *Whom. For Whom the Bell.*"

"*¿Qué?* That book I liked, but *The Old Man and the Fish,* that book I did not like."

"Sorry."

"I'd like to ask you, what the fuck were you doing? It's like a book for my grandchildren."

The guy might've been thirty-five. Hemingway didn't want to do the math.

"Well, that was a stylistic choice, you see, I was —"

"Did you write it in English?"

"Of course."

"I read in *Español.* Whoever translated your book . . . fucked it up!"

The men all burst out howling to this, repeating *fucked it up!* to each other and overall losing whatever self-consciousness they'd had about displaying their bad teeth.

"Really. I'll look into it."

"You look into it! Really, I mean, 'the *hombre* does this, the *hombre* does that, the *pescado* does something else.' It was fucking awful!"

Louder laughing. Hemingway smiled, nodded; the situation was well on its way to defusing. But then he had to, he absolutely had to, say something else.

"You know," he said, pulling Omar up and shoving him toward the door at the same time he pointed a big finger at the cockfight crowd, many of them now gasping for breath in their laughter, and drinking happily from their bottles again, "the Nobel committee understood what I was trying to do! They love that book in America!"

They laughed more now. Mr. Oyster Knife wiped his nose, grinning. "Maybe, Mr. Hemingway! All I'm saying is, whoever translated it for you . . . fucked it up!" Gales of derisive cackling.

Hemingway pushed Omar ahead of him and hobbled out in a huff.

18

Omar's room was above a smelly, mildewy cantina, which meant that the two men didn't make it upstairs but sat drinking cold Canadian beer, obtained probably off the back of a midnight boat, at the corner table on the ground floor. Omar, spindly and nervous by nature, was still quaking, guzzling the beer like an oasis pilgrim, pictures of his throat slit open still running mad behind his eyes.

Hemingway, for his part, took silent pride in how quickly and easily he sloughed off the bruising literary criticism dished out by a roomful of drunk, homicidal, semi-toothed Cuban cockfight gamesmen. He'd never mention it again, he resolved, never let anyone know if it bothered him. *Fuckers.* Instead, the substance of his agenda rose in his mind, buoyed by the beer's excessive carbonation.

"Omar, I need some information."

"From me?" The conversations the two men had had over the years never began like this; Omar suddenly got the shivers all over again.

"I need to know something about some smuggling. Or at least I think it's smuggling. Something crooked."

"What, for a book?"

"No, this is real."

"What the hell . . ."

"A friend was murdered."

"So? Look, I don't want to appear ungrateful, but I don't want to almost die again so soon, you see?"

"Just some basic facts, everybody down here probably knows —"

"I don't know anything. *Anything.*"

"Don't hand me that idiot peasant crap. You know *everything.* Everything that comes in off the Gulf, you try to get a piece of. That's the way it's been since before the war — I've *been* here, Omar."

"Whatever you say, Papa. But you also know it's better to know nothing, when . . ."

"When things get scary."

"When things start getting bigger and more important than people's lives. When people's lives fall in the shadow."

"It is the Castro boys, isn't it."

Omar looked around the bar. He was as

unhappy as Hemingway had ever seen him, which was almost exactly as unhappy as he'd seemed in 1949 when he'd narrowly lost an oyster-eating contest in Playa and then found he was the only one of fifteen contestants to contract septicemia, which nearly killed him in a five-day fever.

"It's not just Castro being another mountain crook or rabble-rouser, Papa. It's bigger than that, it's stronger."

"You fear the Twenty-sixth of July."

"You know what, I respect them because they'd kill me; I respect Batista's police and army and spies because they'd kill me, too; I respect the R.D. and the C.I.A. and the Mafia and everyone else around here, because people get killed, and I'd like to respect them with my silence."

"I should hand you back to *la pelea de gallos,* you're so afraid of everything."

"Papa, you're the only man in Havana I'm not afraid of. Are you sure you weren't followed? Who knows who in here is watching us?"

Great. Watching? There were only two other human beings in the place: the twelve-year-old boy sweeping up last night's cigar ashes and sawdust, and the bartender, who though conscious sat with his head huddled on the bar quietly moaning, in the grips of an unenviable hangover. Omar was clearly being paranoid, which was understandable under the day's circumstances. Hemingway knew that if he kept applying pressure, the sugar crystals of Omar's determined silence would shatter and crumble. He knew this because he knew Omar, who might be the least principled man Hemingway had ever known, and who, however terrified he might be, would always be waving his antenna looking for an exploitable opportunity to present itself.

"So dangerous? I don't believe you."

"Tu eres muy candido, señor."

"Then what the fuck were you doing in a cockfight stuffing peppers up your chicken's ass, man? You're not so scared that you'll sit home and not try to scrounge a *peso.*"

"Scrounge . . . You'd have me cut cane for a slave's wages."

"No I wouldn't. Let me ask you: who do you fear more?"

"Who I fear more. It doesn't matter, you see: the Twenty-sixth of July is getting money from Mexico and from Irish mobs in Chicago and San Francisco, Batista is bankrolled by the Mafia out of New York and the C.I.A. in Washington — you could read about this in *Time* magazine — the army is funding itself by attacking villages and looting them in the guise of being a revolutionary group, Batista himself has deals with Chiquita Banana and M-G-M pictures and J.P. Morgan. It's not just about who's the worst. They're all connected in their bloodstreams."

"I don't think that was in *Time.*"

"Look it up." New beers unexpectedly came, Omar gulped with élan. "I'm an ant in this. Looking to not get squished."

"So, Omar, off the record, you don't think the Twenty-sixth of July have a point, that Batista should be dumped?"

"I didn't say that. You're asking my opinion now? That I can give. Batista is a wealthy pig who should be gutted. Castro and Guevara and those *hombres* are, I think, self-serving assholes who are, right now, convinced they're going to help the poor people of Cuba. They might, somehow. So I'm for them. Saying so will not get me killed."

"Yes. Opinions are free, right?"

"Right. And harmless."

"Coming from the likes of you."

"Right."

"So what if the information I was looking for helped the cause? What if the death of my friend — who was found with a 60-pound harpoon pushed through his chest by the way —"

"Ach! Jesus."

"What if Cuthbert's death had something to do with the revolution, with fighting Batista, and if I found out what it was about, maybe . . . maybe it's important. I think it has something to do with Ferenc Galko."

"Galko. I've heard the name."

"Hungarian."

Omar was thinking, you could see the rusty gears turning. "So you're pro-Castro, too?"

"Uh. I think so. What you said before made sense."

"Papa, you should not goat-shit a goat-shitter."

"Really."

"You're a rich American!"

"Look, I've got a long record of Communist sympathies! I helped the Republicans in Spain! You should check with the F.B.I. guys who kidnapped me the other day, they seemed pretty convinced. Jesus Christ, I was just there trying to tell them that I'm not a Red, and here I am trying to convince you I am."

"*Señor,* you are a muddle."

"God, I'm so tired. Omar, I'll lay it out straight for you. If you don't know who

Galko is or who Cuthbert was, then all I can ask you is: who's doing the shipping work here for Castro? From the Keys. I'll go ask them whatever I can."

"And when they ask you how you found out who they are?"

"I'll tell them Cuthbert told me."

"That's thin. It could get you killed."

"It could work."

"Why should I say anything."

"Because it's the right thing to do."

"Maybe. But I don't see how you can be sure of that. *That* sure."

"For my friend's sake, I am."

"The name I know is Aníbal Desanzo."

"How do I find him."

"The phone book."

19

Desanzo was indeed in the Havana phone book, not as a resident but as a business — Desanzo Taxidermia, no address given. Hemingway discharged Omar to his upstairs flat, where the man would presumably draw the shades and drink himself to sleep, and began pouring *centavos* into the cantina's dented WWI-era pay phone. The number rang, and a man answered, saying only *"Qué."*

"I'd like to speak to Aníbal Desanzo, *por favor.*"

"The taxidermy is closed."

"It's not about that."

"Who are you?"

"Not important. I have just a few questions. Private, off the record."

"I'm waiting for you to say something."

Hemingway began racking his mind for possible code words.

"Harry Truman."

"No."

"Antonio Machin."

"No."

"Guantanamera."

"C'mon, jeeez."

"Pepe Le Pew."

"*Señor,* how many chances do you think you'll get?"

"Look, fuck this. The matter has to do with Ferenc Galko. I'm an American but I'm not a cop or a fed. I'm just a nosy friend of somebody who got hurt."

"Just nosy."

"That's right."

"You know Galko."

"I do."

"Hey, you sound just like Ernest Hemingway — you're Hemingway, aren't you?"

"Oh for the love of God. What, have you people been following me since I landed?"

"Following you? He thinks we're following him!" A snort from the background. "No, I heard your voice on the radio, that Miami station, you read something. Just last week."

"Must've replayed an old interview or something."

"*Si.* So, what's your business, Hemingway?"

"I told you. I want to talk to Desanzo."

"Okay. Be at the bar in La Mina at five."

"Gracias."

It couldn't be that simple — and yet, Hemingway knew that maybe it could, maybe his mission would end right here, with some Cuban crook telling him yeah, Cuthbert ripped him or Galko or the shore police off and got run through for his troubles. What would Hemingway do then? Then he'd have to write, quit avoiding it, which he realized is in a concrete sense what he'd been doing. This was just another lion hunt, or typhoon plane voyage, or war zone observation, or Alexandria brothel dive. All of them distractions from the cold demands of the blank page. He'd been so good, so dogged, in his earlier years, writing wherever he was, centering the calendar around the five to seven pages he thought he needed to do each day to earn his supper. But as life bore on, it became easier to put those pages off, to take the successes for granted, to trick himself into thinking, as only he could with his learn-everything-for-real-leave-50-percent-out formula, that whatever fool thing he was doing was all for the benefit of the work.

The trouble with this last presumption was, of course, that sometimes it was true. But too often these last years it just wasn't.

Had he spent an entire week racing — and crashing — boxcars in Atlanta for the sake of a story? That four-week binge in Majorca had no earthly use. Hunting elk with his new nitrogen-purged rifle scope was powerful business, but you couldn't write about a hunt like that without the protagonist coming off like a jackass. Why'd he even go water moccasin hunting in the Everglades? For fun, not for fiction. Or, perhaps more accurately, as a parry *against* fiction. As a defensive evasion, or a flanking maneuver. Somewhere in Hemingway there had begun the sense that fiction, his fiction, seemed less a discipline or mission any longer but simply entertainment to his readers, as if he was a juggling clown or a radio writer. He was a servant, a retail provider of popular culture.

Anyway, write about what — this? Peter's story is a brick wall, no matter what Scotty M. had thought back in the bar days ago. Maybe, he thought, mine? The assbackwards investigation? A troubled, aging . . . what, retired colonel, on an angry, self-gratifying yet righteous campaign to find who killed his good-for-nothing friend, half-knowing all along that the answer will be no real answer at all. . . . Maybe with a woman, a divorced aristocrat . . . From Majorca . . .

Nursing a small but fiercely blue inner pilot light, Hemingway took a car to La Mina, a run-down restaurant fashioned out of a colonial-era girls' school on Plaza de Armas, at three, equipped with a pad of legal paper and a pencil. He sat at a back table, ordered mojitos, and set upon the page.

The coroner shrugged, strolled vaguely over to one of the three cots presently occupied, and pulled back the sheet, all the way.

The body was buck-naked and the color of blue candy-tray mints. The gaping wound in his chest was just that — torn skin, blue, and a dark hole, no gore.

"You drained him already, where'd you do that?" The man tried to sound merely curious.

"We've got a draining table out back," the coroner said.

"No autopsy?"

"We know how he died, Howard."

"Where's the harpoon."

Ach. Too Chandler.

The body was naked and the color of blue candy-tray mints. The wound in his chest was only that — torn skin, a dark hole, no gore. The man stood over the body and lit a cigarette. The coroner came up from his paperwork with a bottle of wine he kept cold with the bodies and samples.

"Señor Howard, here, the day will be long."

The man took the wine in a broad sink glass and drank it. "Angelo, this is dirty business. This isn't the war."

"Si, señor. This is no war."

The reflexes were stodgy, the ideas covered with drying glue. And how to keep it from being a mere mystery?

Hemingway spent the time scribbling out false starts, smatterings of dialogue, place names intended to invoke in later rewriting a particular geography or real event fit for describing, questions he couldn't answer about the story's larger intentions, words he didn't want to forget to use (like *haymaker*), words he didn't want to forget to avoid (like *schadenfreude*), and doodles. He realized he'd have to research the history of harpoonery or change the murder weapon entirely, which wouldn't be bad; he'd have to give his new heroine a history and persona that was markedly different from the gals in *The Sun Also Rises* and *Across the River and into the Trees,* and he'd have to find some middle ground — oh but how he hated middle grounds of all types — between the more ordinary three-dimensional storytelling of *Across the River* and the bones-only fable tone of *Old Man.* Middle ground, or some other voice, some other extreme, altogether?

Then the man sat down across from him. It was then that Hemingway realized he'd already had at least nine mojitos, which went down like spring water, and was feeling both thoroughly reckless and slightly unstable.

"Buenos dias."

"Desanzo." The man nodded. He could've been any Cuban man in his forties, sunburnt, dentally troubled, scarred randomly, muscly-thin as a cheetah. He had a jacket on, which in this heat probably hid a weapon. He didn't blink and was clearly all danger and business.

"I liked *Old Man and the Sea* very much."

Hemingway was not expecting that. "Thanks . . . I'm proud of that book. Can I call you Aníbal?"

"What do you want?"

"I'm . . . looking for information. A friend of mine was killed on Key West. I think it had something . . . I think you might be able to help me figure it out. Or at least if it has something to do with the Twenty-sixth of July."

"Why?"

"That's not an unreasonable question, and I can't answer it straight. Let's just say I need to, for myself. No one else cares, and, if you give a shit, I'll tell you that maybe I'm feeling like I was one of those people, the ones that don't care, for too long."

"You're right, I don't give a shit."

"You asked, though."

"How did you get my name?"

"He told me. My dead friend. Mentioned it once."

"Convenient. We'd like to help you, *señor,* but there's no way we can trust you. Even if you are Ernest Hemingway."

"I just want to know who killed him. And why. If he was moving something for you, buying or selling for you or the revolution, then you should want to know, too."

"Why should we care? Cuthbert was nothing, a smuggler."

"So you know who I'm talking about."

"Of course."

"How do you know."

"Omar told us."

Hemingway went cold. Obviously Desanzo could see it on his face.

"Don't sweat it, *americano,*" the man said. "We have not hurt Omar. We like Omar. He's safe as long as you turn out to be who you say you are and do what you say you are doing. If we smell anything on you, Omar will die."

"Are you holding him somewhere?"

"No!" He laughed. "He's home. If we want him, we can find him, anywhere."

"So, what about Cuthbert? What was he doing? Why was he killed?"

Desanzo paused. "I'm going to tell you one thing."

"What."

"I am not Desanzo. I work for him. We will get in touch with you."

The mojitos made his mouth move. "Goddamn. You little crook."

"Hold your tongue, old man." Getting up.

Hemingway stood as well. "Don't call me at my house," he said, trying to seem stern. "I'm at the Hotel Sevilla."

"Whoa, you are keeping secrets, too!"

"Shaddup."

The conversation left Hemingway with a sour gut and an angry lack of purpose — waiting around for someone else's phone call was not his idea of a day or even an hour well spent, which is why he'd always had so little to do with Hollywood. So, his probably-worthless fistful of pages in hand, Hemingway took the ordinarily-twenty-minute walk on Calle Obispo, slowly, by cane, to El Floridita. He probably should've laid off the high-sugar cocktails at this point, but the bar's specialty double daiquiris, specialty because Hemingway had forced the tenders to make them that way, years before, were on his mind, and there were few places he liked better for thinking than the end of that bar, looking out at the sunshine on the street, the aromatic hum of rum and lime filling his nose and throat.

This whole adventure might come to a big fizzle, he thought; in fact, it probably would — and wouldn't that be a relief. Walking in the early evening heat and sweating like a bull, Hemingway again wondered if he had caused an ordinary boulder to roll down the mountain by digging around it a little too much. At El Floridita and tired, he let himself get lost for a while in the luxury of the happy gin-mill experience, with its worshipful bartender, the cool and wonderful drinks, the rise of intoxicated buoyancy, the appearance of lovely young girls to look at and talk to, the occasional hand-shaking with a respectful fan. What could be wrong?

Not much, until Stanley Lynch appeared at the bar three stools down, several hours into the evening. What the? Wait — Kwaak had said he was in Cuba. Lynch still had the same straw hat on and linen jacket, though both were a little rumpled by now. He was also wearing a neck brace that cradled his jaw like two-minute egg, with stiff wires reaching up and into his mouth.

He already had a drink in his hand when Hemingway saw him, and was moving the straw to his constricted lips when he spotted Hemingway.

His eyes bugged and rolled to the ceiling, and Hemingway got to his feet and came closer.

"Hey Lynch! What're you doing in Cuba?" Hemingway's first thought, a thoroughly drunken one, was about looking for an opportunity to pop the weasel again; his second thought was consumed with alarm at his own ignorance: Who *is* this guy? What team is he playing for? *What are the teams?*

"Don't get near me, Hemingway, I already have a lawyer coming after you."

"C'mon, Lynch! A spat between men! Besides, you can't lawyer me. You provoked me, and besides, Billy Bolitho was the only witness. You think he'll back your perspective, you're nuts."

"See you in court, that's all I've got to say."

"Had some medical bills, huh."

"Obviously."

"Well, I'm sorry. I'll pay them. It'd be only right."

"You'll get a chance to, don't worry."

"Fine. Be that way. In the meantime, what're you doing down here? You know, I spoke to a friend at the F.B.I., and they're watching you."

"You're so drunk you're hallucinating."

"Don't insult me, boy, or I'll double your lawsuit and put you in traction. I'm not making it up. They knew you were fresh out of Georgia State."

"Well, I guess that makes them geniuses."

"But I'm still trying to figure how you're hooked into Cuthbert's death."

"I'm not. Leave me alone. I'm just trying to . . . make a buck, somewhere. Like everyone. Like you."

"I'm not trying to cash in." Hemingway laughed. "I'm just doing the right thing. Kickin' the dog."

"Is that right." Lynch said it with a contemptuous, almost pitying exhalation. He put down his cocktail and walked out of the bar.

20

The next morning, which was muddy-shady from stormclouds, the air heavy and viscous with the threat of downpour, Hemingway awoke in his room, ordered an omelet from downstairs, performed his usual anti-hangover rituals as best as he could away from home, and tried to recall all of the details from the day before, which got increasingly hazy as the afternoon's memories turned into the night's. There weren't many details worth noting, as it turned out; the phone call from Desanzo, or whomever, was still forthcoming.

Now that he was in Havana, something unremembered but struggling to surface kept at him, and while he was wishing he'd ordered a cold white wine with his omelet it finally emerged: Hemingway had brushed shoulders with Castro a few times in 1945 and 1946, while Castro was a penniless lawyer for peasants and was ranging around trying to gather communal action against the government and American corporate intrusion into Cuba through one semi-Socialist organization or another. Hemingway had heard him hold forth in taverns and cafés, and he was an entertainingly zealous firebrand then, full of bounce and humor and also pigheadedness. Castro's minions had at several points tried to enlist Hemingway in their cause, or at least solicit funds from him, which never worked because by the end of the war Hemingway was far beyond the stage of joining things or holding much faith in organized social change. But none of that is what Hemingway had forgotten — he'd forgotten that once a pretty Castroite girl named Simona had given him a hard sell at Finca Vigia when Mary was out, virtually offered to sleep with him for a promise of support, and then had left her papers behind in a flustered snit. Among the flyers and petitions were lists of names and addresses and even a few Miami bank account numbers, so Hemingway never threw them away, just stuck them in a paper stack on a bookshelf in the library. If she had come back for them, he'd've handed them over, but she never did. Or, at least, she didn't while he was home — Mary might've told her to hit the Dixie highway, figuring she was an aspiring mistress. Hemingway didn't know and certainly wouldn't ask. But the papers should still be where he'd put them, under the unfinished stories and tax bills and newspaper clippings about Spain. They might lead him somewhere, or make a connection clear.

Hemingway dialed the house — if Mary answered, he'd hang up. No, he'd tell her he was still in Florida, but was coming home in a day or two.

She didn't answer; Carlos the seventy-year-old houseboy did, who said Mary had gone into Old Havana to hit the farmers' markets. Hemingway told him to never tell *señora,* but that *señor* will be popping by immediately for something, and then will officially return home some other time, soon. Carlos shrugged with a *hmpf* and said *si.*

On the street, Hemingway got a car and headed out to the house, slouched in the backseat for fear of passing Mary coming from the other direction. The decaying city melted away into the overgrown tropical suburbs where suddenly the houses became purposefully hidden by vegetation, and wealthy Europeans outnumbered the locals.

Finca Vigia loomed, all coddled in palm

and giant ferns; Hemingway paid his driver and snuck around the side, humping over a low and mossy stone wall by lying on his belly on top of it and throwing his legs over first, coming within millimeters of walking into a brown widow web spread between two nance trees, and creeping around the back toward the servants' entrance. Before him, the mango-cluttered slope of the farm's wild acres dipped down, and the jungle landscape spread out toward the sky.

As he stepped from the bush, he saw that right in front of the door was Carlos holding a chicken and a hatchet, leaning over an old maple chair — with Hemingway's first step, the hatchet came down on the chicken's neck, its head fell to the soil, and the body, released, began to run. It ran in a fast loop and headed smack into Hemingway's right leg, spraying blood straight up his trousers and across the palm-patterned button-down shirt he'd bought in Hawaii in the 1930s and which Mary maintained probably hadn't fit him right since 1941.

The chicken's headless body, its last gasp finished, fell over prone. Hemingway turned red.

"What the FUCK are you doing, Carlos, slaughtering animals in my house?! We don't have a farm here, ferChrissake, we buy meat!"

"*Señor! Por mi familia!* I was going to clean up!"

"Are you going to clean up *this?!*"

"Quick, *señor,* undress, I'll get the club soda."

Hemingway was soon standing in the kitchen in his pale blue boxers and undershirt, as Carlos and Zazie, the fiftyish maid, went about maniacally scrubbing his shirt and slacks in the sink, with brushes and club soda and cold dishwater. After more than five minutes, it seemed a lost cause, and Hemingway went upstairs to his room to get dressed in something else, a safari shirt and khaki cargo shorts, half-forgetting his initial subterfuge and neglecting to cover his tracks. Then he remembered that he was supposed to be leaving already, and hurried over to the library, shuffling through the many papers — Mary, a compulsive discarder of other people's effluvia, had been ordered not to touch anything on the book shelves, and now Hemingway was beginning to regret it. Paid delivery bills, newspaper recipes, issues of the *Saturday Evening Post* that didn't even have a review of one of his books in them, typing paper with scrawled phone numbers belonging to people he'd never remember, fan letters, pages ripped from old African Baedekers, envelopes from Patrick or Gregory without the correspondence they arrived with, advertisements for new Havana casinos.

There it was: Simona's list, scripted out sloppily in pencil on the back of two cruise-liner flyers, Spanish names and addresses from all over the island, from the Malecón strip to Baracoa, and only a few Miami bank listings, none of them revelatory. Hemingway scanned it quickly, planning on calling each and every number later, and found no mention of Galko, or Lynch, or Tcheon. But there she was: Matilde Pirrin, listed as having resided in Havana, on Alambique, ten years ago. Was she working for the Communists now, under Galko's nose? Or does Galko know, and do his interests coincide with theirs? (There was as much chance of Ferenc Galko becoming a full-on workers'-rights Red as Hemingway had of becoming Johnny Weismuller.) Or is Galko being set up?

Or, maybe, Matilde, that wicked panther of a woman, might be betraying the movement from the inside, an idea that depressed Hemingway as he stood in his shorts. As this speculative shadow occupied him, he heard a moment too late the sounds of

Mary coming in the servants' entrance, hustling and bustling.

"What the hell happened here? Carlos, no more chickens, I told you that! You're washing your chicken-blood-stained clothes in *my* kitchen sink?! Wait, these aren't yours — what the fuck are *señor*'s clothes doing here covered in blood?! Carlos?!"

Mary could see the front door from the back of the house where she apparently stood, haranguing Carlos; Hemingway was cornered. Couldn't even lope upstairs and drop off a balcony, which would likely bust his ankle all over again. He folded the list and stuffed it into his pocket. He sidled silently toward the front hallway — he'd need only two or three seconds to scoot out and onto the street ordinarily, but with the cast he'd need more. He listened.

Mary was still yelling: "You don't *know* how you got chicken blood on *señor*'s clothes?! Were you dressing up? My God, why am I waiting one more second to fire you?!"

Hemingway heard Carlos muttering, and strained his ear: something about "*señor* was here, earlier, and left."

"Earlier?!" Mary howled. "I've only been gone twenty minutes! Why would he do that?!"

"When you were at the Van Hursts'," Carlos lied through his teeth. Mary had coffee with the next-door Swiss bankers, Hemingway knew, every morning when he wasn't home.

"How did *señor* know I wasn't here?"

"He called and asked and I told him."

Mary got quiet, stewing. Hemingway inched toward the front door, listening for a sound that indicated Mary's movement out of the line of fire — to the bathroom, or up the stairs. He thought he heard it, finally — a creak of bathroom door. He went to the door, touching his cast down quietly on the rugs, and started to open it as quickly as he could without it making a sound. When Mary, after having spotted him several seconds earlier, spoke up.

"Jesus Christ, man, what the fuck are you doing?"

After his blood pressure spike burned his eyeballs for an instant and then subsided, Hemingway turned and smiled lamely. Stammered, flapped his arms sheepishly.

"Hey, Pickle."

"Ernest," she came closer, following him back into the library, "what the fuck is going on? Why are you sneaking into *your* house? Why are you avoiding me? Holy shit, look at that cast. You weren't kidding about that, were you."

"No, I wasn't —"

"How'd you manage that?"

"I, uh, trying to fix those tiles up on the roof?"

"You fell off the roof?!"

"No! Just a little."

She was tearing up now, but her voice remained strong and furious.

"Papa, what's with the skullduggery? Tell me, are you skulking around arranging for another divorce and another marriage? Trading up, as they say? Yet again?"

"No, no, no —" He sat down, rubbing the knee above the cast, which ached. "Listen, Mare, it's nothing like that —"

"I thought this was it, I thought we were different, *you* said it was different!, you said you were finished chasing after women and looking for the perfect man's woman — *your words!* — because you knew she didn't exist! And she doesn't, goddamn it! You want to be in love and be married, you have to cede half of your time and your energy to that other person, right? You said that, right? You were done chasing after daydreams!"

"I know, I know, Mary, it's not like that at all. There's no other woman! Goddamn it!"

"Don't you *dare* get indignant!"

"Sorry! Fuck! But — But, I'm serious, it's

not like that. Men *do* have to be on their own sometimes, though."

"We're back to that again, are we?! You know perfectly well that's an excuse for you to go off and do any silly shit you want to without someone responsible nearby to put a damper on it."

"And what's wrong with that? If that's what I want to do, I will sometimes do it, and it doesn't mean I don't love you, it doesn't mean I don't want to stay married. It just means . . . whatever it means!"

"Do you hear how dumb that sounds?"

"Mary, look, I don't care how dumb it sounds because, honestly, this isn't like that anyway."

"Really."

"Yes. It has to do with Cuthbert."

Mary's hands flew to her scalp and grasped huge haystacks of hair.

"Are you *kidding me?!* Ernest, you've brought that bullshit to Cuba? Why would you want to get involved with people like that?"

"First of all, Pickle, I didn't bring it to Cuba, it brought me. Second, 'people like that' means, what, poor men, smugglers, crooks, revolutionaries —"

"Murderers!"

"— murderers, feds, whatever, right?

Guess what, Mary, I'm already involved. I've always been involved! I've known these guys on every continent my whole life! This is part of a man's life, a real life. You're faced with decisions and matters of honor and loyalty and prairie justice and you can't back down, because if you do you shrivel and die. Damn it, I'm not just a writer and a husband and a homeowner, I'm a man grappling with the real dangers of a real world. Life is a matter of life and death."

"You've been saving that up."

"It's true, anyway."

"It's out of your novels — no, worse, it's out of *Green Hills of Africa.*"

"Bullshit, I never write like that."

"I'm talking ideas, meathead. You're trying to live up to these ideological notions you've picked up and used in your books, which is fine, but life just isn't like that, *Ernest.* Life is actually about responsibility, about living with other people and doing the Christian thing as far as you can and doing laundry and paying bills and eating and screwing and looking for contentment and peace and satisfaction with yourself until you die. It's not about putting yourself at preposterous risk for the sake of a vague Spartan idea about honor and machismo."

"Maybe not for you. Maybe not for

women. But for me, those ideas are important, *that's* how I look for satisfaction with myself. In the end." Was this true, or was he just arguing?

"That's like saying the only route to happiness is to be miserable all the time."

"The Buddhists would say you nailed it."

"Oh fuck all of this, I give up."

Mary stormed upstairs. Hemingway sat, rubbing his knee, wondering how much of what he'd said he actually believed. He wasn't, truth be told, following a noble ideal in wanting to know how Peter died; he just wanted to know. Didn't intellectualize, didn't philosophically reason it out, just felt it was his duty. But where'd that come from, this duty thing? Who knows — as much from Hemingway's experiences in idealistic war zones, surely, as from the brotherhood of drinking buddies, a bond formed between men when they are at their most vulnerable and asinine, and therefore the most trusting.

Hemingway had been having a variation on this argument with one wife or another ever since 1929, after his father had swallowed a gun barrel, and after Hemingway and Pauline had moved to Key West. He never argued with Hadley in this way, he didn't think; he was too young and their life together then was too tremulous and fresh and forward looking. But with Pauline, Martha and Mary, this kind of gender battle had arisen regularly, like bouts of athlete's foot. A big differentiation, Hemingway always thought, between a man's perspective and a woman's is that women most often can grow to maturity in civilized countries without ever knowing what it's like to get hit in the face so hard your nose bleeds. Every man knows. Certainly none of Hemingway's women ever experienced such a mundane thing, at least as far as he knew, though he did come close to belting Martha once in London after a long day of whiskey and after Martha had called him "dickless" in front of Robert Capa.

It's not as if Hemingway *really* wanted his wives to have understood what living a dangerous life meant; for that, they'd have to be men. What he *really* wanted was for them to be a refuge from that life, a warm base camp that provided a human meaning to the risks and wounds and sacrifices. Romantically, or maternally? Hemingway didn't know; he'd avoided trying to explicate his own feelings about women his whole adult life, for fear of it being either finally inexplicable or infantile. That he always felt a need for them, and often for a new one instead of the old, only depressed him more — there was no solution, no happy retirement village at the end of the journey where all of the questions would be answered and all of the worries expunged. Short of spending the next few decades in Freudian analysis, which was never a stomachable option, Hemingway has only one choice: ignore it, be as kind as he can but otherwise let the woman's world take care of itself. He would always have one foot in it, never two.

Hemingway saw no reason now not to sit back and ask Carlos for drinks, which he did. Mary crashed and raged upstairs. He took out the list once more, studying its faded pencil scratch, looking for familiar house numbers or names that might be aliases. He was doing this and inserting a bamboo backscratcher into his cast and drinking a Cuba Libre that Carlos had made with real mint growing outside when the door was knocked upon, and a clutch of Batista's military police began to let themselves in.

21

What they didn't understand, none of them, from Miami to Havana, was the more they tried to muscle Hemingway around the more he became convinced that his personal, prickly, whimsical campaign was in fact righteous and inevitable.

Whatever trifling patience Hemingway had for American feds was monumental beside how much he could muster for the Batista forces, composed as they were completely of opportunistic, amoral bullies and sociopaths. Hemingway didn't remember getting up from his chair, or stuffing Simona's list into his pocket, all he remembered later, holding ice to his forehead at the kitchen table, was immediately being at the door, cast or no cast, grabbing the first policeman there by the hair and punching him flat across the nose three times like machine-gun fire, and glimpsing a spray of blood.

Until a nightstick, coming from behind Asshole Batista Cop #1, came down on Hemingway's head and sent bolts of pain deep behind his eyes. Hemingway reached up, grabbed the stick, wrenched it back, bringing the arm of the cop holding it shooting uncomfortably into the room, as he fell across the slumped figure of the first cop, and Hemingway yanked the stick away for real, placing his cast leg back a ways on the floor as if he were going to throw a touchdown pass, and raising the stick in preparation of a sound pounding.

Until Mary, not presumably wishing to see her husband land in Gunanajay for manslaughter, flew off the foot of the stairs at Hemingway and grabbed his arm, throwing him off balance — *wha?* — as a third policeman stepped over the first, shouting something in Spanish about a search warrant, but not holding one, and about Hemingway going quietly with them, *por favor!*

Until Hemingway grabbed him by the front of his collar as Hemingway was falling backwards, which is where Mary was pulling him trying to get the nightstick out of his hand so he wouldn't kill anyone with it. The three of them fell together, over the other two in a kicking tangle — there were, Hemingway saw, at least three more outside on the steps — and when Hemingway landed on the floor, on his ass, with a house-joint-loosening boom that could be heard up the street, his hand did let go of the stick, and Mary threw it toward the kitchen, thinking as she did that there were too many guns in the house for anyone to feel safe. Imagine, she quickly thought, if this had been the evening, and Papa had already drunk enough to make him a menace under the best circumstances.

The third policeman fell on top of Hemingway, his skinny knee slamming into the larger's man groin like a wrecking ball into a church roof. *"AH GOD, FUCK YA!"* Hemingway howled, kicking, viciously kicking with his right boot the third policeman off and the second policeman, who'd only stumbled and lost his nightstick, in the eye. He began to scream.

Mary was the first on her feet, her fight response hot under her skin but reasonably positioning herself between Hemingway and the various guns elsewhere in the room, on the walls and in the closet. "Papa, c'mere, I've got you," she cooed, going to grab his armpits, but he wasn't having it — he thrashed away and got to his knee, and then to his feet, cursing the whole time, and then, for good measure, turned and hauled off and swung his hard plaster cast at the skull of the third policeman, who was then rising from his hands and knees. The cast hit his face with the sound of a shovel hitting wet dirt, and the man flopped like a scarecrow off the stake, falling onto his back. Finally Hemingway stood, more or less in control of himself and his home. Three Cuban policeman lay on the floor moaning and bleeding, and the other three outside stayed outside, for the moment, cowering. Seven seconds had passed in total.

"Hemingway, you've screwed the pooch this time." Mary sat down and downed the rest of Hemingway's unfinished Cuba Libre.

They arrested him in any case, or seemed to, with handcuffs, taking Hemingway down to the crumbling Picota y Paula station, where he sat waiting on a wooden bench, fuming, dehydrating, trying to ignore a monster headache. Eventually, not soon enough, Hemingway's Havana lawyer, a certain Germinal Riquenes, strode in.

"About time. Mary called you."

"*Si, señor.* How are you? It's been a few years!"

"She must've called you two hours ago."

"*Si.* I had lunch," he said it smiling. "You know as well as I do that no one respects a lawyer who doesn't always seem to have something of equal or greater importance to do than to solve your particular problem." He paid no notice to the angry bump, sticking out like a gopher hill, on Hemingway's head.

"I'll respect you, you mole. I'll do it without gloves on."

"Ah, then, Hemingway, who would you call for help when I have you sent to jail?"

"God, if only there were another competent lawyer in Cuba."

"Ha! There is none! Except Castro!"

Always wearing a sky blue suit, off-white shoes and blood red tie, Riquenes was so universally loathed, and, frankly, inherently, unavoidably loathsome, that he did get respect, and even a certain degree of affection, from the city's moneyed classes. Of course he got the business. No one ever, ever, speculated as to his real nature, his sexuality, his past, his hobbies or his restaurant habits. No one ever wanted to know.

"First things first," Riquenes said, standing before Hemingway and facing the front desk's officers and the long hallway of interrogation rooms behind him, raising his voice in Spanish, "UNLESS this entire platoon wants to explain to *El Presidente* why the American F.B.I. has been COMPELLED, against its wishes, to LAUNCH an official PROBE into the dealings of MR. MEYER LANSKY," his voice rising to a strident, terrifying siren, "WITH THE GOVERNMENT!, THEREFORE JEOPARDIZING AMERICAN AID and the TRAFFIC WITH AMERICAN CORPORATIONS like AMERICAN SUGAR! and UNITED FRUIT!, WHO OWN MORE THAN 80 PERCENT OF FARMABLE CUBAN LAND!, unless this seems DESIRABLE to *el capitán,*" the voice now lowering to a mere definitive declaration, "then I would suggest getting Mr. Hemingway out of irons. Immediately."

The grandstanding was nothing new, but the mention of Meyer Lansky took Hemingway by surprise: is the Mob's presence in Havana so prevalent now that you can bellow about it in the open spaces of police stations and not raise an eyebrow? But a few eyebrows did apparently arch, out of view, down that hallway, because after some stirring a potbellied officer came from one of the distant rooms, jangling keys, uncuffed Hemingway without a word, and beckoned both men to follow him. Bruised and weary, Hemingway was about as disgruntled as he could ever remember being, and couldn't wait, frankly, to sink his teeth into an authority figure as soon as he had the opportunity.

The room was stark and grim, naturally. A large, conspicuous mirror occupied the western wall. Riquenes and Hemingway took two of three folding chairs opposite the tin desk, behind which sat a captain who introduced himself as Miró.

"Like the painter," Hemingway said. Silence.

"El capitán," Riquenes began, "I'd like to first point out —"

The cop cut him short with a finger in the air. "*Señor* Hemingway," he growled, "I'm sure you do not want to be sent to a Cuban prison, yes? No? What a horrible thing for your publicity."

"What kind of threat is that?" Hemingway howled. "Didn't you hear *his* threat?"

"What, about Lansky?" He couldn't suppress the smile. "Hemingway, we could find a whore's body with your thumbprints on her throat, if we wanted to. What would you do about it? Write a letter to *The New York Times Book Review*?"

"You just said that in front of my lawyer!"

"So? The same could happen to him."

"Holy shit!" Hemingway just didn't know how seriously to take this arrogant little slug's mouth, as much as he wanted to wreck the place. "What the fuck is it you want?"

"Ah, I'm glad you asked. You had to ask — you see, I couldn't just say, Hemingway, do this, tell us that. You had to volunteer."

"Don't get carried away, I'm still deciding whether to beat you to death with this cane."

"That temper! Seriously, we want . . . to know where it is."

"Where is what?"

"The thing, the thing you are smuggling or preparing to smuggle for Castro, the thing you are using *Señor* Gargallo for, the thing you met about in La Mina. Right now against you we have conspiracy against the government, resisting arrest, assaulting a police officer on three counts, fraternizing with known pedophiles —"

"What?"

"At the cockfight, *señor.* One in the crowd." Hemingway looked at Riquenes. Riquenes shrugged.

"Look, I don't what you're talking about, what 'thing' you're looking for."

"Where is Castro?"

"I don't know. You don't know?"

"We thought he was in Mexico. But now we have reason to believe he's in Cuba, right now. We need to find out where."

"Go ahead and find him. It's not a big

fucking island."

"Where is Castro." Miró repeated himself with was intended to be a menacing deadpan. Riquenes yawned.

"I told you, I don't know. Don't fucking ask again."

"This thing you're smuggling, we know you were partners with Kovarick —"

"What?!" Hemingway rose to his feet. "How do you know that name? This has nothing to do with Omar or anything else, the fucking C.I.A. had you on my ass the minute I entered the harbor! Is my fucking house here bugged, too?!"

Miró fumbled for a response, and the door flew open. In quickly walked an utterly calm, clean-shaven American man in a gray government suit, pointing to Miró. "Alright, you, out."

Miró shuffled out of the room, apparently disgraced. The American sat down and chinked his tie gently. Smiling.

"Hi! Sorry about that, these Batista guys, they'd check to see if a rattlesnake was sleeping by kicking it. My name is Anderson, Andy Anderson. And I am, in fact, a field agent with the Central Intelligence Agency. I'm honored to meet you, Mr. Hemingway. A big fan!" He leaned over the desk with his hand out, still smiling. Hemingway shook it and sat down. No effort was made to acknowledge Riquenes's presence.

Anderson continued. "No, Finca Vigia is not bugged, but your Key West house is. Full disclosure! Just protecting American lives and liberty, right?, and sometimes overdoing it, but no one's hurt."

"Cuthbert."

"Yes, well, we didn't do that, we think he probably managed that on his own. We sure weren't surveilling him! Ha! Imagine. Anyway, we certainly didn't mean to have you threatened or anything. Honestly, that thing about the thumbprint!" He shook his head, grinning, looking for a shared moment, and didn't find one. Riquenes was checking his manicure.

Hemingway was stewing. "So, you're going to reassure me that the C.I.A. is working in my best interest."

"Exactly! Well, and yes, we're probably going to keep an eye on you — nothing obtrusive! — a little until we figure out what's going on with the Twenty-fifth of July. Cool, right?"

"Twenty-sixth."

"That's right. And we figured, actually, that you could help us. You seem to be on some kind of crusade — and go for the gusto, by the way, good for you — that seems to be, shall we say, leading you toward Castro. We can help!"

"For the love of God, I don't want the C.I.A.'s help."

"Well, OK, but any info you have could help us, y'know, keep things down here nice and copacetic."

"I told everything I know to your boys on the Naval Reservation. And I haven't learned anything significant since, except that the C.I.A. must be a gaggle of retarded peckerwoods to let Batista's cops ever do their dirty work for them, and to ask someone like me to help them find what must be the most notorious man in the hemisphere."

"So you'll help us? Tell us what you find out, who you meet?"

"Sure. And while I'm doing that, I want a written guarantee that you'll debug my house, and stop surveillance on me on every level."

Riquenes spoke up. "Can't do that. It won't be binding because what they're doing isn't legal to begin with."

"That's right!" Anderson chirped. "We don't need written contracts and stuff like that, no, no, no. You have my word, though! Swear to heaven!" He stuck out his hand.

Hemingway shook it, but just as he had

absolutely no intention of telling the C.I.A. anything at all he might find out about Castro, he knew Anderson was a worm and that Hemingway's every move would continue to be carefully monitored and documented.

"But I have a question," Hemingway said in a measured way that made Anderson sit at attention. "What's to keep me from suspecting, and even maybe getting someone I know at the *Miami Herald* to suspect, that Cuthbert, or Kovarick, was killed by the C.I.A.?"

"Gulp!" Anderson said the word, did not perform the action.

"Or the F.B.I.," Hemingway went on. "But I think C.I.A. I mean, you guys haven't left me alone from the minute Cuthbert's body got found on the docks. I've been threatened, bugged, lied to, interrogated, brawled with, incarcerated, had guns pointed at me, I've been accused of being anti-American and blackmailed with preposterous murder frame-up scenarios. . . . I don't need to do anything but look at you guys and the shit you've been pulling to think you had something to do with it. With Cuthbert."

Anderson was forcing himself to chuckle. "That's ridiculous, Mr. Hemingway!"

"But you tell me. What's to keep me from drawing that conclusion?"

"Conclusion?" Anderson got grave, which on him looked almost spooky, if not totally convincing. "You don't have any proof of anything, that's what. No newspaper would publish that story, or if they did, the story would be 'Ernest Hemingway Goes Paranoid in the Tropics, Suspects the Government of Murder.' "

"You tell your story, I'll tell mine."

"Fair enough! No, really, look, Mr. Hemingway, I'll tell you something you don't know. Your friend Cuthbert wasn't always smuggling when he was shuttling back and forth on that little green New Englander of his." Green? New Englander? *The second boat?* Hemingway stayed still. "You don't happen to know where that boat is, do you, Mr. Hemingway?"

"No."

"Well, anyway, whatever else he was doing, he was working for Batista."

"You fucking liar. Your buddies in Florida said they thought Cuthbert was a Communist. Which is it?"

"We're not certain, he does seem to have been a conflicted fellow. But he was on Batista's payroll, I could show you the logs. He gave info about smugglers, and about the American military. And probably, we're thinking now, about the Twenty-sixth of July."

Hemingway believed him; the detail about the boat, which did not suggest the boat of Cuthbert's everyone in Key West knew about, cinched it. Where *was* that boat?

"Jesus," he said. "I didn't know he was making that kind of money."

"It wasn't that much, to be honest with you. Batista does not give money away. But you see why we think whatever trail you're following is of importance to us. We don't want Cuba to be destabilized, or go Communist, God forbid."

"Of course."

"And we don't want you to get hurt either. You're a national treasure, Mr. Hemingway!"

Hemingway stood, ready to go, and waved one hand — *no thanks* — politely squelching whatever brownnosing Anderson was gearing up to do.

"Whoa, one more thing, Mr. Hemingway, if we could — We wanted to discuss with you someone we have in custody, maybe you can fill us in a little." Anderson went to the door, caught someone's eye and gestured with two fingers, and went back to the desk, smiling reassuringly. A moment later two cops came in with Stanley Lynch, who despite his neck brace had a freshly bloodied nose, and his eyes were teary. Sat him down in the third chair, to Hemingway's left.

"Christ, Lynch, you're a bad penny."

Lynch looked to Anderson.

"So you know this fellow," Anderson said toward Hemingway, his voice flattening. "Could you tell us what you know?"

"The F.B.I. has notes on him, I know that. He came snooping around Key West after Cuthbert died, claiming to be next of kin."

"And you're the one that broke his jaw?" Anderson chuckled heartily.

"Dislocated it," Lynch spat wetly.

"Yes, that was me. Lost my temper. I've already apologized."

"Well, Mr. Hemingway, did you know that Mr. Lynch here has worked, and still works as far we can guess, for Ferenc Galko?"

"I didn't. But I'm not surprised."

"*El Presidente* doesn't like *Señor* Galko, I understand —"

"The club dues are probably too high for Galko."

"Ha! I see what you mean, very clever. Mr. Lynch has been caught here with raw coca, suitcases of it, trying to leave the country."

"So?" Hemingway didn't see it right away, he didn't see why in a landscape filthy with smugglers this particular idiot was arrested and slugged and brought in here in front of him like a state's witness, a scapegoat of some kind.

"Smuggling coca is illegal, Mr. Hemingway, you know that." Anderson did not change his manner in any detectable way, but suddenly his glib salesman manner was apparent as a connivance, and he became quietly, unmentionably chilling.

"Right." Hemingway was becoming helpless, he could feel it.

"We also think Mr. Lynch might be the murderer you're looking for."

"No, that's not —"

"The circumstantial evidence is compelling."

"Has Captain Squiccarini been in contact with you? Because —"

"It's not relevant, Hemingway" — the "mister" was gone — "Lynch won't go to Florida to be interrogated by your sunstruck flatfoots, he's first going to face the situation he has here in Havana . . ." Hemingway glanced at Lynch, and the man's eyes were red-rimmed and bulging in their sockets, and then at Riquenes, who was looking down at his lap . . . "Which, being a professional criminal and Communist and drug smuggler, makes him an enemy of the state." Anderson was standing now, taking a pistol from one of the two cops, cocking it, "Hemingway, you appreciate the C.I.A.'s sensitive position on these things," putting it to Lynch's forehead and pulling the trigger.

A teacup-sized wedge of Lynch's skull hit the back wall, and blood spewed and gouted in fast jets in every direction, spraying Hemingway across the shoulder and back. Riquenes was spotless. Lynch's head snapped back, out of the neck brace, and his body convulsed enough to tip his chair backwards, so a second or so after the bullet went through him and lodged in the floor twelve feet away, Lynch fell on his back, wasted and still. The blood spray lingered in the air like mist.

Hemingway didn't dare say a word. He hadn't been that close to a man felled by gunshot since Spain. He was always amazed at the physiological chaos that bullets can perform on the human body, like they're unleashing a suppressed inner frenzy that, once escaped, hits the air like a mad electric storm. He thought he might have a heart attack, the blood was pumping so loudly in his ears.

My God. What was this? Lynch was another nowhere man, hardly worth the theatrics and the trouble of covering up an illegal cold-blooded execution. This was clearly for Hemingway's benefit. And Riquenes's.

"Mr. Hemingway, so sorry for the mess, but you can go now. Really, I hope we haven't inconvenienced you terribly. Good luck with your investigation!" Hemingway had stood up without realizing he had, and Anderson was escorting him and Riquenes out into the hall, around the body, which was already being rolled in a rug by the two cops.

Down the hallway to the lobby, Anderson kept talking. "Sorry about all this, but you understand, right? It's important to American interests to keep Cuba democratic and open for business. Right? You could say we're exporting democracy! And you'd be surprised how much damage one gangster, or one fool criminal, can do when things are politically rocky in a place like this. Can't let the balance be upset, even if it is just for one man's crooked lust for profit, and not for some misconceived higher purpose. Which, I'll be honest with you, I can admire, sacrificing yourself for the benefit of a righteous cause, a revolution or such, but by the same token we have to defend our interests, come hell or high water. I mean, this is man's business, and it's a hard day we live in, and sometimes difficult things must be done and done without pity. You understand, right? Of course, you do, you're Ernest Hemingway! Look who I'm talking to! I don't have to tell you about a man's responsibility in a dangerous world, right? You know all about it! Hell, you've made it a point of pride, haven't you, for us all!"

They reached the front steps, and the sun was hot. "Good luck, Mr. Hemingway, really!" Anderson shook and patted and waved and walked backwards into the building. "And hey, when're you coming out with a new book? I can hardly wait!"

The man and his lawyer stood alone in the heat. "The C.I.A. just killed Stanley Lynch," Hemingway muttered.

"Si," Riquenes answered. "No mystery to solve there."

"Was that a threat?"

"I think it was, among other things."

"I don't know what to do now. What're you going to do?"

"I'm going for a swim."

"Huh. Thanks for coming down, Germinal."

"No problem. I'll send you a bill."

Riquenes walked on down Picota, into the busy city. Hemingway supposed as he stood that he was in some kind shock, he couldn't make a decision. So he thought of looking for a cantina. He didn't quite remember to worry about the Desanzo phone call, but it didn't matter — while Hemingway was in the room with Anderson, Mary had already called around to the handful of hotels she knew he liked, counterbribed the right concierge, and had his things messengered home. At about the time Hemingway stood on the steps thinking only of gin, because he couldn't quite think of anything else, the phone call from Desanzo had come to the hotel, where it was mentioned that Hemingway was by then officially residing in his own house. So "Desanzo," or whoever it was, made a second call, and whoever was on the phone spoke to Mary, who told them to go to hell.

22

It took a few hours and many drinks, but Hemingway regained his bearings, and as night fell Mary lured him to bed and fucked him hungrily, which Hemingway himself was surprised he was capable of doing and doing well, after the day he'd had. He told her sparingly about his encounters in Havana so far; he left out Omar, and the threats of *el capitán,* and the midday meeting with the faux Desanzo, and Anderson's suggestion that Hemingway become, essentially, an American spy. But he had to tell her about Lynch, that just wouldn't stay buried.

She'd listen and groaned in frustration, but then looking through the belly hair caught in the moonlight from the window, after she'd gone to the kitchen naked and got them cold wine from the icebox, she remembered that someone shady had called, asking for him.

"They said, talk to Bernadette. Who's Bernadette?" Mary was lounging, nude and half soused, trying to sound unconfrontational.

"Bernadette? I have no idea. Great, now what."

Hemingway knew perfectly well who Bernadette was, and instantly knew why the name was mentioned — since 1949, he has known a young whore in a brothel on Calle Panurama named Katrina P., whom he had nicknamed Bernadette. He'd only screwed her twice; the third time he went to her, half in the hat, he found that all he wanted to do was talk and pretend to spoil her like a wealthy sugar daddy — after that bringing her books and licorice and wine, and laying out a 75 percent tip when he left. He wasn't proud of those detours, but he liked Katrina a good deal and wanted to help her, and figured if he was in her bed gabbing, no other brute fool was in there smacking her around or fouling her in places she didn't want fouled.

Here was the thing: Hemingway had labeled her Bernadette because she resembled Jennifer Jones, big black almond eyes, and cheekbones the size of Cadillac bumpers, but with shorter, auburnish hair. He had not told anyone else about his nicknaming, nor had he called her Bernadette in the company of others. She had always seemed embarrassed by the name, and had always made pains to keep Katrina in the brothel business at large, but the moment the two were alone, then she'd whisper, "Bernadette." Hemingway had even suggested that she should take the nickname as her *nom de bordel,* Katrina being her birth name. "But I have no family to shame," she'd said matter-of-factly, and instead wanted to be Bernadette only in the intimate presence of *señor,* the World Famous Book Writer.

So, if the Castro people knew her nickname, either they tortured her for it — not out of the question — or she is allowing herself to be used by the revolution, perhaps legitimately for political reasons. Hemingway didn't think that Katrina read newspapers, but maybe he was wrong. He hoped he was wrong. He did not savor the prospect of someone else getting hurt or worse because of a relationship with him, especially not someone he actually liked.

Mary wouldn't want to help Hemingway get any deeper into this mess even without the disclosure of a history with a Havana prostitute thrown in for good measure. So he played it mum, and would go to see Katrina tomorrow.

"Now what? Forget about it, Papa. Let's go to Zanzibar."

"It's not that simple, Mare."

"It is, it absolutely is. The C.I.A. is watching you, the Castroites are watching you, all waiting for you to do something else. So do nothing."

"Nothing."

"Or hit the road. C'mon, let's go a-safariing."

"I just got back a few weeks ago. I'm tired of that crap, Mary. Y'know? I do that to keep from having to write, and to have something to write about when I do write, which isn't working much anymore, so it's just distraction and indulgence and doesn't *mean* anything. It's fun and I love it, but I'm beginning to feel like a big, fake water buffalo con artist, walking around basking in fame for some sentences I wrote two or ten or twenty years ago. I need to do something that has some kind of intrinsic value."

"Like save a life."

"Yeah. Well, I'm obviously behind on that score."

"You didn't get that Lynch guy killed, please. You were just the audience. You could still save your own skin. And maybe mine."

Hemingway eyed her, stretched out naked,

sipping wine, her forty-eight years hardly showing on her from the throat on down.

"Who ever said you're in danger? I'm serious, I can't save Peter, but I can figure out the Truth, with a capital T."

"Didn't Sartre tell you himself that that existentialist stuff was just a way to piss away your time alive?"

"No, he said that *writing* about it was."

"So you're going to answer the big questions now."

"No, I'm just going to find the truth."

"I wouldn't be so sure if I were you, Papa. The truth? I think you're overestimating how clear it'll be when you find it, and you're overestimating how much anyone else on the planet cares."

"That's the journalist in you. I'm not suggesting that anyone else will care. It's pretty clear no one does. But I think it'll make a difference to me. It'll make me feel better."

"That'd be nice. But it could bite you in the ass."

Hemingway was falling asleep, with Mary still talking, about the *real* things, the redecorating the downstairs needed, the fact that Carlos was making a habit of slaughtering livestock in the backyard, the ridiculous paternity lawsuit their New York lawyer had called about, filed by a woman in Dallas with two fifteen-year-old twin girls who, reportedly, look just like Hemingway, and had he ever been to Dallas, ever?

Never been to Dallas, he dreamed, and then he was sitting on a bench in the Tuilleries, watching dozens of identical Little Lord Fauntleroys running around with balloons and balsa airplanes, and beside him was Ezra Pound, eating peanuts out of a paper bag. The dream-Hemingway had a memory, of having just returned from seeing Jean Renoir's *Nana* at Le Champo with Pound, who bought the peanuts there.

"Ernest, what you're writing now, it's a murder mystery? Like Conan Doyle?"

"No, no, I'm actually not writing anything right now — well, I am, but pieces of things. I haven't settled down on anything." Pound was his spry 'twenties self, Hemingway noticed, while he was his 1956 size.

"Then what is it, if not a book, this thing you're doing?"

"It's real. A real story."

"And the ending?"

"How could I know the ending if it's real?"

"My dear boy, you're writing it, aren't you? You're making up the questions, sifting the answers, coming up with the ideas, perceiving the characters a certain way, fueling it with your own motivations, aren't you? Would there be a story, real or not, if you didn't decide to create it?"

"I guess not."

"But it's not a book."

"No."

"Then, perhaps, a quest."

"That's what I told Mary. But I didn't use that word."

"You're not Odysseus."

"I certainly am not."

"You're Oedipus, avenging a royal death yet —"

"Please, enough Greeks."

"Then what's the quest for?"

"What's any quest for? Peace of mind."

23

In the morning, Hemingway had to lie to get out of the house and away from Mary, and he knew that an overly innocent-sounding or even practical-seeming lie would not wash with his wife, who could smell honest deception like a doe sniffing a fire coming up the mountain miles away. So he told her he was meeting the chief of police, who would be flattered to be asked, for a good deal of hard drinking; he wasn't going to say where, in hopes of bribing the creep and therefore getting a little otherwise-classified C.I.A. poop from Cuthbert's file. Realistic, low-stakes, and convincingly drunken. She yelled for a few seconds, and then threw her hands up and returned to haranguing the staff.

He believed Anderson when the TV-shill sociopath said that the house wasn't bugged, if only because it would've cost him nothing to admit it was. So Hemingway had Carlos call a cousin that lived near the Cementerio de Colon to come and pick him up for five American dollars, not at the house, which would be watched, but on a dirt road half a mile away, which Hemingway would get to by sneaking down through the mango trees at the back of his property, and across one of his neighbors' yards and then a stretch of private guava plantation. It was a bit of walking on a cane, and he left in plenty of time; he didn't want to be soaked in sweat before ten in the morning, or have a heart attack. He figured that what he wore was irrelevant, given his body profile, his beard (which he never gave a thought to shaving off) and his cast and cane. But still, he tried to mitigate his Hemingwayness at least a little, with sunglasses and an old baseball cap of Carlos's and a plain denim shirt.

The cousin, a grinning boy who appeared to be fourteen at the oldest, drove a wheezing 1932 Ford pickup that looked like it had survived a mortar attack, arrived on time and took the cash with a spirited laugh. Hemingway slumped down in the backseat out of view, and so the trip was without incident, and soon he was dropped off on Panurama at Lombillo, where he vanished quickly into the unmarked doorway leading to the brothel.

Little expense has ever been paid to the dark, cheap office-panel interior — this was not a rich westerner's hangout — with the exception of the requisite red lightbulbs; Hemingway had always supposed that this distinctly unsexy cliché was perpetuated by pointless tradition alone. The madam, who called herself only *Señora* Carmichael and played only Hoagy Carmichael on the turntable in the lounge room, greeted Hemingway with the rehearsed fanfare rich and famous men get in brothels. Tense and trying to think ahead of himself he paid her no mind, asked for Katrina, was braced with a 9:45 A.M. gin and tonic he didn't even have to ask for, and was then led down the thin hallway to her room.

Katrina sitting cross-legged on her mattress, reading a Mexican paperback with a painting of a gun on the cover; Hemingway sighed silently when he saw that she was not only unhurt but vibrant and relaxed. The building around them was quiet, the brothel almost empty this early. Hemingway kissed her on the cheek, took a shawl hanging on a chair and put it over her back, covering up her transparent slip, and lay down next to her. For a while she read aloud, in Spanish, what sounded like a bad translation of Chandler at his most pickled

— *fucked it up!* — and then he stroked her thigh with one fat thumb and said, "Bernadette."

Katrina got solemn, put the book down, and began to cuddle up, speaking in an excited whisper.

"Señor, we are comrades!"

"My God, *conchita,* have you become a Communist?"

"*Si,* why not? They came to me, *el Movimiento veinte-seis de Julio,* from the mountains, mostly college boys, they paid with bottles of Scotch! They would tell me all about the workers, the capitalists, how the poor are always been fucked by the fat cats." She picks up the stack of thin books on her nightstand, and under the pulp is Marx's *Manifesto,* translated into Spanish.

"I'm surprised."

"Don't be too much. I never told you, but my father was a rifleman for the army, and he was killed in 1933 when the officers rose up against Batista at the Hotel Nacional. I was a baby." Her eyes were large and dark brown and wet, like uncreamed coffee.

"No, you never told me."

"So these men, I was sympathetic to them."

"I hope they were nice."

"*Si,* they were very polite and clean. Che

didn't come, though."

"You like him."

"*Si,* who doesn't?"

"How long has this been going on?"

"A few months. But more in the last week, I don't know why. They've been here a lot. A lot of bottles of Scottish."

"Bernadette, do you think it was all a plan? To use you to get to me?"

"Oh, I don't know, *señor,* why?"

"Because a few weeks ago something happened in Florida, a friend was killed, and it has led me to the Twenty-sixth of July. Once I'm here, suddenly they know that you're Bernadette."

"Maybe they did, plan it, but so what? I told them, it was my idea to tell them. They said they needed to convey something to you secretly, that you were helping in the cause but you were in great danger, and was there any safe way I could contact you? That the C.I.A. couldn't understand. The C.I.A.! *Señor,* you are being so heroic."

"Oh ferChrissake Bernadette, I am not."

"So I said, yes, there is a name only he calls me, in bed, and I've never told anyone."

"Alright. We can never use it again, you understand."

"Why not."

"Because now all of Castro's people know it, and if they've been infiltrated the C.I.A. knows it, too. It's out there now, there's no getting back. And that means they know about you, too."

"That's *if.*"

"You should assume there's an American mole among your revolutionary friends. It's the safe thing to do. And anyway, I wouldn't trust these guerrillas with anything. They may have been nice to you simply because they had a use for you."

"Well, I'm used to that. But I believe in them. For now."

"OK. Now what."

"Ah! This is my top secret message to deliver! Be on Malecón, *numero doscientos treinta, manana* at eleven in the morning."

"Back there? The *pelea de gallos.*"

Katrina shrugged. "You know it, then."

"*Si.* Not my favorite spot. What'll they do with me there?"

"I don't know, Papa bear. Nothing bad, I'm sure. If they think they can use you somehow, then they'll be nice."

"The law of the universe."

"You are a powerful man. Perhaps you could talk to the Americans on the revolution's behalf."

"Perhaps they'll kidnap me for a ransom."

"Don't give them big ideas, Papa."

"I'll keep my mouth shut. Bernadette, what if they find out about you."

"They? Batista? I'm just a whore, what do I know? My father died fighting, how could anything worse than that happen to me?"

"The classic rationale of the naive revolutionary."

"It's only naive, Papa bear, if you have a great deal to lose. For you, it'd be naive. For me, there's no alternative."

Hemingway left Katrina two twenty-dollar bills, eight times her fee, kissed her and left. There were many other things he could have asked her, could have done for her, ways he could've maybe rescued her from a life she frankly didn't seem to hate very terribly. But Hemingway had seen this paradigm play itself out before — the struggle between the moneyed and the powerful, and the property-less peasants, and the individuals ground up for hamburger in the process: the opal-eyed young whores, the red-cheeked schoolboys, the mothers realizing that the price they'll pay for teaching their children self-respect and justice is to bury those children, the schoolgirls who deserve to be chaste for good husbands but end up surrendering their virginity years before they should to lovers going to combat and then end up raped later and not caring very much because their lovers are dead. Everyone knows who pays the price of history. Hemingway had too often been at the heart of things and had too often come to know these people, the mass-grave and assassination destined, these ideologically hopeful nobodies who may, if they survive, see the fruits of a revolutionary spring but will just as likely know the chokehold of a new oppression. These are not epic, romantically tragic lives, but tiny lives that vanish in the dawn wind like ash. Maybe there's the book, he thought, maybe he could write about Katrina. . . . But to make it real and true and passionate without imparting to it a sense of grandeur? To find the truth in her pitiable, disposable historical role? Would that be too Remarque?

He'd stew on that — but fiction seemed to be exactly what he didn't need clogging up his head at the moment. The problem did present itself, as he prepared to exit *Señora* Carmichael's: what to do with the rest of the day, with the C.I.A. and probably the Castroites examining his every burp and fart. He should act normally, he thought, and go to El Floridita. Cocktails for lunch.

He hit the street with his hat brim down

and quickly hobbled a few blocks, hoping to not be noticed in the brothel's vicinity, before fielding a gypsy car and heading east. At the bar, Hemingway spent only about an hour appreciating the daiquiris, the midday light through the window, the buoyant bartender, the mild traffic, the high rump of a new waitress who wore heels to be noticed. Then, he began feeling the need to takes notes, not for fiction, but because the details of the situation he was trying to ignore for a while were fighting like mad to be forgotten in a rum haze, perhaps never to be found again.

He grabbed a menu and a ballpoint pen from the bartender, and began scrawling. Trying to stake things down to the ground in a flood. As best as he could reason it, the Twenty-sixth of July people were on one side, gearing up for a coup, in cahoots with that Matilde woman (perhaps) and Galko, who could only be trusted to rampage after the money, wherever it was, and the Batista–U.S. feds nexus, which supposedly included Cuthbert the Notorious Communist, were on the other, looking to keep Cuba open for business. Hemingway was, naturally, smack in the middle, potentially a helpmate or a liability to both combatants. What about Tcheon? Were either Squiccarini and

Omar Gargallo genuinely neutral? Larcenous rat that he was, Omar had to be. Who exactly did Cuthbert work for really, if not only himself? Had he been trying to play both sides, *Red Harvest*–style?

Hemingway looked out at the sunlight baking the street and felt the earth shift under his step. A menacing vibe of addictive grandeur. He'd done it again without meaning to, strolled-tripped into the war machine, become a protagonist in a story that involves peoples and nations and maddeningly complex issues of justice and power and history being written and rewritten as it happens. He apparently could not help it: whenever Hemingway had smelled the fuel for such a fire, he had sent himself to the front, perhaps only because being there imparted an electrical primacy, an intoxicating sense of belonging to a vital human moment too large to envision at one time and of it belonging to him, which backfilled the smallness Hemingway saw in himself when he sat on the toilet or ate breakfast or walked down the street. History itself, and his tendency to become embroiled in it, allowed him to feel like the man he thought he should be.

He filled up the backs of five menus in a furious scrawl, at times attracting a few bystanders delighted to witness Hemingway actually writing something, but he was oblivious to them, drawing diagrams of connections between people and places in the Cuthbert Matter, but also writing out an entire nine-paragraph beginning to a story, about a young whore getting involved with the Twenty-sixth of July Movement, for love and righteousness, and never being quite aware of how much danger she was in or how much her intervention mattered. He tried not to make her heroic, not even in her modesty or guilelessness, and knew he had more work to do on her. But it was the first happy thing he'd written in months, hard and filled with sadness between the words. He'd had eleven double daiquiris in the meantime.

From there, the afternoon and evening was something of a blur. Though Hemingway wouldn't remember the details the next day, he had, after bouncing to two other bars, ended up in a restaurant bar and was blabbering with an American businessman about Joe DiMaggio, when said businessman, who was also lit like a cherry bomb, introduced him suddenly to a smallish, thin Jewish fellow in an open-collared shirt, who was, he said, also a New Yorker, and whose name was Meyer Lansky.

Even with enough ethanol in his system to run a farm tractor, Hemingway knew to be scared and respectful. The Mafia, through Lansky and with the greased blessings of Batista and the C.I.A., were ridiculously powerful in Cuba, getting away with murder and gambling and smuggling right and left, no holds barred. They had their hooks into the country for at least a few years before Hemingway moved there in 1939; no matter who the official president was, or what office the ever-present Batista held, the Mob was there, their casinos and whorehouses were there, and the American tourists were there, in ever-increasing numbers as the years passed.

Hemingway could only figure they'd be opposing Castro and Guevara, though he had no way of knowing if deals were cut both ways. It was possible. Standing beside him in that where-ever-it-was barroom, he didn't know how much Lansky knew about what Hemingway was doing, or if he cared, or if he knew that some slick and creepy lawyer had barked his name down a police station hallway the day before, and Hemingway could hardly think straight enough to reason it all out in any case. So he said nothing. Imagine the obedient puss of a first-row high school student.

Lansky smiled, Hemingway remembered, and said he'd liked *The Sun Also Rises* a good deal but hasn't read much since. He talked vaguely about Cuba and how wonderful it was, and how it's strange, isn't it?, they'd never met before. Hemingway could only nod. Lions didn't scare him, women didn't scare him, the U.S. government didn't scare him, but the Mob scared him. They eat their young and in public, they massacre at the drop of a lost profit, they care nothing about bad publicity or public opinion or breaking laws or even celebrity fame. Hemingway had heard a good deal over the years, from corporate executives in fishing trips and local bureaucrats and reporters and crooks, and he knew Lansky's world did not accommodate the dance-around-the-grave gentility of politics, but rather the conscienceless will of predation. Not that Lansky and his partners did things much worse than, say, the Rothschilds did prior to the Great War, buying the entirety of the British banking industry when the manipulated stocks were down, and virtually lighting the wick of the war — Lansky, it was rumored, had already bought his own Swiss bank during World War II. But with the Mob, in the grand scheme and case by case, nobody was inviolate.

Hemingway remembered Lansky chatting about Cuban women and about Batista and other things in such a vague, relaxed manner that Hemingway became a little friendly, venturing a joke or two, no telling what about, until Lansky mentioned Castro, what a dangerous thug, et cetera, which was when Hemingway shut up again. Lansky did say, "J. Edgar Hoover," and damn it if Hemingway, later on, could not remember why. How Hemingway bid Lansky adieu, or how he got home, he had no idea. Part of the large sections of the conversation Hemingway couldn't remember went like this:

LANSKY: I understand you met my friend Henry Elam.
HEMINGWAY: Did I?
LANSKY: Yes, in Key West. He's C.I.A.
HEMINGWAY: Oh. I don't remember him.
LANSKY: He's bald.
HEMINGWAY: Oh yeah. The guy who said he knew John Dos Passos.
LANSKY: I love Dos Passos! The *U.S.A.* Trilogy is something else.
HEMINGWAY: Ugh. Dos Passos.
LANSKY: I found those books to be very revealing.
HEMINGWAY: I thought you said you

didn't read much anymore?

LANSKY: I said I haven't read anymore of *you.*

24

The hangover was perhaps the worst Hemingway had experienced since 1945, when Marlene Dietrich met him in Berlin and helped him drink an entire bar's worth of schnapps in celebration of VE-Day, which then had them both vomiting in the ruins until dawn. Hemingway had even burst a blood vessel in his eye with all of that extreme heaving; Dietrich merely went to Czechoslovakia the next day to a spa. In any event, he couldn't at least remember any hangovers that were worse than this; in fact, he began to worry about how much he didn't remember, period, beginning with the night before. He woozily hoped Lansky wasn't involved in any way with Galko or Cuthbert. He wasn't stomach-sick until he took a Bloody Mary with breakfast, then he was. The usual remedies — aspirin, chili peppers, lime juice, raw egg — didn't work, his headache compounding with each additional thing he ingested until it tolled in his head like a cast-iron cathedral bell. Mary would have nothing to do with him and left to shop. What was he supposed to do, where was he supposed to be? On Malecón, at 11. It was 9:35 now. Definitely not enough time.

Not enough, certainly, even for Hemingway to clear his head enough to figure out a new way to get to Malecón without being seen by the surveillance teams presumably staking him out. Would Carlos's cousin drive him again? He would, Carlos told him after a quick call, but that scenario meant Hemingway had to walk another half mile down the mountain and through the lowlands and gardens, in a cast, with his stomach wracked as if harboring a giant sea urchin and his head screaming like an air raid alert. Instead, he called a cab from the phone book, got dressed in khakis and denim, took some cash from Mary's top dresser drawer, and launched out.

The unassuming cabbie, wearing a yellow cap, pulled up, Hemingway got in with, he felt, the world's eyes upon him, and said, the zoo. The trip to the Parque Zoológico took twenty minutes or so, and there, at the front gate, Hemingway quickly hailed the most ramshackle of gypsy cabs among seven. The rail-thin middle-aged driver turned, grinning at Hemingway's bouncing, secretive leap into his backseat, and Hemingway thought, this is my man.

"*Por favor,* drive like a madman north." The driver looked puzzled while never letting his smile drop, and Hemingway made zigzagging hand gestures to indicate fast, erratic driving. "Till your hat floats."

"¿Qué?"

"¡La policia. Vámanos!"

Ah, the driver gestured and pulled out with a squeal. Hemingway looked back through the shoddy sedan's window, saw that there was none, just jagged glass edges, and that's all he saw: beyond the cloud of dust his driver kicked up from the road, Hemingway could discern little, and what little he saw — desultory traffic, pedestrians — gave no indication that he was being followed. Or could have been, really — the car shot down unpaved side roads, up easterly through Arroyo Naranjo, like a torpedo plowing through reef and fish. Hemingway could hear the arthritic shocks of the car screech and grind with every pothole and propulsive landing; the driver, relishing the imagined chase, turned so many times, and often on two tires, that Hemingway began to feel nauseous all over again, and completely lost his sense of direction. *"Norte,"* he choked out a few times, and the driver just waved, *"Si, si!,"* and swerved again, tossing Hemingway across the smelly backseat. Soon, countless abrupt turns and miles of flying cityscape later, he began to worry that they might very well be headed back south, or out west, and that being at the Malecón address by 11 A.M. might not be in the cards. It was already 10:20. As Hemingway looked up from his watch, his car hairpinned left onto a side street and skidded, its tail swerving sidelong and smacking into a telephone pole. The car immediately stalled, and the driver tried in a panic to start her up again; as he did, a few residential natives came out into the street to yell at him, and as they did the pole, already old and weather worn, creaked and began to fall over, bringing wires ripping through the tree branches. *"Jesus Christ!"* Hemingway exhaled, still hiding, as the engine turned over finally, and the driver tore off like the damned on holiday, leaving the pole blocking the road behind them and wires straining and dangling everywhere.

A few more blocks of this, and Hemingway'd had enough — flashes of the last plane crash in Africa began to haunt his headache — and he realized he could very well die this way; it was not out of the question. *"¡No más loco!"* Hemingway hollered, trying to make it sound approving and not angry, with his hands up in a slow-down gesture. The driver shrugged and slowed to a mellow 30mph, winding his way through the boulevards.

And then they were at the Malecón, just like that. The driver headed east, to *numero doscientos treinta.* Hemingway paid the man and tipped him robustly, stepped up and knocked. A voice from behind cleared its throat and the eye-level slot on the door slid open. No one was visible.

"¡Contraseña!"

Shit, what was the password?

"Zapata!"

The slot began to quickly shut, but Hemingway shot his right hand into it as it did. It slammed on his palm, but the fact of that and not the pain was enough to ignite him, and so with a single motion he braced his casted leg against the door, gripped the sliding hatch with his hand, and just ripped it and its frame right out of the door, splinters everywhere. The open hole in the wood revealed only the ill-lit hallway.

"Bolivar, goddamn it. Open up!" A little harumphing, and then the doorknob jiggled. The door had to be fought with from the inside to open; Hemingway had knocked the door off plumb and loosened its hinges.

The same old man Hemingway had seen a few days earlier stood holding the door, looking down with a dismissive air, and then left shuffling for the kitchenette.

Hemingway made his way down the hall, quiet, and realized his hand was bleeding. His headache had reached blockbuster-bomb proportions; it had begun to make him feel nauseous, with a different gastrointestinal menace than hangovers or psychotic car rides can produce. So of course someone crept behind him, making less noise than the explosions inside Hemingway's skull, and in a flash pulled a burlap bag over his head and cracked his head with a pipe, turning out his lights.

He didn't dream, not even of suffocating.

Hemingway woke up, he eventually figured, more than a half hour later, and though the bruised surface of his skull hurt and the inch-high bump on it was too tender to touch, his headache was gone. He sat up, no sack on his head, and found he was in the backseat of a Willys MB jeep, clearly U.S. Army issue, driving pell-mell, but not recklessly so, down the peasant roads outside of the city. Where, toward what province, he had no idea, of course. He found that the cash he'd taken was still in his pocket; now that he was out in the hinterlands, he took it and stuck the thin wad deep into his sock.

In the front seat were two fatigued guerrillas, *escopeteros,* Hemingway assumed, with black berets, sunglasses, kerchiefs over their noses and mouths, and old Browning Automatics, not blunderbusses, in their laps. He didn't ask them anything, he just watched the jungle pass by, watched the villages come and go in their increasing squalor, the farther he got from Havana the more he saw huts with mud floors, children shitting in streams, Cuban men sitting with no work, other men packed shoulder to shoulder in the back of pickup trucks to go cut cane or pick fruit, adults sleeping on the dirt ground, cars without wheels, butchered donkey carcasses left by the roadside. It was a brilliantly sunny day, but the tropical sunshine wasn't about luxuriating or relaxing or fishing now, now it was about owning nothing and eating little more than what you can find in the jungle, about worrying all day about your children's hunger, about the sun growing your face older by three years for every year you spend under its barrage.

The sun was brutally overhead but Hemingway thought it was leaning behind him, which meant they were heading east, southeast, down the island, into the foothills and mountains. The rough ride took hours, four, maybe five. The afternoon breezes off the hills smelled like hibiscus. Eventually the Escambray Mountains loomed, and the jeep went straight up into them.

They stopped at a village planted on the mountain right as the slope began to get seriously steep. The *escopeteros* hopped out and lazily gestured that Hemingway follow them, which he did, after a full minute of stretching his back and knees and setting his weight upon his cane so he could walk. There were only seven shacks with a mud flat between them; more huts were built higher up, deeper into the forest. Chickens, sleeping dogs and an uddered pig. Around him, the children instantly flocked, fishing in his pockets, tugging on his belt; he turned out his pockets to show he had nothing to give them.

He followed the soldiers as closely as he could, as they spoke quickly to two women at the door of one shack, gestured to him again, and tracked past the houses into the woods, some five hundred yards. Over a small crest, and to a cloaked ravine framed by ficus and jocuma and young palms. Hemingway caught up after what felt like a solid half hour, and without saying anything one *escopetero,* the driver, pointed into the ravine, so Hemingway would look.

They moved out of his way, and he looked. It took a second to differentiate in the shadows and vegetation, but quickly it was apparent he was looking into a mass grave, an open dumping ground. How many bodies were down there he couldn't tell; he saw fresh ones on top, with clothes and hair, and beneath them bits of skeleton. He might estimate he could see remnants of ten corpses down there, but he didn't want to look any longer to figure it out any better.

"Who —. *Quién lo hizo.*"

The two men looked exasperated. "Batista," the driver said. *"Por ocho o diez anos."*

"Cuántos haya . . ."

"Nosotros encontramos treinta y nueve."

Thirty-nine bodies, some perhaps a decade old . . . Like everyone, from Eisenhower on down, Hemingway knew Batista was a soulless bastard whose political and business enemies often disappeared and were assumed murdered; Hemingway had just never bothered to think on how, or where their corpses ended up. Nor did he normally choose to think about the degree to which the C.I.A. did his bidding this way, or how much Batista's forces were reliant on U.S. arms and training. The soldiers walked back to the village, and Hemingway followed, wanting to hurry but actually moving very slow, as if his gears were gummed up. There hadn't been many times in his adult life, even in Africa, when Hemingway felt quite as guilty about his bulletproof station in the world, his wealth, his complacency.

They climbed back into the jeep and waited for Hemingway — apparently, they'd been instructed to show him the site, to give him some perspective. Perhaps Castro assumed he was a typically selfish American, apolitical and unempathetic and thinking only of his own bottom line, and he'd be both right and wrong about that. Right, maybe, where it counts.

The jeep ride from there headed at first down the mountain, and then east along a ridge, and as he jostled and bumbled along roads that were barely roads, Hemingway could see the green stretches and mangroves of Sancti Spiritus and beyond that, faintly, the blue line of the Caribbean.

The roads did vanish altogether, and the jeep took paths through jungle that were only wide enough for an ox, leaving the car to sometimes slow down between close trees and squeak through. Time was being eaten up, and evening was no more than four hours away — Hemingway realized he'd be spending at least the night up here, no question about it.

Within another hour, along a stretch of hair-raisingly narrow mountain pass, the jeep hit an impromptu road block of cut palm tree trunks. As it stopped, *escopeteros,* a dozen or more, emerged from the woods carrying tommy guns and Brownings, wearing a rummage sale amalgamation of fatigues and brand-new Army boots, to a man, to nod at the jeep's driver and go about the business of moving the trunk, which they had down to a science but still took another ten minutes. On the other side, the jeep wound up a little into the trees and reached a camp. It was as dark as late evening, completely covered in shade and presumably unseeable from the sky. Dozens of soldiers and peasant refugees bustled about, doing laundry, mending uniforms, and cooking a pig over an elaborate campfire. Hemingway saw no militarization, no bazookas, no large shipment of guns. Walking from the jeep, he almost asked the driver, is this it for the 26th of July? But he didn't.

Then a man came at him in a straight line,

his hand extended, and it was Castro. In combat greens, neatly trimmed beard, Army boots. He was thin. In his other hand he held a whisk, and he was wearing a kitchen apron.

"*Señor* Hemingway!" Shaking hands. He looked fresh faced, his fatigues clean but for a spatter of grease on his left breast pocket.

"*Señor* Castro, I'm delighted."

"Oh, I think Fidel! And you, Ernest?"

"Yes."

"Come." They walked back to the fire, where on a plank table Castro was apparently preparing a salsa-ish-glaze for the pig from jungle fruits. Hemingway congenially stuck his nose in it and looked quizzical. Castro pointed. "For dinner! My grandmother taught me about cooking, with the jungle. Here I've got guava, mango, some oranges. And mint, you can find that here, and cardamom, saffron, *bijol,* allspice. And chilis, can't neglect the chilis!"

Seated at the other end of the table on a stump, splitting papayas with a machete, under a sulky beret, was Che Guevara, who looked up, smiled for half a second, and then looked down.

"You'll stay for dinner?"

"C'mon, Fidel, where else am I going."

Castro laughed, shrugged, and took a

massive slug from an unlabeled bottle of mescal. Handed it to Hemingway, who was thinking he'd never offer, and who drank enough, an extra gulp or two, to place him almost immediately in the frame of mind that could enjoy a camp-out with revolutionaries in the jungle, with gourmet-peasant barbecue and raw native mescal and loaded, ping-pong banter with an authentic lawyer-turned-guerrilla leader. He assumed he was not at risk, and got further and further away from questioning the good sense of this assumption the more he drank.

"Ernest, I must tell you, *The Old Man and the Sea* is a masterpiece. I've read it three times."

"That's a lot."

"He reads it," Guevara piped up, sullenly but with a sardonic smirk, "on the toilet."

Castro blushed bitterly and resumed whisking his salsa. "Not something the Nobel Prize–winner needed to know."

"It's his book," Guevara barked — the two of them seemed to be in the middle of an argument that had volleyed on long before Hemingway showed up — "you flatter him, but the truth is a little less . . . sweet smelling." He had his own bottle of mescal and sipped at it.

Hemingway instantly disliked Guevara —

what a snitty little prick.

"Che," Castro was whisking angrily, "it hardly matters where the fuck you read a book, especially, if you're reading it over again, to savor it, am I right, Ernest?"

"That's right."

"And I'm sure *Señor* Hemingway is man enough to not be shocked by you. *Hijo de puta.*"

Guevara looked up. "Jesus, Fidel, I was only joking."

"But it's true. Right? Even if there is no toilet in the jungle! So it's not a joke."

"But *you* do it, not me! OK, not a joke, but, what do they call it in Guatemala, *mamar gallo.*"

"Whatever. You're not having respect for our guest."

"*Ay, ay.* I am apologetic."

Their English was schoolboy arch, but it seemed to force them into being exceptionally cordial. Hemingway sat down at the table, shrugging, happy to have them bickering about something meaningless. Grabbed the bottle again.

"So, Ernest," Fidel said brushing his salsa onto the pig with a camel-hair paintbrush and turning its spit. "I understand you wanted to see us."

"Uh . . . yes, I suppose so."

"Suppose? I hope we weren't wrong to fetch you up here! We are only here for a little while, to make a few deals, a little fund-raising, before we must flee again to Tuxpan. Before we are caught!" He was chortling. "Very soon, Ernest, we will be making a venture back to Cuba, though, and we are going to unseat that maggot Batista and establish a genuine people's state!"

"So I've heard."

"But not now, now we're just in preparation. Were we wrong?"

"With me? No, I guess not. I'll be precise: I've just been on the trail, so to speak, of a murder. A friend of mine was killed, brutally."

Guevara looked up, drank. "He must've been like a brother to you, to bring you this far."

Hemingway was given pause. "Actually, I can't say that he was. No. Just a friend. That nobody cared a shit about."

"Did you?"

"Not enough, I'd say, before he died."

"Oh *Señor* Hemingway, you are trying to absolve the past?" Castro was seated now, drinking, captivated and earnest.

"No, no. Dammit. I'm just trying to fix the present."

"You cannot help other people, don't you know, from their own problems."

"I know that. But finding out what that problem was would satisfy me."

"How can we help?"

"I think he was smuggling for you."

"Ay, ay, ay."

25

"You tell me, Ernest, if you being Ernest Hemingway gives us more reason to trust you than if you were, say, Omar Gargallo, *señor*-average-Cuban-idiot-alley-weasel, or less, or, maybe, no reason at all."

Night had fallen, and they had all eaten the pig, which was pink and moist and might've been the most dizzingly delicate pork Hemingway had ever eaten anywhere — Castro's glaze was fruity and tart and spicy and not overpowering. They had rum with it, mixed with fresh lemons, and roasted sweet potatoes right out of the mountain's soil.

Hemingway had mentioned Cuthbert's name before supper was ready, and that froze the conversation until now, when everyone was full-bellied and lubricated with liquor. Some *escopeteros* slept under lean-tos, others huddled together drinking at their own fire, others left into the darkness to stand guard. Hemingway sat with Castro and Guevara on tree stumps around the cooking fire, which had burnt down to fierce embers. Another bottle was passed between them.

"You mean, because I'm famous. I can't have a conversation with anyone anymore without the substance of it eventually coming around to that. My motivations, my conclusions, are always suspect, because I won a goddamn Nobel. I'm getting a little tired of it. But out of all the living writers you could name, I'm the one who's the most interested in trying to remain an ordinary man."

"See," Guevara said, "I doubt that. I can't help it, you're Ernest Hemingway, you can have whatever you want. You live the life most people want to live."

"I know what you mean, but most people are wrong, that's what they think because they learn about me from *Life* magazine, not from me myself. If they walked in my shoes, they'd be a little disillusioned." Hemingway had come to like Guevara better with the passing hours and rum consumption; he was a wary and savvy man, not easy to like, which is always something Hemingway found easy to like.

"I think if they walked in your shoes,"

Castro burped and fisted his chest, "they'd be delighted. Most people have to piss away their every day working just to have the right to a place to sleep and food to eat so they can get up and do it again the next day."

"Working. Who should complain about having to work?"

"No one, but neither should you complain about a life in which you do not work. You pay others to do even your housework, yes?"

"Yes. What should I do? Give up writing and haul crabs instead?"

"Yes!" Guevara was laughing.

"But who would that benefit?"

"No one," Castro admitted. "But don't complain."

"I'm not. I'm just saying no one trusts me to be just a fellow. I should instead be buying them a big dinner because I've sold a lot of books, or I should instead be lunching with the President and shouldn't pretend I believe in the working man, in fishing, in fighting an honest fight, in struggle. But I do believe. And as for my employees, I'm sure my butler here in Havana likes answering my door and making my beds better than he would cutting cane for fourteen hours a day, for one-fifth the wages."

"Good God, Hemingway, are you a socialist or not?" Guevara laughed again, and Hemingway saw his point.

"I don't know. It's not my fault people like my books and the hard little toil I expended on them over the years has now put me in the position of, what, betraying my own principles. If that's what I'm doing. I'm not a monk on a mountain top. I'm not Jesus Christ."

"I am!" Castro roared.

"Ernest, for real," Guevara got intent, "we must know first what you know about Cuthbert."

"He was my friend, I know lots of stuff. But not much that's pertinent to how he died."

"About his work."

"Was he smuggling for you or not?"

"No."

"My God, you're lying." Hemingway said this with a broad smile, a grin shared between drunkards in the throes of a buddy-buddy binge, and he hoped it would be received jovially, because if it wasn't it could instead be a line that shouldn't have been drawn in the sand.

Guevara smiled briefly and then sulked away to piss in the jungle. Hemingway didn't know what to think.

"Obviously we knew Peter," Castro allowed. "We were wondering why or how he disappeared. But we still cannot trust you, no matter how much we drink and pat backs and cry on each other's shoulder about being misunderstood by the world."

"But you've just told me, both of you, in your reactions, that Peter died because of what he was doing for you."

"You should know better than to leap to such outrageous conclusions. You should know that life is more complicated than that."

"Don't tell me you had him killed."

"Ernest, you're pushing when you should let yourself be pushed. The rules of good wrestling. If we killed him, would we sit here drinking with you? Would we be talking about trusting you?"

"I don't know."

"First things, first," Castro said, casting an eye on Guevara returning, his hands still buttoning his fly, "you are an American, you've been talking with the C.I.A. and Batista's police, you are asking many questions of many people and no one knows exactly why."

"I told you —"

"Yes, yes, your friend, your duty, some kind of personal matter you must settle for your own good, *que será será.*"

"Hmpf."
"That reason, my friend, no one can truly swallow."
"That's not my fault. It is what it is."
"But you can see why we'd think you're nosing around for someone else, right? That your 'personal' reason," fingers quoting in the air, "is a little thin, a little airy, and unprovable. It makes far more sense to conclude that you are working for the U.S."
"But I'd never —"
"You did during the war, didn't you? What was that called —"
"The Crook Factory," Guevara chimed in.
"Right!" Castro. "They sent you money from Washington for that, didn't they?"
"C'mon" Hemingway sputtered. "We were looking for Nazi U-boats, ferChrissake! Sure the State Department funded us, bought us some boat fuel and some hot lunches, so what? It was the fucking war!"
"Of course," Castro said. "You did the right thing. But once you have those connections, they're always there."
"A lot you know about American bureaucracy. Talk about something that's a lot more complicated than you think. I had a liaison, yes, but only one and now he works for the F.B.I. So what. He's busy trying not

to look busy, probably trying to prosecute the Mafia while not being allowed to do exactly that by his superiors."

"Maybe." Awkward silence prevailed for the three men. The bottle got passed around, as if all three were stewing on a logistical problem.

"Matilde Pirrin," Hemingway said finally.

Castro sat up and looked at Guevara. "Yes?"

"You know her."

Castro nodded slowly. "And you?"

"Yes," Hemingway said, treading carefully, because he still didn't know if that woman was earnestly anti-Castro after having been pro-Castro, or if her name on that long-forgotten list of comrades — where'd that list go? — revealed only that she'd tried to infiltrate the movement, or if she was lying to Hemingway about her pro-Batista position to lead him away from Galko, or . . .

"We've been looking for her." Guevara.

"She is pro-Batista, yes?"

"Yes." Castro took a deep breath. "Pirrin has been working for Batista since before the war. In 1948 she informed on a cadre of protesters and they were all executed. She is an agent of oppression."

"Are you sure?"

"Of course."

"I can tell you where she is. If I do, can I then be trusted?"

"Yes. Yes?" Looking at Guevara.

"Yes," Guevara said.

"She works with, and lives with, Ferenc Galko. In Key West."

Guevara and Castro looked at each other.

"You know Galko?" Castro.

"I'm afraid I do, a bit. We live in the same town, our paths have crossed occasionally, mostly because he's so good at being a horse's ass in public."

"And Pirrin?"

"She . . . I guess she was dogging my steps in Florida, ever since . . ."

"When?"

". . . Since I walked into the Key West morgue and said in front of a friend of mine, who's a cop but is also officially F.B.I., that I wanted to know how the dead man died."

"This other friend, the cop, do you trust him?" Guevara.

"Yes. As far as I can throw him. Which is a little ways. I trust him to do his job."

"But he's F.B.I."

"Yes. I haven't told him much about what I've been doing, and haven't spoken to him at all since I left Florida."

"So," Castro scratched his beard, "Pirrin

works for Batista's people, who of course talk to the Americans."

"It would seem."

"That means she's betraying Galko," Castro said. "Does she share his bed?"

"Yes."

"How do you know this?"

"She told me, before fucking me."

This gave both revolutionaries pause. Guevara blurted, "Who wouldn't want to live your life, Hemingway!" And they both guffawed righteously, and Hemingway had to nod and grin.

"So, Galko runs for you," Hemingway said. Castro looked wounded, his smile fading; he'd let that slip.

"Galko runs for anyone," he said. "But yes, he has run for us."

"It seems that you trust me now. So what was it that Cuthbert was wrapped up in? It's time, *compadres,* to let it loose."

"OK!" Guevara stood up and paced, sipping in his way from the bottle. "We'd heard his name only, through Desanzo, through our other men on the Havana waterfront, through Tcheon. We OK'd the deal. It seemed dubious, from where we stood. We were still in Mexico."

"Uh-huh. But."

"But, it had a decisive flavor to it. We

couldn't say no."

"Excuse me — Tcheon?"

"Yes, he was ours, undercover as an unofficial 'operator' hired by your feds. You broke his face, you know. He's in Guatemala now, hiding."

Hemingway squeezed his eyes with his fingers, he couldn't keep the interfaces straight. "OK, the deal . . . Couldn't say no. To who?"

"Cuthbert. He came to the movement with the idea."

"Which was."

"Which was," Castro took over, "a certain amount of uranium-235, isotopes, stolen. With which we were supposed to make a kind of 'dirty' bomb, some kind of low-yield *macanas,* that we'd decided right away we'd use as a threat against Batista but never set off."

"Holy shit."

"Si."

"But . . . But how did Cuthbert get mixed up with that?"

They both shrugged. "Galko, I'd imagine," Castro said.

"But, where'd it come from?"

"Who knows. We assume it was American, not Soviet."

"Assume?"

"We never saw them, the deal never happened, Desanzo said forget about it. Cuthbert disappeared. The isotopes disappeared."

"Desanzo said . . . What'd he find out?"

"He didn't find out anything, Cuthbert was supposed to meet him, probably at sea at night, and never showed. No one knew why. Next thing he heard, Cuthbert's dead in Key West."

"Who told Desanzo?"

"Tcheon."

"How do you know there were any real isotopes?"

"We don't." Guevara. "We just said yes, bring them in, we'll buy if we don't get the sense we're being cheated. Good thing it fell apart, we would not have known, really, what to do with them anyway."

"How much would they have cost you, if you don't mind me asking."

"A hundred thousand American dollars."

Hemingway sputtered, weighed down by the drink and the complexity of the past. "For nondetonating radioactive material? Where'd you get that kind of money?"

"That's what we've been doing in Texas, and Mexico, raising money. Many wealthy exiles have been screwed by Batista," Guevara said simply. "We'll be frank with you, we've gotten support from the American Army and Navy, too, artillery, et cetera."

"And you're blasting away at me for having a fed connection."

"We have to trust you, you don't have to trust us."

"True. But. But, how could you use this isotope thingamajig as a threat unless Batista or the C.I.A. were sure it was authentic and that you were in possession?"

"We hadn't gotten that far yet, we were waiting to see if we would buy it first. Have a scientist friend in Havana look it over, whatever."

"But then what. What were you going to do, to spread the word?"

Castro and Guevara looked at each other. Castro took the bullet. "We would've had to inform on the smugglers, yes, and let the feds trace it back to wherever it was stolen from."

"You would've had to hand over Cuthbert."

"*Si.* I'm sorry, it would've been necessary for the revolution. As it was, he'd have been better off if we had. Yes?"

"Not if Batista's apes got ahold of him. He'd be laying in that mass grave you made sure I saw coming up here." Hemingway and the rum were brewing red-faced rage like a bull with knotted balls. Guevara saw it.

"Maybe," Guevara said, his chin stuck way out. "No difference to him in the end. We're all prepared to die for the cause, Hemingway, which is a commitment you've never made. A war zone journalist! But this much is true: we needed Cuthbert alive, otherwise the isotope would probably have been useless. It could've been a rock in a box, for all Batista would've known. So you know this much, that we didn't kill him. In fact, if the whole scheme had played out, we would've paid whatever we needed to to keep him alive."

Hemingway was quieted, it made sense. They drank a little more in silence, before the men, almost in unison, lurched for the water barrel and drank like camels and stretched in the moonlight. Then the Cubans took out cigars and the three of them luxuriated in the campfire moment, like hunting-trip pals.

"This all still doesn't tell me who killed Cuthbert," Hemingway said, suddenly weary and also a little self-dramatic in the realization that his windmill-tilting has not finished.

The three then handicapped the suspects, with Galko emerging as even money, the

C.I.A. coming up close with two-to-one, Squiccarini pulling five-to-three, Lansky and the Mob — if Squiccarini and the F.B.I. had a chance at knowing about it, then the Mafia could've known, too — netting ten-to-one, the Revolutionary Directorate army and Comandante Felix Torres falling in as long shots. More likely than any of them, it seemed, was the prospect that it was someone they didn't know, crossing paths with Peter in ways they hadn't figured out. All three men knew well how these dark harbor lives are lived, how money draws the hounds, how news of the merciless opportunity can travel like light particles on an unrippled plain. To presume to know how a body became a body on the boats and beaches of the last American miles and beyond is to presume to have the eyes of God.

Hemingway slept in an Army sleeping bag that smelled, strangely, of mulberry. The scent, cramped by mildew, reminded him of his grandfather, who drank a mulberry-anise tea most evenings in the Oak Park house, and who told Hemingway when he was only eight about how once when he was wounded with a wrecked knee on the scorched fields of Chattanooga he'd crawled over and cut a Confederate soldier's throat with a mess fork, how hard it was to do and how he'd regretted it right away, since the battle was mostly over and the soldier was not threatening him but just trying to act dead. It's my burden, Grandpa Hall said, ever since. My payload, my tribulation.

26

When Hemingway awoke from the usual slumber cannon fire couldn't interrupt, Castro and Guevara and the *escopeteros* were gone, the camp packed, the fire doused. Only a lone soldier remained, sitting in his jeep reading a Cecilia Valdes paperback. Jeez, are all of these revolutionaries college boys?

On the long, teeth-rattling ride back across the Escambrays and northwest to Havana, Hemingway was at a loss in his own head. What now? Just confront Galko? What about Peter's second boat, the *Em* or some such crap, that apparently the feds know about but can't find? The answers he wanted might not, in the end, be available, no matter how he threw his reputation around or big-brained it like Maigret in the tropics. He had thought at one point that finding out what Cuthbert had been involved in would satisfy him — as if the nature of the criminal venture would be enough, and it didn't matter what scheming bastard did impale Peter on that spear that night, all scheming, impaling sons of bitches were more or less the same, and it happens, murder, in those circles often enough to let it be shrugged over by everyone except the police, whose job it was to sift through details, however pointless. One lowlife scofflaw is more or less like another, what does it matter which one?

But that's not how it turned out in Hemingway's dehydrated skull, where it became more imperative than ever to grip the throat of the actual man responsible, be he arch-bastard or mere henchman or rogue crook or fed agent or dirty cop. They might be all worthless cutthroats, but Hemingway didn't care. He should've known: as with any investment, the further you go, the less inclined you ever are to count your losses and go home. He was in too deep, he knew too much to consider it another fruitless adventure and move on. He'd dream about it for the rest of his life, in nagging, itchy narratives he could never resolve.

By the time the jeep dropped him off in a blind alley near Malecón, and a gypsy drove him back to Finca Vigia, where he spotted a top-heavy toucan fly-leaping from one mango tree to another on the edge of his property, Hemingway knew he had to go back to Key West. Back to Galko. Back to Peter's second boat, wherever it was.

"Back from the brothel?" Mary sniped in the kitchen, without turning around from the counter where she was instructing Zazie on how to slice onions, on a slant and with the knife point touching the board at all times, which she clearly had no interest in learning because, it could be presumed, she had her own homegrown method, passed down from her grandmother, that worked just fine.

Hemingway was jolted by the brothel comment — *Bernadette* — before he realized that it was a generalized insult-slash-fight-starter that she'd used before, sometimes correctly, when he disappeared overnight.

"Very funny. When you're civil, I'll tell you where I've actually been. It's a swell story."

"I couldn't give a shit."

"Well, I have to go back to Florida," and she turned fast, with a large Spanish butcher knife raised in her hand.

"You creep, you fucking liar, what kind of husband are you? What do you think a marriage is, just a shed to throw your things into while you're off doing whatever you want alone? No wonder you've been through four wives, and I'm guessing you're angling for a fifth now, am I right?, looking for someone else's patience to exhaust before they get so fed up they want to take the widest knife they can find and stick in your belly while you sleep!"

Hemingway had walked away after the first dozen words, upstairs to pack, and Mary followed him, hollering. "I don't want to know what you're doing, what I want to know is why you keep getting fucking married!"

In the bedroom, Hemingway was calm and low: "You know very well that my other wives didn't leave me, I left them. Nobody got fed up with me."

"And this you're proud of?!"

"I didn't say that."

"All that means is you've picked weak, pliant women — I knew Pauline, she was a pussycat, and Martha talked tough but she needed a daddy. It comes down to you, buster. You are an irresponsible lout! You don't care about anyone else's feelings. You shouldn't've gotten married once, much less four times."

"The fuck all you know about it," Hemingway said. "You just see your needs being met or not. And you've jumped ship on two husbands before me, so you've got no high ground to stand on. Are you done shouting?"

"Yes, and I'm done listening, too. Go fuck yourself in Florida."

Hemingway packed alone and had Carlos drive him to the ferry, in full view and with no attempt at secrecy, figuring it was useless to try, the feds would surely spot him at least by the time he landed. Anyway, so what if they follow him? Back on American soil, Hemingway would again breathe easy in the no-assassinating-celebrities zone. And if the C.I.A. had something to hide? Like culpability in Cuthbert's death and in the fate of stolen radioactive isotopes? They'd more likely just muddy the waters, destroy the paper trail and call him a Commie than do him any real harm. Perhaps.

But the Mob? They'd kill anyone, anywhere. If Hemingway caught one more whiff of them, he thought, he might have to beg off and lay low. That was not a pot he wanted to stir, regardless of how badly his conscience bothered him. The questions might have to go unanswered.

27

He disembarked on the Key West dock, the anole lizards road-running under his feet as he limped to the cars and grabbed a cab home, interrupted the staff's drunken midday canasta game in the den, and took a long, long shower. He decided that today he would drink nothing, give his aching kidneys a break, clear his head.

Getting dressed. He knew he had to talk to Galko, but he knew it would be risky. What does Galko know about what he's been doing? Lynch might well've told Galko about seeing Hemingway in Cuba, and word must've gotten back to Galko that Lynch had been executed while in police custody, and maybe even that Hemingway was present when it happened, depending on where the inside scoop came from. There was no telling what info that Matilde woman might've passed to Galko, working against him as she seemed to be. Then again, Galko did make payments to the State Department to prevent extradition, as Kwaak had mentioned once in passing — maybe he got information back for those payouts, maybe he knew that Hemingway had penetrated, so to speak, the 26th of July. Hemingway remembered Galko's bodyguards, how they were tensed and poised for violence — maybe just the fact that Hemingway was *still* pursuing Cuthbert's killer two weeks later, and after Galko had kicked him out of his house in a flurry of evasions and vaguely veiled threats, would be trouble enough.

Maybe. There was hardly a way of finding out what was what without charging into the shadows. Hemingway decided he'd simply go to Galko's house and let the chips fall. Should he bring reserves — and put his guileless bar cronies in jeopardy? He'd call Kwaak, but doubted he'd even get him on the phone this time. There was no one to help. Hemingway looked for a weapon but could only find hunting rifles and an old Astra M400 he'd found on a Nationalist's corpse in Valencia. He checked that it was loaded and stuck it in his belt, under his shirt. But he knew if there was shooting, he with his cast would be as hard to hit as a sleeping cow, and his little Spanish pistol would do little good. He brought it with him anyway. He didn't feel quite up to walking up Whitehead as he had weeks earlier with the college girls and decided he'd scooter, despite the absurd visual detail he knew it added to the story, however bloodily it might end and however it would be told when all was said and done.

He was downstairs, jamming a piece of good Spanish sheep cheese into his mouth, when someone knocked on his front door. He listened: Marisol answered, and it was Squiccarini. He jockeyed over, invited the man in.

"Can't, Papa. We have to go to the office." Which is what he called the station house on Jose Marti Drive.

"We? Vinnie, you're arresting me?"

"No, no, just for questioning."

"Who the *fuck* is going to question me now?! I didn't think there was anyone left who *hasn't* had their nose poked up my hairy ass!"

"That was the C.I.A., Papa. Write your congressman. I'm sorry. C'mon."

The Captain did look genuinely forlorn about his task. The two rode in Squiccarini's state-issue Chevy across the island, and as Hemingway boiled about being "picked up" for the fourth time that spring, he also thought he might be able to use Squiccarini and the F.B.I. to his advantage — at least for protection. He only wished he'd lit a stick of dynamite under Galko's chair *before* the good Captain had fetched him into custody.

In the station, which was decrepit and so ill-kept that the window seams were wide enough for anoles and palmetto bugs to come and go like rush hour traffic, Squiccarini surprised Hemingway by opening the small holding cell door and pointing offhandedly to the bench inside.

"What the fuck, Vinnie."

"Or stand, Papa. It's the only place to sit down. It'll only be a few minutes."

Hemingway looked around — he was right, not a seat in sight. "FerChrissake, buy a few folding chairs."

"Why don't you do that, as a gift to the police force."

Hemingway sat down in the cell, the door hanging open, thinking he would in fact buy some chairs for the station, but they'd be pink and fragile and covered with images of bunny rabbits or something. Squiccarini, distracted and mopey, disappeared into the offices.

It wasn't a minute, it was in fact almost a half hour, during which time Hemingway paced in and out of the holding cell, yelled

Squiccarini's name a few times, stepped outside into the blaring heat and then thought better of it, and began to think that deciding not to drink at all today may have been rash. Maybe he'll wait until five. Alright, three.

Eventually he just sat down again, and mused to himself that this was a spot Peter knew pretty well, having been dragged in on drunk-and-disorderlies a few times, and at least once on assault, along with the Brazilian sport fisherman he'd supposedly assaulted, meaning it was a barfight and no charges were ever brought.

While he was alive, Peter had seemed to be a fairly simple guy, with a few large secrets, but by now Hemingway wondered if he'd known him at all, had even had the merest glimpse into what kind of man he was, what he thought day to day, what he wanted out of life. The more questions Hemingway asked, the more Peter became an impenetrable mystery, a perfect stranger. Maybe that's the way Peter had meant it to be, leaving essentially all of his past out of every conversation, playing the cynical, life-beaten Key West drunkard-fool to a tee but as a disguise, a contrived identity protecting what or who he really was.

Hemingway sat just as Peter would've

done when he was here, as anyone would in a drunk tank, thoughtlessly, selflessly, all decision-making operations switched decisively to off. Across the hallway on the wall was only a large, de rigueur map of the Keys; nothing else to look at, nothing else to see, nothing at all to observe and think about. Hemingway looked at the map for too long, as anyone else would sitting on that bench, and saw how the words "MONROE COUNTY" arc down the islands like giant letters in the clouds high above the water, beginning angled out into the Gulf past Key West and curving up through to the mainland.

He sat, bored, and counted the spots in the Gulf and in the Caribbean where he caught swordfish, and the spots he thought he'd seen a Kraut U-boat during the war, and the one spot where he actually did, and Peter was with him, and the Crook Factory had its glory moment in the conflict, though it was immediately dubbed top secret and everyone was sworn to secrecy. Hemingway also dimly recalled a trip he'd made with Peter, Rick, and Johnny Otshenko out past the Mullets, where Peter swore up and down he'd found a galleon wreck, but the men found nothing in their tentative dives, and drank rum until diving took too much energy and life became too funny to consider doing more than lying in the sun and appreciating the tropics. That was where, Hemingway supposed, the map's large *M* sat, above Little Mullet.

The Em? The *Em?* It sat northwest of Little Mullet, sure enough, marking off within it about six or seven square miles of open sea — the *Em?* For the love of God, is that what the crotchety old dolt was talking about? That's where the fabled second boat was? Like that movie, with Franchot Tone — *Five Graves to Cairo.* There it was, twenty-five minutes or so, if you were moving at a clip, north-northwest from Little Mullet, just as Rick remembered. How'd Peter expect anyone to decipher that, unless they got thrown into the drunk tank? Or, more likely, Hemingway thought, he didn't expect anything, he was soused, Rick was soused, and Peter forgot he said it less than a minute later. Jumping Jehoshaphat.

Hemingway spent a second calculating the downside of hightailing it out of the police station as fast as his plastered limp could propel him, heading downtown, somehow reconnoitering a boat, maybe from Rick or Jean, and heading out past Little Mullet, right goddamn now. But that's when Squiccarini emerged and with a whistle and a head tilt, beckoned Hemingway into another dingy office, onto another rickety chair, across from another tin desk. Hemingway prayed silently to a deity he didn't really believe in that he wasn't in for a replay of Lynch's date with the C.I.A.

"Papa, this shouldn't take long," Squiccarini said, as both men sat down facing the desk, where a lanky fed wearing a black suit and the half-lidded, saturnine glower of a mortician sat.

"Good morning, Mr. Hemingway, thank you for coming in."

"Don't mention it." No smile. He was itching to get out.

"My name is Esper, and I'm an agent with the Federal Bureau of Investigation," showing his I.D., which is more than anyone else had done so far, "and we have just a few questions."

"So do I."

"Hmm, yes. We understand you've been looking into a friend's death."

"Murder. Yes. Captain Video here has made it very clear that the Bureau's not taking it on."

"No, we're not."

"I could've used the help. Though frankly after seeing the American bureaucracy in action lately, I might be better off without

your help. Anyway, I'm done with all that."
Squiccarini shot a look.

"You found the killer?"

Hemingway stretched a little deliberately. "No, but this guy, my friend, he was just a crook and was tangled up with lowlifes, and so something like that would've happened sooner or later. I'm a busy man, gala lunches to attend, lions to shoot, I can't be bothered any longer."

"I see," and it was not obvious that Esper recognized the sarcasm, but nothing about him was obvious. He seemed to just ignore it. "So what was the last trip to Cuba all about?"

"I live there."

"Yes, but. OK, please tell us what you can about Stanley Lynch."

"He's dead. You should know that."

"We do. What do *you* know."

"I saw it, a C.I.A. spook named Anderson put a bullet through his head. In Havana, a few days ago. Investigate it."

"Papa," Squiccarini said.

"Are you willing to make a statement to that effect?"

"Testify against the C.I.A.? Sure. I can't believe this is news to you."

Esper didn't move a muscle. "Lynch was undercover for the F.B.I., Mr. Hemingway."

Hemingway fought like a bear not to look surprised and had no idea if he succeeded. But with a beard scratch, he finally chuckled.

"Oh, that's rich. The C.I.A. and the F.B.I. killing each other's drones. Don't mind if I save my derisive laughter for later."

". . ."

"Did Anderson know Lynch was with the Bureau?"

"We have reason to believe that he didn't know, no."

"Typical. You guys are all half-cocked."

"It appears that the Agency thought of Lynch only as a smuggler and a mobster."

"So? Your boy in Havana was killed for being a criminal? Or for maybe working with Castro on the wrong side of the divide?"

"The latter, apparently. We'll find out."

"No you won't. You're just tying up loose ends, aren't you, that haven't been rightly tied up. A spook executes a fed spy in front of a roomful of witnesses, and you're not investigating it, right?, you're just talking to whoever was present, make us all think it's being taken care of, maybe get us to sign a little statement that'll then get consigned to a locked file in a cellar, if it's not just burned in a pail somewhere. You're just housekeeping, that's what you're doing."

"Mr. Hemingway, why are you in the middle of this, anyway? Why are we compelled to interview the most famous fiction writer in the world about the felonious pursuits of a few petty Caribbean criminals?"

"And spies."

"Yes."

"Well, lots of reasons, Aristotle, and you must know most of them. One was Tcheon."

"Tcheon . . . Yes, I believe Captain Squiccarini apologized for that. He was a contract agent and no longer has an affiliation with the Bureau."

"Did you know he is Twenty-sixth of July?"

Esper stopped. And stared.

"Really. And you know this how?"

"That's the word in the cantinas in Havana. Heard it around."

"Are *you* Twenty-sixth of July, Mr. Hemingway?"

"Me! I'd sooner be a priest."

"Your actions have been . . . suspect, of late."

"That's what my wife says. Hey, this is all about that uranium, isn't it?"

Esper was holding a file and now put it down. And stared. Squiccarini put his hand to his eyes and gently rubbed, exhaling.

"Now, you're going to have to tell us how you heard about that, Mr. Hemingway."

"How? You stun mope, every Cuban in Havana has heard about that debacle. Castro was going to make a dirty bomb, or something. Do you have agents in Cuba that actually speak Spanish?"

"Very funny. But really."

"Really, Mr. Esper. Cab drivers, barkeeps, hookers, everybody. A shoeshiner told me he thought Castro had a hydrogen bomb. But I've also come to understand that Peter probably had something to do with that uranium whatever-it-was, the smuggling of it, anyway, and the reason no one, and I mean no one, has deigned to investigate his murder, or Lynch's for that matter, was because you and the C.I.A. and everyone else have only been concerned with covering the whole shebang up and playing it down and shoving it in the closet, probably because if it went public it would mean somebody wasn't watching the store, right?; or worse, someone in the fucking F.B.I. or the C.I.A. was actually involved in the sale or theft or whatever the fuck it was, in ways a newspaper-reading public wouldn't quite like. And if *that's* true, then maybe you guys are responsible for Cuthbert's death, too, and from the moment it happened everyone's been covering their asses about *that.* How do you like them apples?"

"That's an incredible accusation," Esper was icy calm, almost droll. "You'd need a little proof."

"I know Castro didn't have him killed."

"How do you know that?"

"Gut feeling."

"I'm going to have to write in my report that you didn't cooperate with questioning, Mr. Hemingway."

"Oh you go right ahead and do that, you fucking truant officer, and I'll be happy to see the F.B.I. in court when I get my Fifth Avenue lawyers on the docket," Squiccarini had him by the arm, standing, escorting him to the door, "and charge the Bureau with harassment, that's what! — and do it over lunch at *The New York* fucking *Times*!"

28

"I don't know what the fuck it is you think you're doing," Squiccarini said on the station house steps, somewhat sadly. The sun bore down.

"Vinnie, I'm calling their cards. I'm fed up. They've been tailing me for days anyway, I might as well give them something solid to talk about. I don't think they can hurt me, but if they try, they'll find a brawl."

"You can't brawl with gunfire, Papa. Remember Huey Long?"

"Huey Long? I thought that doctor shot him."

"No."

Squiccarini gave up, went inside.

Hemingway was far beyond paying heed to warnings of state unscrupulousness by now; all he wanted was to find a boat. But he knew he couldn't do so easily — he'd be followed, closely. As he walked down Truman, he felt eyes and turned, and there were two plainclothes Florida cops about a hundred yards behind him, one on either side of the street, in light sport jackets and trousers and sunglasses; when he stopped, they did, too, and just watched.

There was no way he could outrun them in any sense, with his cast; he'd have to lead them around, as if on a leash, and maybe wear them down. Hemingway couldn't hit the usual gin mills and slips and run the risk of implicating his friends, in particular Rick and Jean Fumereaux, in more F.B.I. business. Or could it be Lansky's minions, working hand in hand with the feds? It was getting so that the only powerful man Hemingway could trust was Galko; while everyone else was tied in and dirty with someone else, and it was impossible to know for sure who, Galko was just dirty.

No harm, Hemingway figured, in heading down the block, at a relaxed pace, to the yacht club in the old bridge-tender's house on Garrison Bight, to see if a vessel could be scared up from among the island's tonier guests and residents, few of which, he assumed, could resist a show-off jaunt on their million-dollar toys with Ernest Hemingway.

He hobbled, affecting a Sunday-stroll casualness, and his hyenas followed at their measured distance. The Key West Yacht

Club didn't look terribly ritzy from the outside, an antique municipal building deliberately left to look a little salty, beside the bridge ramp; the array of Mercedes Benzes and Ferraris outside were the only indication of the depth of the pockets inside. Galko was a longtime member, despite his ignorance about his own vessel (a 1930 Camper & Nicholsons 110-footer) and the fact that it officially flew a Syrian flag, and he was accepted for his money but otherwise privately loathed. Hemingway himself was no stranger to the club, but despite the board's strenuous efforts over the years to land him as a member, he'd steered clear — these were not people he loved to spend time with, corporate types and magnates and old-money heirs who generally don't have the slightest idea how to talk about something that doesn't involve their bottom line or bragging-rights lifestyle. The thick aura of insecure, mercenary smugness in the air of the place had, on more than one occasion, gagged Hemingway and sent him scrambling south to a real tavern, where no one proves anything to anybody, except, maybe, how well they can take a joke.

Checking once for his police friends, who stood stock still on the edge of the parking lot when he turned and looked, Hemingway went inside, where it was unnecessarily dark, past the abandoned front desk, the fifty-gallon fish tank swarming with lion fish, the never-used cloak room, and to the bar.

There were a handful of golf-shirted millionaires standing there, tanned and potbellied and smelling of aftershave, their hands wrapped around Manhattans, a bartender, and a busboy in the back of the room, dressing tables. Hemingway nodded, ordered a Manhattan as well, and looked to the other patrons, no more than three feet away, silhouetted against the bay windows looking out onto the bight, and expected a conversation to cordially begin, as they always seemed to, with only a drink and a nod. But the moment came and went, and Hemingway, having taken only a sip of his cocktail, realized that something was wrong. The other men shuffled uncomfortably and kept their backs to him in a way that was unusual enough to seem outright unnatural. No one met his eyes. Then the phone rang, the bartender answered, also turning his back. Suddenly, the busboy was gone. The men at the bar finished their drinks in an unpleasurably rushed slurp and left, never looking at Hemingway, two heading for the front door, one heading to the back, without a word.

"What the fuck's going on?" he asked the bartender, an athletic-looking fiftyish ex-boatsman Hemingway had seen before but never spoken to beyond drink orders.

The bartender looked him briefly in the eye, and it was a look intended to be steely and express nothing, but of course expressed menace and fear and doubt all the same.

"Well?" Hemingway said bullishly. The bartender put down the glass he was drying, walked around the bar and disappeared into the kitchen. "Hello?"

He refused to entertain the idea that he was being set up, as Squiccarini had warned, that he'd walked into a trap of some kind, that the bar had been forewarned and emptied out so that some assassins, maybe the cops-of-unknown-fealty outside, could slay him in solitude. It wouldn't make any sense for anyone to cross that line, even now, after all the trouble he'd gotten into. Would it? Would the F.B.I. want him done away with because of, what, hanging with Castro people and barking, however loudly, about the feds being responsible for murder and stolen isotopes? Or would it more likely be the C.I.A.? Was there a significant difference?

After having been made to witness the execution of Stanley Lynch, which was a kind of warning and a sharing of culpability both, it would appear, why did Hemingway think his every move *wasn't* being weighed and deliberated upon on a serious level, and that those deliberations couldn't again end up in violence?

Still, it seemed preposterous, the costs were too high, he was too famous, he'd been too much of a loudmouth these past weeks. He looked around the bar and listened — not a peep. He walked over to the front doors, pushed them open, squinting in the daylight — the parking lot was empty, even of the cop escort. Where'd those boys go to? Hemingway went back inside, slugged the rest of his Manhattan, and pushed open the kitchen doors.

The busboy stood in the middle of the room, lit by fluorescent, quickly wiping down a steel countertop, and when he saw Hemingway he froze. And then finished mechanically, hanging his towel up, never taking his eyes off Hemingway. Hemingway didn't budge and wasn't sure if the door he'd opened had made much, if any, noise.

The busboy, with burning dread in his

large eyes, then pointed with just one segment of his right index finger, hidden to his side and close to his stomach, to his left, where Hemingway couldn't see due to the industrial freezers against the wall. Someone was there, it would seem, hiding in the corner of the kitchen, waiting, and waiting with enough of a threatening demeanor to give this kid, who must've been Cuban, the serious willies. Hemingway nodded, didn't move. The busboy then exited, dashed, out the kitchen-staff door, almost without making a sound.

Hemingway began to sweat — in or out? Confront or run? If they were crazy enough to come after him, both scenarios seemed dire.

"Hel*lo?!*" he boomed into the kitchen, figuring that he should act clueless. "Make my own fucking drink!" And huffed out, back into the bar.

Where he quickly stuck his cane through the loop handles of the kitchen doors, making them impossible to open without a full-court, cane-snapping charge. He then limped quickly over to the front doors and twisted the inside lock.

The phone, behind the bar. But who to call? Hemingway actually began to panic — was there another way out? He could not rely on the local law enforcement. No one in Miami could come to his rescue. None of his friends in town deserved to be shot up and unloaded into a sump somewhere just because they were his friends.

The cane rattled.

Hemingway reluctantly took the Astra out of his belt and checked with his thumb to make sure the safety was off. If he was forced to use it, a gun that hadn't been fired in twenty years, he'd be lucky if he got one ill-aimed ricochet off before being pounded by bullets. But he had nothing else.

This is suicide, he thought. But wait — so what? Why not just seize the opportunity, one he's been courting and considering for thirty years? What else was he doing, running down the middle of the street in Madrid during a Fascist raid, or trying to fly a plane, his first, over Kenya drunk as a skunk? How many more ways can he find to *avoid* finally doing it? Let's just let them take me, he mused, let them come in firing away and blow me away after a good fucking fight, and that will be goddamn that.

But damn, Hemingway remembered feeling at times as if he'd wanted to die, innumerable times, but right now, he couldn't play that record. He rummaged around his brainpan for a few seconds, looking for the little gremlin that nestled there feeding him black thoughts about dying all too often. But the bastard always seemed to be on a coffee break whenever a genuinely dangerous opportunity presented itself. Whenever death threatened and became a palpable reality, all Hemingway could think about was what everyone else thought about: more life. His body and brain chemistry were probably trying to tell him something, electrified as it all was right now with fight-or-flight adrenaline. More life. And maybe it was also righteous egoism again, beating the gremlin down — if I die by misfortune, it'll be on my terms, not at the hands of some corrupt government flunkies in sunglasses. They will go *fuck* themselves.

Hemingway quickly, too quickly, made himself a perfectly awful Manhattan behind the bar and downed it in a gulp.

The cane rattled a total of three times, the first two quiet and exploratory, the third insistent and angry, and then nothing. Whoever it was would be heading outside now, around the front first.

Hemingway began to make his way to the back door, hoping it had a lock, hunched over, beneath the windowsill edges, stumbling, his spinal discs wincing and then snapping meanly at him.

There was only a key lock, unlocked, with no key in sight. He shoved his pistol back into his pants and began to push tables across the room to block the door. Then, scrambling back to the bar area, he began feverishly searching for an out — an air duct, a drainage vent, something, and hopefully something he wouldn't clog and die in like a rat in a sewer pipe. There must be a way to the roof — there can't be a basement — and in either case he'd be cornered.

He dashed into the smoking room, off the dining area, which was small and, he was reminded, had only one door. It was there, before he turned to leave, listening to his heart pump in a stampeding panic, he saw the harpoon — the *same* dumb, clumsy, old, sixty-pound whale harpoon. It was sticking straight out of an old leather chair, having been thrust through the seat, as if it were impaling prey. What the, Hemingway thought, irritated by the timing, now that he was scrambling to save his own life, but there it was — did Squiccarini donate it to the club or some such idiocy? What soused moron killed the chair with it? Whoever did it, it was apparently deemed by someone worth saving, and the arrangement had been shoved into the cluttered corner of the room; the club, it seemed, wasn't quite what it used to be.

But — Hemingway glanced up, and saw: over the blocked-up fireplace hung a giant marlin head emerging out of a wooden plaque (why couldn't they just mount the whole fish?), and on either side of it were conspicuously blank sections of wall, each with a pair of large hanging hooks, and faded-paint outlines above them — of harpoons, it would appear, one aiming west, the other aiming east. The spear sticking up from the chair was one of a pair. Hemingway'd noticed the marlin head the few times he'd been in that room before, but never the harpoons. Somehow, the second of the two had traveled all the way from its age-old position on the club's smoking room wall to the center of Peter Cuthbert's torso, the bulk of Key West away.

Which narrowed the suspects down to Club members, he supposed, and he salted that nugget away for later, when he wasn't being stalked by assassins. He hobbled in a hurry back out to the lobby and scanned the place for exits: closets, bathrooms (windows too high and too small) and the cluttered staff office — which used to be the original building's kitchen, before a renovation in the 'thirties. And which harbored, Hemingway found, between a dry sink and a row of file cabinets and over cardboard boxes of old pamphlets, a dumbwaiter, its door closed.

Oh no goddamned way. Hemingway slid the door up, and did a half second's survey of the equipment — the cables were wool rope, ferChrissake, and the waiter itself barely big enough to seat a ten-year-old. It'd probably hadn't been used in thirty or more years, and only then for cases of rum. Where did it go? There were no cellars in the Keys; it must've been used for deliveries right off boats, small boats, he assumed, because they had to come in under the docks, under the building. Smuggler's boats.

It smelled of mold, its platter sat under a quarter inch of dust, and it looked like it wouldn't hold the weight of a bottle of beer. Jesus H. There hadn't been a more fecund opportunity for disastrous foolishness presented to Hemingway in some time, and since he'd fallen off his own roof only a few weeks earlier, he did not feel as if the time was quite ripe for another boondoggle. He'd already had a devil of a time keeping his head straight about which stories he should tell in public company, and which were so embarrassing he shouldn't divulge them to a single soul, and lately the second category was outpacing the first. Besides, it might kill him.

But he heard his cane rattle again in the main room, with a menacing measuredness, and anonymous noises outside the windows.

Hemingway looked up into the dumbwaiter's tiny closet and could see the gears — they were rusted and might not turn at all. Another indignity-saturated scenario: the assassins break in and find him sitting there, stuffed into the cubicle like a zealous gradeschooler playing hide-and-seek.

A crash rooms away, and Hemingway heard the cane snap. His father's cane. He propelled himself into the cavity of the dumbwaiter with a single leap, left knee first, ass squeezing in on one side, the contraption heaving and shaking uneasily; then he managed to sit, sort of, his head crushed down and forward by the waiter's frame, his right leg folded painfully beneath him, his left leg bent at the knee and pressed against his chest, so the cast settled flat on its sole, his right shoulder and arm left sticking out and then pulled gingerly but forcefully in, causing Hemingway to fold down and to the left in a way that made his back explode in novas of nerve-whipping pain. His left hand reached up and yanked the sliding door shut.

Darkness. The dumbwaiter wasn't creak-ing, it was screaming under the stress. Hemingway couldn't guess whether or not you could hear it out in the office. But he did hear footsteps, maybe in the office, maybe in the lobby. How close? He realized it was preposterously hot where he was, and that sweat was already stinging his eyes. Hemingway reached up with his left hand and tested the cable, and then tugged at it a little, to try to lower the waiter down. But it didn't budge. His back pain was making him dizzy. He decided to pull harder, why not, just as he heard a chair get overturned in what had to be the office on the other side of the door. Then the waiter gave out.

Hemingway fell. He fell for what seemed simultaneously to be hours and milliseconds, and because he could see nothing, he had no idea how far. But it couldn't have been more than twelve, fifteen feet all told, eight or so to some kind of floor, made up of rotting marine wood that splintered with a fleshy splat under his catapulting girth, but which sent a hot lance up his spine nonetheless, and then another six or so, maybe, with an epic splash, to the water of the bight. Which was warm and smelled of crab shell.

Hemingway quickly bounced off the silty bottom, and his back instantly started seizing up in high-voltage knots, which did not abate even after he found he could stand, the water coming right up to his chin. What kind of hellish racket did he just make? No way of knowing: he ducked down and started to walk and paddle westward, thinking as he went that the plaster of his cast would quickly begin to soften and dissolve if he didn't get it out of the water as soon as he could. Wouldn't it? Would it matter if it did, to his ankle? Hemingway didn't have a guess to that, either, and realized he'd never spoken to the doctor who put it on, and so didn't know when it was supposed to come off.

Moron, he thought, skulking around under the dock, disappearing underwater every now and then but otherwise keeping his nose low to the water and half-swimming all under the surface. The cast got noticeably heavier with each minute it spent submerged.

He made his laborious way past the bridge ramp and tried to hurry toward the docked boats on the other side, low and out of sight of the club and the road. It might've taken him ten minutes. Soon he reached moored boats he knew, and eventually asked Tony Buglion ("pronounced 'bullion,' like the soup"), a Miami banker who never read fiction and who was at the moment cleaning the weather off his eighteen-footer in its slip, to throw him a rope ladder and make him a cocktail. On Buglion's deck, saturated with Gulf water and holding a highball, a thin trail of wet white plaster drips behind him, Hemingway propped his cast up on a stool to dry in the sun; the plaster was oozing, but firm. Buglion, when asked, said he thought the cast should probably stay on for a month or two, at least. Then he silently wiped up the plaster residue with a rag. Hemingway tried to be discreet, but scanned the horizon over by the Club, through the docked masts, and saw no evidence of cars or plainsclothesmen. It did already in fact look shuttered and abandoned.

He lied to Buglion, of course, said he'd fallen in, four docks over, off Herb Tiptree's new Nova Scotia schooner, and decided to float, since he was drunk and Herb was napping. He knew that even the most gullible of the bunch at Joe's would raise their eyebrows in doubt if he told them the dumbwaiter story, or tighten their lips shut in derision because they did in fact believe it. He'd have to save it, just as drinking with Castro in the mountains would have to be something he'd reserve for a memoir, or maybe an *Atlantic* piece. Or that new one,

The Paris Review. All the same, he should write the pertinent facts down and put them in a sealed envelope and sock it away with his will, to be mailed upon the event of demise to, maybe, Cy Sulzberger at the *Times,* maybe with a bottle of Scotch, to insure somehow that Hemingway's mysterious death on American soil, if it happened some time after this, wouldn't disappear under a cover story but would blow up, with details about Castro, Cuthbert, Lynch and the C.I.A., on the front page of the Old Gray Lady. Hemingway knew, though, that Sulzberger was dirty with the feds himself. So it might be pointless. He wished he knew another high-profile *Times* reporter, or even someone at the *Washington Post.* He might have to resort to the masturbators at the *Herald.*

But he wasn't dead yet. He was sitting on a docked boat, drinking expensive single malt with grocery-store ice that made it taste tinny, and talking about Whitey Ford with a calm banker in shirt sleeves and discount deck shoes.

29

The Audubon House was quiet, with two Isottas parked on the street, when Hemingway pulled up, checking his sad little pistol as he paid the cabbie, and with all the solemn dignity he could muster walked to the door and knocked. He didn't think he'd been followed but had to assume it.

The same day: he disembarked once Buglion began to get antsy about not cleaning his boat, and once the cast seemed sufficiently dry. He decided that he'd find a boat later and talk to Galko now, as he'd meant to do when Captain Video came calling. He took only an hour to shower, his cast stuck out through the curtain, and change before he called a car. He rehearsed questions to ask Galko, questions that said nothing explicitly but were loaded with covert meanings. Or he hoped they were loaded. Who knew how much Galko understood of what was said to him. Hemingway still wasn't sure he wasn't just walking right into gunfire.

A houseboy he'd never seen before opened the door, and Hemingway politely, with a slow push and a smile, let himself in. "Please tell Mr. Galko that Mr. Hemingway would like to speak to him."

The boy nodded and left. Hemingway heard nothing in the house except some walking and some murmuring. The front rooms were still chockablock with shippables of dubious provenance in and out of crates.

The boy returned, and led Hemingway to the western room, with tall windows, that Galko used as his office. It was filled with every imaginable high-priced import item, apparently selected by Galko as things he'd rather keep than sell from amidst his product stream: a gorilla-hand ashtray, a blue-porcelain-elephant table from India, a seventeenth-century Chinese silk standing screen, a polar bear rug, no less than six jeroboams of 1900 Château Margaux standing on a side bar. Galko was behind the desk, on which were numerous open log books and legal pads filled with presumably illegal information. Galko sat with his hands in his lap, staring at Hemingway as he came in, and the look was predatory. Hemingway caught out of the corner of his eye, standing to the side behind the open door, one of Galko's barrel-chested goons, Tibor or Jacint, the one without the newly broken nose. The houseboy vanished.

"How are you, Ferenc, thought I'd —"

"Sit down, Hemingvay."

Hemingway sat. Galko was not in his congenial, sparring, shooting-arrows-through-foxes mode; Hemingway had always assumed the Hungarian had another manner in which he conducted business, given the nature of his business, and here it was.

"Ferenc, I've come about the isotope."

"I know." Galko searched his teeth with his tongue. "You've been meddling all over the map, haven't you. You even vent to Castro."

"Yes. And the C.I.A., and the F.B.I., who you'll be happy to know have been plotting out how to kill me. They hate me now more than they hate you. I even spoke to Meyer Lansky."

"Lansky!"

"Yup. So far the body count is two, and I've had at least three serious threats to my life, only one of which may've been yours." Eyebrows up. "So I'm thinking it's about time to settle this shit before another stiff hits the pavement."

"Let me make this clear, Hemingvay, though I thought you'd know this already — I operate just under the sonar of the authorities, and my operation is large and various and involves a great many people, none of whom knows very much about the operation at large, and many of whom pay off to the authorities so they can conduct business without being harassed, which they do unless circumstances force the authorities," his voice rising, like a fire alarm, "to do what they're paid to do anyway, despite the bribes they've taken, which means my people get focked twice, and you my fat writer friend have made the authorities SWARM LIKE FOCKING BEES ALL OVER ME!"

"Me? What'd I do?" Hemingway lightened up; he liked the bellowing Galko better than the saturnine Galko.

"You tell me! You've mentioned my name to everyone in the focking hemisvere! Theese uranium ting was just a botched deal, a mess, forgotten already, but *you* made sure every branch of the focking government would investigate it!"

"That's where you're all wrong, Ferenc — they're not investigating it, they're burying it. They're implicated somehow. Or they're embarrassed. That's why they've been trying to scare me."

"Implicated? How? It was my deal!"

"I don't know, maybe at the source."

Galko waved his hands around in frustration. "All I know is I have eyes on me, I have IRS agents calling for audits, I have bugs in my house — bugs! — I have the F.B.I. demanding more bribes, those *fockers,* I have boats from Africa stalled at customs no matter how much I pay, I have people that owe me money held in Coast Guard stockades somewhere, no lawyers."

"My house is bugged, too."

"Mine is no longer, I hired this Israeli spy to debug. Took him all day yesterday."

Tibor or Jacint sat down in a wing chair off to Hemingway's left, and lit a cigarette. Hemingway glanced at him — the readiness stance was gone.

"I'm not the enemy, Ferenc."

"You're no focking help, Hemingvay, you're no partner, you're not bribable, you don't want what other people want, you just want to be goddamn nosy. You are just a roach in my kitchen, and God help me I vant to step on you."

"Then go ahead you crazy Hunkie, step on me, see what it'll get you. But I'm not just being nosy, I'm trying to figure out what's going on around me. Like why the C.I.A. blew Stanley Lynch's head off right in front of me."

Galko grew more relaxed with the tough talk, as Hemingway hoped he would. He of course knew Lynch was killed. "How'd you know it was the C.I.A."

"The guy told me."

"So?"

"He couldn't've been anything else, Ferenc."

"OK, I'll tell you vot, meester Big Brain. Then you go take a nap or write a focking story. Lynch is the one that stole the uranium from New Mexico."

". . . Los Alamos."

"That's right. One of my people brought him to me, I say, sure. Dey told me he had a brother-in-law that worked there or someting. He had a lead box, and if you opened it you'd die. I had sent some German and Soviet guns and shit down to Castro, so I thought maybe he'd vant to buy this thing. Those Cubans have money to spend."

"And how was Cuthbert involved?"

"He had the boat, and he knew the Castro connections vell enough."

"What went wrong?"

"I don't have the slightest idea, I told you. All I know is, I didn't put any money up for it, so I did not lose. Dat was Lynch's mistake."

"You told me? You've lied about everything else."

"Excuse the fock out of me, Hemingvay, I'm trying to stay out of trouble. I don't have any obligation to be a boy scout vith you."

"So Cuthbert was the only one to speak to the rebels."

"Yah." Hemingway was trying to sound offhand, but the questions are inching toward the danger zone. "And they said they'd pay how much for this lead box?"

Galko paused, chewing on his tongue. "One hundred thousand."

Hemingway couldn't read the Hungarian. This was no help — if Cuthbert had tried to rip Galko off, and Galko had found out and killed him for it, then naturally Galko would know how much Cuthbert was asking from the Cubans. But: the harpoon.

"When did you hear that the deal went south?"

"About de same time you did, I expect. Day later, two days, whatever. I vas in Miami."

"What happened to the uranium?"

"Dat's a good question. You know, if you could find out, wit all deese people you've talked to, I vill buy it from you."

"I'm not looking for a new line of work, Ferenc."

"Forty thousand, in cash, tax-free."

"Besides, I don't think Castro wants it anymore."

"Fock Castro, I'll sell it to de Algerians. Or North Korea."

Hemingway shrugged. "Didn't it bother you that if the revolution had used this thing you'd be selling, a lot of people would be dead."

"No, it didn't. My scientist friends told me it'd kill maybe a dozen people on a crowded city street, less than a few grenades. But it's a lot scarier, and therefore a lot more expensive. Anyway, I figured those Latin mountain men would blow themselves up first."

"Still." Scientist friends. What a cesspool the world has become. Hemingway felt like he was out of cards. "I wonder . . . if Matilde Pirrin knows anything more about it."

Galko's face brightened, and Hemingway didn't like it — it wasn't joy or excitement, it was malice, emanating from him like charisma.

"Vell! Yes! Hemingvay, ve should go find out! Let's go talk to her!" A gesture with his eyes and suddenly Hemingway was being heaved from his chair by the armpits by Tibor or Jacint, and then the other one, Tibor or Jacint, appeared and grabbed the other arm, and he was turned around and led out of the room so quickly and in grips so bruisingly strong he didn't dare resist. Galko overtook them, practically skipping, and the four men made their way to a back hall and a cellar door, unlocked it, down into the darkness, which smelled to Hemingway, at first, like camphor.

The lights were turned on. The basement was predictably filled with junk, boxes, not-so-expensive importables still in their hundreds of crates. There was a work table in the center of the cellar, and across it lay Matilde, naked and purple with bruises, gagged and handcuffed, a chrome chain running from the cuffs under and around the table and over her belly three times. Cuffs held her ankles, too, and the skin under her ankles and wrists was dark with bruises and dried blood. It was the smell of her urine that filled the room. Which meant she'd been there for a few days. She appeared groggy, semiconscious.

Hemingway could not say a thing. The goons let him go.

"Go ahead, Hemingvay. Ask."

Hemingway looked down, he couldn't

look at her. This is where the search has led him — to the extended torture of a woman in a dank basement, for reasons of profit and crooked business? This isn't the way things go in books, *good* books, god fucking dammit, in books even the louses have a respect for life, because they're fighting for their own, right? This is Fu Manchu shit, this is the arena of the cartoon caricature, not real people, people who have childhoods and mothers and, maybe, children, and women they'd once loved, genuinely, and war buddies they'd die for in a scrape. Who does this?

"Ferenc, who does this?" Hemingway said finally, his bile rising along with his nausea. "Who does this? Who tortures people? You fucking scumbag, I'll tell you who — totalitarian governments, like the ones you've been running from your whole life, the KGB and the Nazis and the Stasi and the AVO. Is this what you've been reduced to?"

Galko was expecting fear, not outrage. "Ach, shut up, Hemingvay, don't lecture me!"

"Lecture you! I've never seen anything like this in my life, and I was in Spain watching good Socialists, *real* Socialists, not those cardboard carpetbaggers that call themselves Socialists in Hungary! I was there watching them kill the innocent wives of Fascists, just as warnings, as terrorism! But this — this woman, what'd she do to you? Don't answer me! I'll tell you — she did or said something that cost you a profit on something, right? Maybe it was the uranium, maybe something else, but it's the money, isn't it, Ferenc? How many more fucking Isottas do you need, you leech! You've been torturing her for, what, what it would take to buy a new English suit, or a new Swiss watch? Right now, tell me how much she cost you, and I'll pay it. I'll buy the suit! I don't care! I'll get you cash on the spot, you monkey, I'll make your big problem, the one you're disposing this woman for, go away. How much, huh, how much?"

Galko, a man of dubious attention span to begin with, was already exhausted. "It's not the money, Hemingvay. It's the principle. Don't be a child. The C.I.A. does it, trying to fock vith the Castros, the Castros do it to scare the Batistas, the Batistas do it to hold on to vhat they have, Meyer Lansky and those guys do it to hold on to vhat dey have, the C.I.A. do it to partners of mine — don't dink dey don't! — this is vhat happens vhen you play with the hard balls, Hemingvay, and I didn't bring you down here to hear you give me a focking sermon, I brought you down here so you vill understand that you are a writer and nothing more and you do not belong focking vith my business. I vill not hurt you, I decided that veeks ago, but this Batista bitch will die, and business vill go on, and you'll go vin another prize or something, or go fock another movie star, and you'll know better your place in the vorld."

Teach me my place?!, he sparked inside. But Hemingway's ire was daunted, he felt the air leak out of him, he felt in the room the inescapable fact that raging around like a rhino with his balls in a twist wouldn't help and might in fact kill him. And the woman.

After a pause. "But Ferenc, you sent this woman after me, you got her involved."

"Big shit, I paid her enough."

"But Ferenc."

"Vhat."

"I know where the uranium is."

Galko looked him over, like he was buying a horse.

"You do."

"Yes." Quietly. "And I can tell the F.B.I. where, and tell them everything I know, which I haven't done as yet, and not only will you not get the uranium, whatever it's worth to you, but the feds will ship you out of the country for good. I'll talk to the *New York Times* to make sure it happens just that way, so you can't bribe yourself out of it. If the feds trace the uranium to you, they'll have no choice."

"I could kill you right now," Galko whispered back, spitting. "You'll disappear. I'll feed your fat belly to the barracudas off the Dry Tortugas."

Hemingway maintained his calm; the whole conversation was so quiet Tibor or Jacint had to lean a little to hear it.

"That'd be a mess, Ferenc. If you could do it without having a few extra bodies on your back. I'll take one of you fuckers with me, and it might be you. I could snap you over my knee like a willow branch. You see, I'm *not* just a focking writer. Not to mention, I'm pretty goddamn certain some branch of the federal government has been tracking me for several days now, which means they know I'm here, right now."

"Think they're vorried for your protection?"

"No, I don't. But that's not the point. The point is, there's a way that would be cleaner, better for everyone: give me the woman and I'll give you the uranium."

Galko stared his Hungarian gangster stare,

which always meant to indicate more craftiness than was actually there. Craftiness is quick, and Galko's stares, like this one, always took upwards of a solid minute.

"Do you know her? She's a whore, and a Batista *közlegény.*"

"Whatever that means. Yes, I know her well." Galko looked doubtful. "She screwed me dizzy," Hemingway added, and Galko appeared to be convinced enough.

"Alright," he said, with a relaxed smile. Tibor and Jacint took the cue and went about uncuffing Matilde. She sat up with help, and Tibor or Jacint threw a dusty blanket over her shoulders.

"Plus the forty thou?" Hemingway said dryly.

Galko didn't get the joke. "No, you bleeder, the voman for the lead box."

Hemingway shrugged. "Get her clothes."

"So vhere's the stuff?"

"I'll let you know, by the end of the day tomorrow." Galko clenched his teeth in momentary frustration, and then threw up his hands.

"Y'know, Hemingvay, after this, never come to my house again." Galko turned his back and went toward the stairs, still complaining, the goons following. "If ever a movie star vants to export me, let her, anything but have to focking deal vith you one more focking time."

They were alone, Hemingway and the woman, suddenly, in the Audubon House cellar.

"Gracias," Matilde said, hoarse and shaky but clear as day. She had not been, Hemingway gathered, semiconscious after all. Hemingway helped her get dressed and upstairs had the houseboy call another cab.

Before they left, Hemingway picked up Galko's freshly unbugged phone in the foyer, Matilde teetering beside him, and called Rick Villareal, again. Would Rick be up for fishing, tonight? Even if it were big fish, dangerous fish? Rick said he would.

Hemingway scoured the street — no visible tails. Which meant nothing. "You should see a doctor," he said in the back of the cab on the way home. She began to pull her hair back and look at her lips and cheeks in the cab's rearview mirror, as if she'd done this everyday. But Hemingway got a closer look at her arms and neck and calves, and the dark bruises and slashing wounds were real, maybe the work of a blackjack and wire hangers.

"I'm alright, Mr. Hemingway. I just need some ice and a bath."

"Did they rape you?"

She looked at him. “None of your business.”

30

After Marisol had poured Matilde a bath, and taken a generous amount of care with helping her undress, and bandaging her cuts and icing her bruises and wiping her tears and feeding her tlalpeno soup with a spoon, and after some time had passed and the afternoon grew late, Hemingway came into his bathroom with two mojitos, and sat on the toilet drinking his.

Matilde didn't want to get out of the tepid water and cried a little more without making a sound. "Mr. Hemingway, I'm afraid I've gotten you in trouble, for saving me."

"No, you haven't. Stay here as long as you want. My doctor's coming by in the morning to look you over. But I have to go soon. I need to know whatever you can tell me about Cuthbert, about what happened."

"I only know what I heard."

"That's why you were in Galko's house, right?, to gather information. And to squelch the deal?"

Matilde sighed. "To squelch any deal with Castro that I could. But Cuthbert didn't need my help, he squelched it good all by himself. He was, of course, trying to rip everyone off."

"Everyone."

"Yes, as far as I could hear, he overcharged Castro, and then lied to Ferenc, and then hid the goods somewhere, trying to jack the price up even more."

"Why did Ferenc turn on you suddenly?"

"He found out I was loyal to Batista, that I worked for Havana. He found out from Castro's people, day before yesterday."

No. Did that news trickle down to Galko from the Escambrays after Hemingway's campfire visit? Did he tip yet another set of suffering dominoes in motion? Hemingway was beginning to feel as if everyone he touched was doomed, one way or another. He instantly regretted calling Rick, roping him in. Maybe I should just find a desert island, he thought, and just sit.

"So who killed him? Cuthbert."

"I wasn't there. But Castro's people were not to come to Florida, Cuthbert was to go to them."

"So it was Ferenc. Tibor or Jacint."

Matilde shrugged. Sipped her drink and

seemed happy to be frank for once.

"What about," Hemingway asked, "the harpoon."

Matilde took a breath. "As far as I could understand, Tibor and Jacint were drunk, which is an assumption if it's past five o'clock, they guzzle vodka together every night, and they were to meet Cuthbert on the docks, check his package, and take the trip with him to Havana. They were drinking at the club, and they were horsing around with these harpoons they found there, and they thought it'd be funny — that's what Tibor said, when he told the story to Ferenc, and then Ferenc hit him in the face with a three iron, full swing, from all the way out here — they thought it'd be funny to take that old harpoon with them, in case they were shanghaied, or whatever. *Pendejos.* When they got there, in their white suits and carrying this harpoon, Cuthbert told them to go back and tell Ferenc that Castro and Guevara would only pay $25,000, and if they didn't get it for that price they'd kill Cuthbert. Apparently, Tibor and Jacint didn't believe him, and they argued on the pier for a while, and it got rough, Tibor and Jacint started scaring Cuthbert. They made him go to the pay phone and call Ferenc, who told him to fuck himself, I was there with Ferenc to hear that, and then they made him call the Castro number in Havana, which he couldn't get through to."

"He called me, too."

"Really. What did he say?"

"The lines were down, I didn't talk to him."

"So, how do you know."

"The cops said he called. The phone company said so."

"They came to Ferenc's house, too, questioned him for maybe five minutes."

"That was their plan. Wrap it up quickly and bury it."

"Why?"

"It was their uranium. Bad publicity, letting it get stolen and sold to Communists."

"Hmpf. Well. Then I think it was Jacint that called Ferenc, who told them to forget the deal altogether, kill Cuthbert and come home. So they shot him, when I guess Ferenc was expecting them to drown him, or something. But then they realized they used those stupid Arab guns, which Ferenc had told them to get rid of months before, because they were traceable and no one else in the state had them. The idiots had bought them cheap in Marrakech, and liked the Arabic styling. They went to call Ferenc again, to ask what they should do now, because they were drunk, but they were out of change by that point, if you can believe that. So they looked for the bullets that went through Cuthbert and realized they'd gone into the water, but the bullet holes in his body might be distinct, and traceable, too, they thought, who knows. So they shoved the harpoon through him and tossed him off the dock."

She took a long sip. "Then they wrecked the nearest boat."

Hemingway had no more questions. It had been everything he'd always said it was, a criminal boondoggle on the docks at night between foolish hoods, that's all, but it was also a tragedy, a petty, pointless fuckup that took a loser down with it, a man who'd already given up everything he ever had because it all spoiled in his grip like treefall fruit. It couldn't've happened that such a man, of a kind Hemingway knew well, and always had sympathy for, might've lived out his last decades peaceably drinking at Mile Zero and ogling the tourist women and watching the boats, harming no one and maybe even acquiring some salty, second-hand respect with the years, from those that knew him a little. Peter never did harm anyone, no one who didn't have it long coming, anyway, and it did seem that the world simply had had no place for him, that the last, dangling corner of America was just as much a place for a last boot in the throat as it was a sanctuary for the valueless. In that way, it was very much like the rest of America, deceptive and Godless and black, despite its promise of serenity.

Dusk was falling, in registers of puce and peach. The Cuban woman went to sleep in his bed. The breezes hissed relentlessly, as always. Hemingway ransacked the house and found a real handgun, an Army-issue .45 from the last war, and asked Marisol for a Pepto Bismol.

31

Hemingway didn't know of a way to sneak out of the Whitehead Street house that would fool anybody, and he didn't know who'd be watching in any case, Galko's huns or the feds or both. So Hemingway took his scooter out, brazenly, and headed for the basin through the back streets, doubling back, cutting through yards, taking every shortcut he knew, his plump frame teetering on the putt-putting scooter like a pachyderm on a circus bike. It took him three times as long to get to the docks as it might've had he walked, but when he did he saw Rick waiting for him, engine primed and ready to go. The sky was getting dark, Hemingway parked his scooter by the harbor master's booth, and leapt aboard.

"Papa," Rick said, gunning the motor and spurting out of the shallows, "you gonna fill me in as to what this is now, aren't ya."

"Yes, Rick. You've fueled up, I hope."

"Si."

"Ricky, this might not be a pleasure cruise tonight, I warned you. People have gotten very hurt, and a few killed."

"I'm not scared, Papa. I'm with you."

"Ah Jesus."

They were tootling along north by northeast, Hemingway telling Rick the whole story, or only its important parts, including his estimation of where the *M* on the Key West police station's map of Florida marked the Gulf itself, for just a handful of minutes before a boat pulled out behind them, and Hemingway immediately recognized it as one of Galko's speedsters, faster than any Coast Guard vessel but immediately recognizable, sleek and arrow shaped, so whatever they had in the way of fleetness they lost by lack of stealth. Hemingway wished he had binoculars, but it didn't matter, he knew who was on the boat.

"Slow it down, Rick, no rush." Rick brought the throttle down, and Galko's smuggling bullet kept its distance, the two boats shuttling along evenly like lovers making a game in the fog.

But it was nearly night now, and the lights of both boats went on.

"It was them, the other time, wasn't it," Rick said listening to their engine.

The trip out toward the north patch above Little Mullet was quiet — the old boys didn't dare speak for the longest time, the two boat engines were hustling along at slow cruising speed, the men's eyes all on each other, the sky silent. Rick sat driving and Hemingway sat beside him, looking fore and aft in rhythmic succession. Finally, Rick spoke up, quietly.

"I brought a gun, Papa."

"Me, too, Ricky."

"*Ay.* That means someone's guaranteed to catch a bullet."

"I wonder if they're drunk. They usually are."

"What if the boat's not there?"

"Rick, that's the best-case scenario. If it's not there, there's nothing to fight about, nothing to betray anyone over, nothing to kill for. Galko won't care about that Cuban woman, and I'll be off the hook."

"And the feds."

"Will close the book. With satisfaction."

"And if we do find it."

"That I don't know."

"Very funny. C'mon, Papa, don't give me dialogue, give me a plan."

"Alright, you sarcastic wetback, let's say it's there, and there's an isotope right on the deck with a ribbon on it, waiting for us.

We don't want Galko to get it, but are you ready to die for that cause?"

"Not really."

"Me neither. The world's full of that shit, bombs everywhere, power plants going up everywhere. So do we hand it over?"

Rick was shaking his head in little jerks. "No, not that."

"Then we have to kill them. Tibor and Jacint."

"Ay, ay."

"And then hand the thing, whatever we find, to the feds. Have them chase Galko out of town. They can at least dump it somewhere so that crazy gangsters don't sell it to Korea."

Rich was nodding.

"At least we should shrug these bastards off and get there first."

He turned off the boat's headlight and pumped the throttle, plowing into the darkness.

Hemingway heard the other boat behind them gun, and the two ships, once again, fire off into the void of the night Gulf, not having a firm grasp at all on where they were going in the darkness.

Not entirely true, for Rick: his radio and gas gauge were still kaput, but his compass and the poles of the earth were still functioning, and Rick knew the stars pretty well, and to his fortune, the moonless sky was clear. The Hungarians behind them, children of a land-locked country, had no such advantage. As Rick forged ahead, smacking the waves in a violent undulation, Galko's boat began to recede.

Another hour, of circling wide around and pausing to look over the constellations and then firing forward and negotiating between northwest and northwest-west and arguing in profane shorthand and reticently turning the headlight on for moments at a time and scanning the ink around them for Hungarians, brought the men to a standstill. They were indisputably north-northwest of Little Mullet, but the sea and blackness were endless in every direction, and frankly they'd lost their intuitive sense of exactly how far they were from the island. Which left them in an abyss.

"Rick, think of something."

"Oh, sure."

Rick began trundling ahead at a medium pace; they both knew that the longer it took for them to search the area, the more gas they'd use up and the sooner the Hungarians would find them. The night around them was monstrous and humbling.

"I think we're going to have to commit to

the light. Keep it on."

Rick turned it on, and no more than forty yards ahead of them sat an old anchored fishing boat, New England in style, vaguely lime green in the darkness, covered in loose tarp from pilothouse to stern, bobbing in the water. They would have ran into it without the light.

"Jesus Christ." Hemingway stood up. "Hit the light."

They approached slowly, and Rick pulled up beside it. The tarp was heavy with rain puddles and gummy with a layer of gull crap.

"Flashlight, perchance?" Rick did bring one this time. Hemingway sat on the boat's gunwales and swung his legs over to the other boat, pulling it in, kicking up the tarp, and scooting over into the boat. Fucking cast. He spent a few minutes pushing the tarp back, and then scanned the deck with the flashlight.

There wasn't much junk, just a few beer cans and cigarette butts, but the boat itself was in awful shape, so weather worn and salt rotted the deck wood felt soft under Hemingway's feet. It seemed on the verge of just collapsing and must've been out here, getting worn down by the sea, for ages. Hemingway poked around in the dank cuddy, where he spotted, oddly for a craft this small, two deadlights in the boat's hull, small, thick windows looking out and down under the water. Peter could've put those in, but some half-assed handyman did. On his knees, Hemingway shone the flashlight beam through one and saw fifteen feet or so through the clear, green Gulf water, and glimpsed floating there a small, dead fish, rising to the top in no great hurry.

Then another, and a third, rising from the darkness, fish souls ascending to heaven.

Hemingway stood up and hit the surface of the water with the light, Rick watching carefully — dead fish, floating spread out around the boat but numerous, some as big as a foot long but most of them small feeders.

"What the fuck?" Rick hissed.

"I think we have radioactivity."

Rick shrunk back into his seat and unconsciously began to scratch.

Then Hemingway saw the first shark, just a prowling shadow that he supposed was a male bull shark, maybe. It was no surprise they'd be drawn to the dying fish, but there might be little left alive for the beasts to feed on now, until they got sick and started dying themselves. If they did. But the boat's arrival and the jostling and the light, out here where little happens at night, had probably brought the sharks in again.

Hemingway made his way back aft and went to his knees, fishing through some collected boxes and crap at the stern.

"C'mon, Papa, this is unhealthy," Rick whined.

Hemingway ignored him and pulled out a burlap sack that suddenly resisted him, steadfast — and he pulled, and realized that it carried a small anvil or something, and looking into it found a box, crate wood on the outside, big enough only for a pair of deck shoes. It must be lead on the inside, he supposed, it must've weighed forty pounds.

It was locked, with a small, rusted old Yale padlock. The next moment had the relaxed, crystalline ease of a math problem having become clear and solvable: Hemingway took the lock key he'd found on Peter's *other* boat out of his pocket's mess of coins, matchbooks, note scraps and spare bullets for the .45, surprised a little that he'd held onto it all this time, and inserted it into the lock, and with a rusty grinding, snapped it open. He lifted the lid, and the box was indeed lead-lined. Inside was an old golfball — to ape the sound and feel of the isotope, had anyone jostled the locked box — and a matchbook from Joe's, on the underside of which Peter had scrawled GO FUCK YOURSELF.

Peter had been thinking ahead — foreseeing his own dire fortune, in which he'd be screwed over and his boat discovered and plundered by blaggarts. Hemingway began to get nauseous, thinking of the radioactivity. He went to the anchor line and tried to make the end of it visible with the light but saw only murk.

"What're you looking for?" Rick was on the verge.

"I think he must've tied it to the anchor, somehow, in a bag maybe. Don't think he counted on the dead fish to give him away."

"Whatever, leave it, Papa."

Rick was right. That was all he needed. Hemingway stood up, finally emotionally finished with the whole affair, with Peter Cuthbert, even with Key West itself.

Before he could even finish his sigh, a bullet tore through the boat's hull six inches from where he stood, missed his calf by a whisper, and exited through the rumpled tarp on the other side, which is when he heard the gunshot. The Hungarians had arrived.

Hemingway lurched for Rick's boat, falling on his belly across both boats' parallel gunwales, trying to flop over and out of view like an oversized fish. Rick, he saw vaguely in the dark, had hit the deck, lying on his stomach. Hemingway completed his flip, landing with a crash, and looked to Rick, expecting the Mexican to be in a familiar state of terror. But this time Rick was neither hungover nor drunk, nor did his movements seem scared — Hemingway heard he was getting his gun out, a ferociously large Colt, and checking the barrel, and inching quickly down to the back corner of the boat, so as not to be seen until the last possible minute.

Hemingway did the same, grabbed the .45 from his belt, checked it, made sure the safety was off, and the other boat came chugging up to it in bottom gear, and Hemingway could hear the two henchmen muttering in Hungarian, coughing, *sshhhing.* It wasn't clear if they were in fact soused, as Hemingway hoped they were, until they drove Galko's boat smack head-on into Rick's, at a low speed but rapidly enough to cave in a hull wall, the cracking and snapping of which both Rick and Hemingway knew, just from hearing it, meant the demise of Rick's already old skiff; it'd scarcely be worth towing to shore.

As Rick's boat reeled from the collision, a

Hungarian hand grabbed the side of Rick's boat, the fingers appearing inches from where Rick lurked hiding his head, and because it was close enough to allow him to just see it by starlight, that's all that the Mexican required: Rick grabbed a machete and swung it out from the darkness, from a thick night illuminated only in the headlight of Galko's boat. When the machete snapped down with authority and took off three Hungarian fingers, Tibor's or Jacint's, the starry sky was filled with shrieking.

And Hungarian curses and gunfire — the Hungarians began firing willy-nilly in the boat's general direction, and the guns weren't Berettas or copies of Berettas but tommy guns, sprinkling Rick's boat with crazy bullets that had Hemingway wondering if the boat would sink from perforation before anyone actually got hit.

But get hit someone would — unless the dumb idiots used up their magazines pretty goddamn soon. One did suddenly stop shooting — the one that was bleeding — and so, like a lizard on a branch, Rick leapt up onto his haunches while the other goon, Tibor or Jacint, was still sending spurts of bullets out in a panic; saw the two dim figures silhouetted against their own boat's light, and with a patient quickness directed his large gun at the one still standing, at his head, and fired.

The tommy-gun fire did cease, immediately. Rick jumped up, and Hemingway jumped up, and Rick leapt into the boat, onto the finger-cut Hungarian, who was helplessly blubbering and bleeding like a chicken throat, and started to lug him up and onto the boat's ledge — to what? Hemingway's mind ricocheted around. To keep the amount of gore that had to be washed from the boat to a minimum? Was Rick thinking this, or thinking at all? But the second Hungarian, the one whose head Hemingway'd assumed had been forcefully emptied of brain a moment before, charged like a bear out of the darkness, grabbing Hemingway by the throat and pulling and rolling over onto him on Galko's boat's deck. Where the man's machine gun had gone Hemingway couldn't guess, but it became clear as Hemingway got sticky with blood that Rick had hit the man above the neck somewhere, and he'd probably lost his gun in the disorienting frenzy created by one kind of heavy-gouting head wound or another.

Rick fired. The first Hungarian that Rick was straddling on the gunwale took Rick's second shot through the nose and was unquestionably dead, the body slumping like dropped sacks of sugar, tripping Rick up. He fell. The second goon — Tibor or Jacint, no one could say, it was still too dark — found Hemingway's windpipe with his hands and squeezed it shut, and Hemingway started seeing pink lights flare up in front of his eyes. His hands roamed frantically for his gun, which had fallen, somewhere.

Then a thump and a shudder, Hemingway couldn't see what, but the Hungarian's grip loosened and his body lightened — Rick had stuck an aluminum fishing gaff, the kind you find stocked on slick, fast boats from which no one actually fishes, through the surviving Hungarian's back, and began trying to lift him off. Gasping, Hemingway heard both men growling-grunting in the blackness, and reached around him for a gun, any gun.

The Hungarian stood up fast, pushing Rick over the splayed legs of the other Hungarian, and the gaff fell out of his back with a clang. Blood sprayed and made everything slippery. He turned, raising a leg over Hemingway, who couldn't see it but caught it by accident as he raised a hand to grab something to hold on to, and the Hungarian immediately lost his balance, falling on Rick and quickly reaching for his throat and eyes in a mortal rage, cursing Hungarian curses, and bleeding so much from his back that Hemingway, who had managed to stand, slipped and went down and rapped the back of his head on the edge of a passenger seat facing aft. But there on the deck again his hands found one of the tommy guns, so he again went to his knee and then his feet, his finger finding the trigger, his panicking thoughts hoping this time for just a few more bullets in the magazine.

The Hungarian had Rick by the throat and his thumb was trying to dig Rick's left eye out of its socket, but Rick kept jacking his knee and shin up to the Hungarian's groin, again and again, in strikes that would've made another man cry and lose consciousness.

Hemingway found the two of them with his left hand, first the Hungarian's wide, bleeding back and then his hair — he grabbed a fistful and pulled the man back only a few inches, it was all Tibor or Jacint would allow, put the tommy gun barrel to his right temple, and squeezed off four or five bullets in a hectic spray, which immediately wilted the man's big body and also made mincemeat of his head in general, as Hemingway was now holding a handful of Hungarian hair attached to a tattered swatch of scalp — the rest had more or less been broadcast over the water.

The two men spent five minutes breathing hard, the sea around them quietly rolling, five more trying to calm their blitzing adrenaline loads, and five more thinking of what to say to the other. Eventually, Rick just said, "My eye, it's OK," and then they stood up, checking for serious wounds.

They had to find Rick's boat, which had drifted a few dozen yards away, with the other boat's light, and Rick had to swim over to it holding a rope, nervously and in a brisk dive, despite the satiated and scattered sharks, and then they tied the boats loosely together. When they did, they saw it was taking on water and sinking, slowly.

"We'll have to tow it out of here, let it drop somewhere else," Hemingway said.

Then the men set about attracting more sharks, letting the two head-blasted bodies bleed over the gunwales for chum, and as that happened they undressed the bodies and sloshed gallons of Gulf water over the deck, trying to rinse away the blood they could see via the boat's fluorescent pilothouse light. After a half hour they couldn't see any more and kept rinsing for another half hour after that, getting soaked to the skin themselves, working around two huge naked Hungarian bodies with their upper transoms dipped over the sides like seriously seasick tourists.

The sharks came, gradually, bulls and makos and tigers, eventually more than a hundred of them, and it took them all night to make well over 450 pounds of Hungarian meat and bone disappear. Rick and Hemingway only checked in on the spectacle occasionally, anxiously, only turning on the light for a few seconds at a time. They could barely stomach that. Hemingway knew it was far from a clean solution, and any trawling of the area might well turn up something incriminating. But he also knew that if something was found, even a set of traceable teeth inside a shark's belly, it wouldn't make the news, or even make it past Captain Video's desk. Everyone had their priorities. He wasn't even sure he was trying to cover his tracks, that he wasn't ready to admit to anyone who asked that he helped kill those thugs and let the sharks have them. He felt as if he was instead just setting something a little right and leaving more questions for Galko than answers.

It was about 3:30 A.M. when signs of the struggle had sufficiently dissipated into the water, and the men towed Rick's boat closer to home, south of Little Mullet, by which time it was half sunk. Rick punched couple more holes in the hull with one of his steel pikes, and they left it to vanish.

Hemingway decided he'd buy the Mexican a new boat, no question.

They arrived at the Basin after four, parked Galko's boat in Rick's slip, with her keys in her. They went home.

32

Matilde was gone. As he thought she would be.

Hemingway waited until noon the next day to even get out of bed, at which point he loudly ordered the works for breakfast, eggs and bacon and bread and coffee, and some German wine, to begin his day.

He had a twinge of pride, just for having completed the unruly, unwriterly task he'd unconsciously laid out for himself. Peter wouldn't ever know or care, and no one was about to thank Hemingway for his efforts. But it was done, and that was something.

But now he had a new secret. The Hungarian whose hair he'd held was the second man he'd killed; the first, in Spain, was for so long Hemingway's most toxic secret, something none of his wives or drinking pals ever knew about. He thought he'd grow old with that memory spawning a blanket of poisonous mold alone in the darkness. But now he had another. If it would, in some time, distribute the weight away from the first killing, it might also burden him in his nights, staring at the ceiling, more than he would be prepared to handle. There was no way of knowing.

He did a few things that morning after getting dressed. He called Rodhizler's Boat Sales on De Kalb and told Oscar Rodhizler to pick out a new, twenty-foot skiff for Rick, and send Hemingway the bill. A cock-and-bull story, half-told and half-suggested, was necessary, about running Rick's old boat into shoals at an ungodly speed, and scotching the hull. Then he called Mary and said he was coming home for real.

"What happened," she growled.

"Nothing much. It will remain a mystery. Probably some scrap over cigars."

"Whew."

Then Hemingway called Kwaak. This time, he got him on the line immediately.

"Mr. Hemingway. I hear you dressed-down a Bureau chief down there yesterday."

"George, honestly, you government men are all goddamned humps."

"I'm not arguing."

"And they sent a few coyotes after me yesterday, and they cornered me in an empty bar."

". . . And then?"

Hemingway didn't want to make it sound as if his life hadn't been in danger, but he didn't want to tell the true story, either. "I got out. Barely. Almost broke my back. Tell you about it sometime."

"Not likely."

"It was *your* agency."

"Don't know anything about that . . . Quite a little excitement down there lately."

"Yes, well, George, I'm not calling to chat about how much I think all government law enforcement and intelligence agencies are little more than rat broods. I'm calling about the Cuthbert, I mean Kovarick, issue."

"Yes."

"It was Ferenc Galko, he had Cuthbert killed."

"Really."

"He had two goons, probably ex-AVO. They shot him, tried to cover it up."

"Galko's gone."

"What?"

"Flew out this morning for Rio. Apparently, when you dropped the bomb about the isotope on Esper, the attitude here toward Galko took a turn, and he got a visit late last night. He was told he was destined, shall we say, for expatriation. We're in the process of seizing the Audubon House as we speak."

"That all must've been after."

"After what."

"After I met up with his enforcers last night, twenty-five minutes or so north, north-northwest off Little Mullet. If you go there — you can find the spot on the Florida map in the station house here, under the big M — you'll find an old anchored fishing boat with deadlights and a large lead-walled box."

"Uh-huh."

"And somewhere on the anchor, past a lot of dead fish, you'll likely find the isotope."

"And Galko's men?"

"You won't find them."

". . . Okay."

"Please see to it, George, that I'm not approached by another federal agent for at least a decade."

"I'll try to make it happen, Hemingway. But you try, too."

"Oh don't worry. I'm cured of whatever plague befell me."

Kwaak didn't chuckle, but the silence served the same purpose. They hung up.

Hemingway finished the wine, and asked Marisol for some Scotch now, with ice, as he looked over the roofs from his veranda and out to the ocean. He told her too to start packing his vitals up, clothes, books, papers, everything — he was going back to Havana. For good, he said to her, I'm leaving the Keys for good, I'm never coming back. He'll sell the house from Cuba — Mary will be happy to see it go — and split the money between the boys. He'll get a Cuban doctor to saw this goddamn cast off. He'll watch the Twenty-sixth of July either succeed or fail, and he'll be a sideliner, a witness, not a participant, not even a reporter. He'll try to exercise — he knows it would help his back, if only he'd begin. He'll fish, and he'll write, and he'll try to stand by his wife, even at home. He'll try to forget the scalp he held in his hand, or the sight of tiger sharks, glimpsed in the flashlight beam briefly, fighting over a wide slab of human thigh. He'll go back to remembering Hadley, and Paris, and maybe he'll decide that looking back isn't such a damn pathetic thing to do. He'll visit Peter's grave one last time before he leaves, to write an end to this bedeviling thing. He'll read something new, see if there's any truth out there.

ABOUT THE AUTHOR

Michael Atkinson is a former film critic for *The Village Voice.* He has written for *The Believer, Spin, Details,* and many others, and has been included in *Best American Poetry* and *Best American Movie Writing.* He lives in Centerport, New York.

We hope you have enjoyed this Large Print book. Other Thorndike, Wheeler, Kennebec, and Chivers Press Large Print books are available at your library or directly from the publishers.

For information about current and upcoming titles, please call or write, without obligation, to:

Publisher
Thorndike Press
295 Kennedy Memorial Drive
Waterville, ME 04901
Tel. (800) 223-1244

or visit our Web site at:

http://gale.cengage.com/thorndike

OR

Chivers Large Print
published by BBC Audiobooks Ltd
St James House, The Square
Lower Bristol Road
Bath BA2 3SB
England
Tel. +44(0) 800 136919
email: bbcaudiobooks@bbc.co.uk
www.bbcaudiobooks.co.uk

All our Large Print titles are designed for easy reading, and all our books are made to last.